LAGOON

ALSO BY NNEDI OKORAFOR

KABU KABU ★ WHO FEARS DEATH
THE BOOK OF THE PHOENIX ★ BINTI

NNEDI OKORAFOR

LAGOON

SAGA PRESS

LONDON SYDNEY NEW YORK TORONTO NEW DELHI

SAGA PRESS

AN IMPRINT OF SIMON & SCHUSTER, INC.

1230 AVENUE OF THE AMERICAS, NEW YORK, NEW YORK 10020

Text copyright © 2014 by Nnedi Okorafor
Originally published in 2014 by Great Britain by Hodder & Stoughton
Map copyright © 2015 by Lonely Planet
Cover photograph copyright © 2015 by Franklin Kappa/Getty Images
Saga Press and colophon are trademarks of Simon & Schuster, Inc.
For information about special discounts for bulk purchases, please contact Simon &
Schuster Special Sales at 1-866-506-1949 or business@simonandschuster.com.
The Simon & Schuster Speakers Bureau can bring authors to your live event. For
more information or to book an event, contact the Simon & Schuster Speakers
Bureau at 1-866-248-3049 or visit our website at www.simonspeakers.com.
Also available in a Saga Press hardcover edition.
The text for this book is set in Plantin.
Manufactured in the United States of America
First Saga Press paperback edition February 2011
10 12 14 16 18 20 19 17 15 13 11
The Library of Congress has cataloged the hardcover edition as follows:
Okorafor, Nnedi.
Lagoon / Nnedi Okorafor. — First edition.
pages ; cm
Summary: "A biologist, a famous rapper, and a rogue soldier become
the honor guard and interpreter of humanity's first contact with an alien
ambassador in this thriller that combines magicial realism and
seemingly end-of-the-world high tension"— Provided by publisher.
ISBN 978-1-4814-4087-5 (hardcover)
ISBN 978-1-4814-4089-9 (eBook)
1. Extraterrestrial beings—Fiction. 2. Human-alien encounters—Fiction. I. Title.
PS3615.K67L33 2015
813.6—dc23   2015010814
ISBN 978-1-4814-4088-2 (pbk)

TO THE DIVERSE AND DYNAMIC PEOPLE
OF LAGOS, NIGERIA—
ANIMALS, PLANT, AND SPIRIT

The cure for anything is salt water—
sweat, tears, or the sea.

—ISAK DINESEN (pseudonym of
Danish writer Baroness Karen Blixen)

Lagos na no man's land. Nobody own Lagos,
na we all get am. Eko o ni baje!
(Lagos is no man's land. Nobody owns Lagos,
we all own Lagos. Lagos will never be destroyed!)

—a protester from Ajegunle District
to local reporters, interviewed the night it all happened

Lagos, the city where nothing works
yet everything happens.

—an American white woman
in the wrong place at the wrong time

Welcome to Lagos, Nigeria.
The city takes its name from the Portuguese word for "lagoon."
The Portuguese first landed on Lagos Island in the year 1472.
Apparently, they could not come up with a more creative name.
Nor did they think to ask one of the natives for suggestions.
And so the world turns, masked by millions of names, guises, and
shifting stories.
It's been a beautiful thing to watch.
My designs grow complicated.

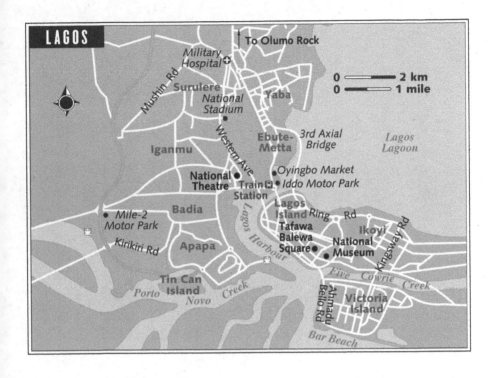

ACT I
WELCOME

MOOM!

She slices through the water, imagining herself a deadly beam of black light. The current parts against her sleek, smooth skin. If any fish gets in her way, she will spear it and keep right on going. She is on a mission. She is angry. She will succeed, and then they will leave for good. They brought the stench of dryness, then they brought the noise and made the world bleed black ooze that left poison rainbows on the water's surface. She often sees these rainbows whenever she leaps over the water to touch the sun. Inhaling them stings and burns her gills.

The ones who bring the rainbows are burrowing and building creatures from the land, and no one can do anything about them. Except her. She's done it before, and they stopped for many moons. They went away. She is doing it again.

She increases her speed.

She is the largest predator in these waters. Her waters. Even when she migrates, this particular place remains hers. Everyone knows it. She was not born here, but after all her migrations, she is happiest here. She suspects that this is the birthplace of one of those who created her.

She swims even faster.

She is blue-gray and it is night. Though she cannot see, she doesn't need to. She knows where she is going. She is aiming for the thing that looks like a giant dead snake. She remembers snakes; she's seen plenty in her past life. In the sun, this dead snake is the color of decaying seaweed with skin rough like coral.

Any moment now.

She is nearly there.

She is closing in fast.

She stabs into it.

From the tip of her spear, down her spine, to the ends of all her fins, she experiences red-orange bursts of pain. The impact is so jarring that she can't move. But there is victory; she feels the giant dead snake deflating. It blows its black blood. Her perfect body goes numb, and she wonders if she has died. Then she wonders what new body she will find herself inhabiting. She remembers her last form, a yellow monkey; even while in that body, she loved to swim. The water has always called to her.

All goes black.

She awakens. Gently but quickly, she pulls her spear out. The black blood spews in her face from the hole she's made. She turns away from the bittersweet-tasting poison. *Now* they will leave soon. As she happily swims away in triumph, the loudest noise she's ever heard vibrates through the water.

MOOM!

The noise ripples through the ocean with such intensity that she tumbles with it, sure that it will tear her apart.

Then the water calms. Deeply shaken, she slowly swims to the surface. Head above the water, she moves through the bodies that glisten in the moonlight. Several smaller fish, jellyfish, even crabs, float, belly up or dismembered. Many of the smaller creatures have probably simply been obliterated. But she has survived.

She swims back to the depths. She's only gone down a few feet when she smells it. Clean, sweet, sweet, *sweet!* Her senses are flooded with sweetness, the sweetest water she's ever breathed. She swims forward, tasting the water more as it moves through her gills. In the darkness, she feels others around her. Other fish.

Large, like herself, and small . . . So some small ones *have* survived. Now, she sees many. There are even several sharp-toothed ones and mass killers. She sees this clearly now because something large and glowing is down ahead. A great shifting bar of glimmering sand. This is what is giving off the sweet, clean water. She hopes the sweetness will drown out the foul blackness of the dead snake she pierced. She has a feeling it will. She has a very good feeling.

The sun is up now, sending its warm rays into the water. She can see everyone swimming, floating, wiggling right into the glowing thing below. There are sharks, sea cows, shrimps, octopus, tilapia, codfish, mackerel, flying fish, even seaweed. Creatures from the shallows, creatures from the shore, creatures from the deep, all here. A unique gathering. What is happening here?

But she remains where she is. Waiting. Hesitating. Watching. It is not deep but it is wide. About two hundred feet below the surface. Right before her eyes, it shifts. From blue to green to clear to purple-pink to glowing gold. But it is the size, profile, and shape of it that draws her. Once, in her travels, she came across a giant world of food, beauty, and activity. The coral reef was blue, pink, yellow, and green, inhabited by sea creatures of every shape and size. The water was delicious, and there was not a dry creature in sight. She lived in that place for many moons before finally returning to her favorite waters. When she traveled again, she was never able to find the paradise she'd left.

Now here in her home is something even wilder and more alive than her lost paradise. And like there, the water here is clean and clear. She can't see the end of it. However, there is one thing she is certain of: What she is seeing isn't from the sea's greatest depths or the dry places. This is from far, far away.

More and more creatures swim down to it. As they draw closer, she sees the colors pulsate and embrace them. She notices an octopus with one missing tentacle descending toward it. Suddenly, the octopus grows brilliant pink-purple and straightens all its tentacles. Then right before her eyes, it grows its missing tentacle back and what look like bony spokes erupt from its soft head. It spins and flips and then shoots off, down into one of the skeletal caves of the undulating coral-like thing below.

When a golden blob ascends to meet her, she doesn't move to meet it. But she doesn't flee either. The sweetness she smells and its gentle movements are soothing and non-threatening. When it communicates with her, asking question after question, she hesitates. It doesn't take long for her apprehension to shift to delight. What good questions it asks. She tells it exactly what she wants.

Everything is changing.

She's always loved her smooth, gray-blue skin, but now it is impenetrable, its new color golden like the light the New People give off. The color that reminds her of another life when she could both enjoy the water and endure the sun and air.

Her swordlike spear is longer and so sharp at the tip that it sings. They made her eyes like the blackest stone, and she can see deep into the ocean and high into the sky. And when she wants to, she can make spikes of cartilage jut out along her spine as if she is some ancestral creature from the deepest ocean caves of old. The last thing she requests is to be three times her size and twice her weight.

They make it so.

Now she is no longer a great swordfish. She is a monster.

Despite the FPSO Mystras*'s loading hose leaking crude oil, the ocean water just outside Lagos, Nigeria, is now so clean that a cup of its salty-sweet goodness will heal the worst human illnesses and cause a hundred more illnesses not yet known to humankind. It is more alive than it has been in centuries, and it is teeming with aliens and monsters.*

CHAPTER 1

FIST

It was an eerie moment as Adaora and the two strange men arrived at that spot, right before it happened. Exactly three yards from the water at exactly 11:55 p.m., 8 January 2010. Adaora came from the north side of the beach. The tall veiled man came from the east. The bloodied man wearing army fatigues from the west. They ambled in their general directions, eyeing each other as it became clear that their paths would intersect.

Only Adaora hesitated. Then, like the others, she pressed on. She was a born-and-raised Lagosian, and she was wearing nicely fitted jeans and a sensible blouse. She'd spent more time walking this beach than probably both of these men combined.

She wiped the tears from her cheeks and trained her eyes straight ahead. About a quarter of a mile away was open water where the Atlantic overflowed its banks. When bad things happened, her feet always brought her here, to Lagos's Bar Beach.

In many ways, Bar Beach was a perfect sample of Nigerian society. It was a place of mixing. The ocean mixed with the land, and the wealthy mixed with the poor. Bar Beach attracted drug dealers, squatters, various accents and languages, seagulls, garbage, biting flies, tourists, all kinds of religious zealots, hawkers, prostitutes, johns, water-loving children, and their careless parents. The beachside bars and small restaurants were the most popular hangout spots. Bar Beach's waters were too wild for any serious swimming. Even the best swimmers risked a watery death by its many rip currents.

Adaora had removed her sandals. It was deep night, and this was probably a bad idea. So far, however, she hadn't stepped on any pieces of wood, rusty nails, broken glass, or sharp stones. Her need to feel the cool sand between her toes at this moment outweighed the risk. Despite its trash, there was still something sacred about Bar Beach.

On 12 June 1993, the day of the most democratic election in Nigeria's history, she'd come here with her father and watched him shed tears of joy. On 23 June, her mother brought her here because her father and uncles were at home cursing and shouting over the military annulling those same elections.

She came here to escape the reality that her best friend was sleeping with her biology professor to earn a passing grade. On the day she received her PhD in marine biology from the University of Lagos, she came here to thank the Powers That Be for helping her stay sane enough to finish her degree (and for the fact that she hadn't had to sleep with anyone to earn it).

Last year, she'd come here to weep when her father was killed along with thirty others during a botched robbery of a luxury bus on the Lagos–Benin Expressway, one of Nigeria's many, many, many dangerous roads. The thieves had demanded that all the passengers get off the bus and lie in the momentarily empty road. In their stupidity, the thieves hadn't anticipated the truck (speeding to avoid armed robbers) that would run over everyone including the thieves.

And now Adaora was here at Bar Beach because her loving perfect husband of ten years had hit her. Slapped her really *hard*. All because of a hip-hop concert and a priest. At first, she'd stood there stunned and hurt, cupping her cheek, praying the children hadn't heard. Then she'd brought her hand up and slapped him right back. Shocked into rage, her husband leaped on her. But Adaora had been ready for him. By this time, she wasn't thinking about the children.

She didn't know how long she and her husband had scuffled

like wild dogs on the floor. And the way the fight had ended, it wasn't . . . normal. One minute they'd been brawling, and then the next, her husband was mysteriously stuck to the floor, his wrists and ankles held down as though by powerful magnets. As he'd screamed and twisted, Adaora had got up, grabbed her keys, and run out of the house. Thankfully, their Victoria Island home was only minutes from Bar Beach.

She rubbed her swollen cheek. Even on her dark skin, the redness would be visible. She set her jaw, and tried to ignore the two men coming from her right and left as she walked toward the ocean. After what she'd just dealt with, she wasn't about to let *any* man get in her way. Still, as she got closer, she ventured a glance at the two of them.

She frowned.

The man in the military uniform looked like he'd already seen plenty plenty pepper. He reminded Adaora of a whipped lion. Blood dribbled from his nose, and he wasn't bothering to wipe it away. And half his face was swollen. Yet he had a hard, unshaken look in his eye. The other man was a tall, dark-skinned scarecrow of a fellow wearing a black-and-white veil. Maybe he was a Muslim. He was scrutinizing the approaching beat-up-looking soldier more than he was her.

Each of them walked in their respective straight lines. Each heading toward each other. Adaora squinted at the man in the veil. *What is it about him?* she thought as she walked toward the sea. *Something.* But she didn't slow her gait. And so the three of them met. The tall man was the first to speak. "Excuse—"

"Tell me this is a joke," Adaora interrupted as she realized what it was about the man. "Are . . . are you . . . Can I ask you a . . ."

The tall man, looking deeply annoyed, removed his veil and sighed. "I am," he said, cutting her off. "But don't call me Anthony Dey Craze. I'm just out for a post-concert stroll. Tonight, just call me Edgar."

"Na woa!" she exclaimed, laughing, reaching up to touch her throbbing cheek. "You wore that scarf on your album cover, didn't you?" After what had happened at home, it was surprising and felt good to laugh. "I was supposed to be at your concert tonight!"

At some point, her husband Chris had changed his mind about "letting" her go to the Anthony Dey Craze concert with her best friend Yemi because he'd barred her way when she'd tried to leave. "Since when do I need your permission to do anything, anyway?" she'd said to her husband, taken aback. Then came the slap.

"Please," the bloody military man said, snatching his green beret off his smoothly shaven head and squeezing it in his shaking hands. "Do either of you have a mobile phone? I must call my father. I will pay you well."

Adaora barely registered his words; she was now really looking him over. Up close he looked not only injured but in deep, deep distress. The blood running from his nose glistened in the dim mix of street and moonlight. She took her hand from her burning cheek and reached out to him.

"Hey, buddy," Anthony said, looking at the military man with concern. He'd brought out his mobile phone. "You're bleeding, o! Do you need help? Are you all—"

"No!" he snapped. "I'm *not* all right!"

Adaora jumped back, unconsciously bringing her fists up.

"Do I LOOK all right?" he shouted. He motioned for Anthony's mobile phone. "I need to *make this phone call right now!* My fam—"

BOOM!

Anthony dropped his mobile phone as all three of them dropped to the ground, their hands over their heads. Adaora found herself looking from the bleeding military man to Anthony in terror. It was *not* the type of sound one heard on Bar Beach, or in any part of Lagos. On Bar Beach, the loudest thing was typically some woman shouting at a man or someone's old car backfiring on a nearby road. This booming sound was so deep Adaora could feel it in her chest, and it rattled her teeth. It left cotton in her ears. It was so wide that it seemed to have its own physical weight. Adaora glanced around and saw that the noise pushed everything to the ground. A few feet away, two seagulls dropped from the night sky to the sand, stunned. Something black bounced off Anthony's head and fell beside him.

"Bat?" Adaora asked. Everything was muffled, as if she were speaking underwater.

Anthony looked at it closely. The bat was furry-bodied and beady-eyed with black wings. It wiggled a bit, still alive. He scooped up the poor creature and grabbed Adaora's hand. He nudged the military man's shoulder as he cradled the stunned animal.

"Come on!" he shouted. "That came from the water! We should get away from here!"

But something was happening to the ocean. The waves were roiling irregularly. Each time the waves broke on the beach, they reached farther and farther up the sand. Then a four-foot wave rose up. Adaora was so fascinated that she just stood there staring. Anthony stopped pulling her and pushing the military man. Blood ran into the military man's eyes as he tried to focus his gaze on the darkness of the water. The wave was heading right for them. Fast and quiet as a whisper. It was closer to ten feet tall now. Finally, the three of them turned and ran. The fist of water was faster. Adaora grabbed the military man's hand. Anthony threw the bat to what he hoped was safety, leaped, and grabbed Adaora's legs just as the water fell at them.

PLASH!

The salty water stung Adaora's eyes and pulled at her garments as it sucked her toward the sea. Her hands scrambled at the sand as it collapsed beneath her, the pebbles raking at her skin, the sea sucking at her legs. She could still feel the desperate grasp of the military man's hand and Anthony's arms around her legs. She wasn't alone. In the blackness, she could see some of the lights from the bars and the nearby buildings. They were flickering and growing smaller and smaller.

Bubbles tickled her ears as she tried to twist to the surface. But it was as if the ocean had opened its great maw and swallowed her and the two men. She couldn't breathe. She heard bubbles and the roar and rush of water against her ears. And she could feel the tightness of her laboring lungs and the suction of the water. *Aman iman*, Adaora weakly thought. The phrase meant "water is life" in the Tuareg language of Tamashek. She'd once worked with a Tuareg man on a diving expedition. *"Aman Iman,"* had been his answer when Adaora asked how a man of the Sahara Desert had become an expert scuba diver. Despite the pain in her lungs now and the swallowing darkness, she smiled. *Aman Iman.*

The three of them grasped each other. Down, down, down, they went.

CHAPTER 2

THE BOY AND THE LADY

Only two people on the beach witnessed the watery abduction of Adaora and the two men. One was a young boy. Just before the boom, his guardian had been standing several feet away having a heated discussion with the owner of one of the shacks selling mineral, mainly orange Fanta and Coca-Cola. The boy was staring at something else. His stomach was growling, but he forgot about his hunger for the moment.

In the moonlight, he couldn't clearly see the creature, but as it walked out of the water, even he knew it was not human. All his mind would register was the word "smoke." At least until the creature walked up the quiet beach and stepped into the flickering light from one of the restaurants. By then it had become a naked dark-skinned African woman with long black braids. She reminded the boy of a woman whose purse he'd once stolen.

She'd stood there for several moments, watching the three people who came from three different directions and ended up standing before each other. Then the strange woman creature silently ran back to the water and dove in like Mami Wata.

Rubbing his itchy head, the boy decided that he was seeing things, as he often did when he grew confused. He flared his nostrils and breathed through his mouth as he tried to focus back on reality. The great booming sound rattled his brain even more. Then came the wave that looked like the hand of a powerful water spirit. The boy saw it take the three people, one who was a woman and two who were men. And just before it did, he saw one of those people throw a black bird into the air that caught itself and flew into the night.

Nevertheless, he could not speak or even process any of this information for he was both mute and mentally handicapped. He stared at where the three people had been and now were not. Then he smiled, saliva glistening in the left corner of his mouth, because somewhere deep in his restrained brain, he had a profound understanding that things around him were about to change forever, and he liked this idea very much.

The other witness of the abduction was a young woman named Fisayo. She was a hardworking, book-reading secretary by day and a prostitute by night. She, too, noticed the creature woman who emerged from the water. And she, too, thought the word "smoke," but she also thought "shape-shifter."

"I am seeing the devil," she whispered to herself. She turned away and dropped to her knees. She was wearing a short tight skirt, and the sand was warm and soft on her shins and kneecaps.

She prayed to the Lord Jesus Christ to forgive her for all her sins and take her to heaven, for surely the rapture was here. When the boom came, she shut her eyes and tried to pray harder. The pain of death would be her atonement. But deep down she knew she was a sinner and there was nothing that would ever wipe that away. She got to her feet and turned around just in time to see the woman and two men snatched up by a huge fist of water. Just before it happened, one of them had released something black and evil into the air like a poison.

She stood there, staring at the spot where they had been and no longer were. She waited for the water to take her, too. The fist had to be the hand of Satan, and she was one of the biggest sinners on earth. Oh the things she'd done, so many, many times. Sometimes it was just to fill her empty belly. She trembled and started sweating. Her armpits prickled. She hated her tiny skirt, tight tank top, red pumps, the itchy straight-haired brown wig on her head. When nothing else happened, she went to the nearest bar and ordered a cranberry and vodka. She would anxiously tell her next john, a businessman from the United States, what she had seen. But he wasn't interested in anything she had to say. He was more interested in filling her mouth than watching it flap with useless dumb words.

But she wouldn't forget. And when it all started, she would become one of the loudest prophets of doom in Lagos.

CHAPTER 3

MIRI

The breeze cooled Adaora's wet back through her drying blouse. She heard people nervously talking, some in Yoruba, one in Igbo, two in Hausa, most in Pidgin English.

"Hurry, *biko-nu*! Make we go from here!" someone said.

"I don' know. Maybe *na* suicide bomb, o!"

There were clicks and clacks from people packing and locking up, rushing to close shop and bar. And there was the sound of the surf. She seized up. For the first time in her life, that sound scared her. Someone touched her shoulder and she flinched.

"Awake," a female voice said.

Adaora opened her eyes and sat up quickly. She tried to stand but fell back to the sand, dizzy and light-headed. "Don't," she muttered. "Don't touch me." Then she saw the other two lying in the sand, still sleeping or passed out or drugged, whatever *they* had done to them. Nearby, a dim streetlight flickered. Most of the other lights were completely out, leaving Bar Beach in darkness.

"I won't," it said. Adaora squinted at it in the flickering light . . . No, not "it," "her." The woman wore a long white sundress and looked like someone from Adaora's family—dark-skinned, broad-nosed, with dark brown thick lips. Her bushy hair was as long as Adaora's, except where Adaora had many, many neat shoulder-length dreadlocks, this one had many, many neat brown braids that crept down her back.

Adaora turned to the water as the breeze blew in her face. She inhaled. The air smelled as it always smelled, fishy and salty with a hint of smoke from the city. But the water was way too high. Nearly ten feet up the beach! Only a foot from her toes. In the darkness, bar and restaurant owners and employees with battery-powered flashlights looked fearfully at the water as they rushed about closing up. All their customers must have fled. *They should be more than a little afraid,* Adaora thought, shutting her eyes and trying to gather her faculties. *How much time has passed? Hours? A few minutes?*

"What's done is done," the woman said. "We are here. Now . . ."

"Now you . . . you people should leave," Adaora said, slurring her words.

"No. We stay."

Adaora looked at the woman and couldn't bring herself to feel irritated. She shut her eyes again, forcing herself to think analytically, calmly, rationally, like the scientist she was. Many things depended on how she reacted, she knew. But when she looked at the woman, an unscientific thought occurred to her.

There was something both attractive and repellent about the woman, and it addled Adaora's senses. Her hair was long—her many braids perfect and shiny, yet clearly her own hair. She had piercing brown eyes that gave Adaora the same creepy feeling as when she looked at a large black spider. Her mannerisms were too calm, fluid and . . . alien. Adaora's husband, Chris, would instantly hate this woman for all of these reasons. To him, this woman would be a "marine witch." Her husband believed there were white witches, physical witches, and marine witches. All were evil, but the marine witch was the most powerful because she could harness water, the very substance that made up 70 percent of an adult's body and 75 percent of a child's. *Water is life,* she thought, yet again.

Adaora grinned. She could easily pass the woman in the white dress off as her cousin. Scaring the shit out of her husband was the perfect way to get back at him. And she had a lab in the basement. She could run some simple tests on this . . . "woman" there. It would be an easy, uncomplicated, private way to determine if what was happening was real and not just some stress-fueled bizarre hallucination.

"What should I call you?" Adaora asked, sighing and rubbing her forehead. She touched her cheek. Still swollen and sore.

The woman paused and then smiled knowingly. "I like the name Miri?"

Adaora blinked, surprised. She'd been thinking this exact name. It really *could* read her mind. The name "Miri" would surely drive her husband that much more insane; it would be the icing on the cake. Still, something in Adaora resisted. The name needed to be more subtle than the Igbo word for "water."

"No," Adaora said. "What of the name . . ." She paused as the name "Ayodele" came to mind. It was a Yoruba name and it would fill Chris with suspicion, since Adaora was Igbo. Also, Adaora had had a childhood friend named Ayodele who'd been killed while trying to cross a busy street when she was eight years old. She'd loved Ayodele. She frowned at the woman. "Do you know what name I'm thinking of right now?"

It . . . *She* smiled. "No."

Adaora's husband would remember her friend Ayodele from when they were kids too. He'd cried just as much as Adaora when it happened. The name would trouble him more than "Miri." Yes.

"You need a place to stay," Adaora said.

"Yes," she said. "I would like that."

"Fine," Adaora said, her voice hardening. "So you are Ayodele, then."

CHAPTER 4

WHAT WOULD YOU DO?

They all went. Adaora, Anthony, Ayodele, and Agu . . . Adaora knew the soldier's name now. His name meant "leopard" in Igbo. Her name meant "daughter of the people" in Igbo, and she told them so. She told them all a lot of things. She knew plenty about both Anthony and Agu, and they knew plenty about her. Adaora drove.

What would you *do if this happened to you?*

The soldier Agu had woken soon after Adaora had given the creature a name. His still swollen face was crusty with sea salt and blood that must have seeped from his wounds and dried after they'd been returned. All he could think about was his family, who he said was in the village. "Please, do you have a mobile phone?" he'd asked Adaora again.

"It's in my car," she said. "Let's wake Anthony up first."

Agu had pressed his head with his big hands and shut his eyes. Images of being in that foreign place under the sea where for some reason he could breathe and had to answer a thousand questions—questions that made him laugh, cry, and think—kept trying to cloud his thoughts. If you were Agu, would you return to your barracks where you'd encounter your fellow soldiers who had just beaten you up after you tried to stop their assault of a woman? When your superior had threatened to send hired thugs to kill the only family you had? He did not wish to return to his barracks, not right away.

Anthony woke as Adaora softly patted his cheek. In the dim, flickering light, he'd looked into her face and thought she was a fish woman because of her ropelike dreadlocks and intense eyes smeared with runny mascara. Then he'd remembered the music from under the sea in the reeflike place and how he could hear it too, and how they'd called him "brother." He had several brothers, and being called one reminded him of home. And this woman looking at him now had been there with him and the beaten soldier. He was glad they were all alive. He was also glad to find his mobile phone in the sand a few feet away.

All three of them stayed together. All three of them were in. It was 9 January and approaching one a.m.

CHAPTER 5

THE LAB

"Hurry," Adaora said, flicking the light switch on and moving quickly down the stairs. "My husband sleeps heavily but my children wake up at the slightest noise." She moved to the far side of the lab and flipped on the lights there, too. This was her personal space, and she felt odd bringing strangers into it, especially one that was *so* . . . strange. Normally, no one but her eight-year-old daughter and five-year-old son came down here. Of late, her husband avoided what he now called her "witch's den" at all costs.

"Shut your eyes," Chris had told her years ago on the evening Adaora returned home from her first day of teaching at the Nigerian Institute for Oceanography and Marine Research. Both of them giggled as he led her down the stairs. When she opened her eyes, she had to sit down right there on the steps. He'd transformed the place.

Chris was a wealthy, very busy accountant for an international textile company. The job took him all over the world. For him to spend enough time at home to gather and work with his equally busy colleague friends to build her a lab was an act of the truest love. There were bookshelves packed with her textbooks, monographs, and journals; a place for her to hang her diving gear; a brand new computer with a huge wide-screen high-definition television as a monitor and a high-speed, generally reliable, Internet connection; a large solid lab table and a powerful microscope, plenty of test tubes, racks and slides; and a giant flat-screen television in the back for when she needed to relax. In the middle of the room, he'd even installed a two-hundred-gallon tropical fish tank full of wiggling sea anemones, darting butterfly fish, busy shrimps, sneaky crabs, and three large confused-looking cowfish.

"The institute can't give you everything you need," he'd said that day. "But I can."

Adaora had been speechless. Back then, he'd loved her so much. But that was a long time ago. Before the children. Before the stress. Before Chris's traveling became too frequent and took him over-seas for more than a third of the year. Before his miserable mother started meddling in their marriage. Before the turbulence-plagued plane flight that scared Chris so profoundly that two days later when he was passing a prayer tent, he decided to become "born again" (something that made even his meddling mother frown). Before the fasting. Before the jealousy and accusations.

The woman Adaora had named Ayodele came slowly down the stairs, Anthony and Agu a few steps behind her.

"Please. Sit down," Adaora said.

Ayodele went straight to the computer and sat in the black leather chair. Anthony and Agu looked at each other and cautiously followed Ayodele into the room, afraid to get too close.

"Nice crib," Anthony said.

"Yeah," Agu said. "What is it your husband does, again?"

"He's an accountant," she said as she rummaged around in her equipment drawer. "I am a professor at UNILAG. So we do okay."

Agu nodded as he looked at some of the books in the cases.

When Ayodele touched the computer's flat-screen monitor with a graceful finger, the background picture (of a menacing dragon-like lionfish in a blue ocean) flickered the slightest bit. "You people have your own"—she giggled, a creepy dovelike sound that raised the hairs on Adaora's arms—"little inventions."

"Yes," Adaora said. "That's a computer. Your, eh, people don't have them?"

Ayodele laughed at this.

"They don't need them," Anthony muttered as he tiredly rubbed a hand over his face and put his veil over his head.

Adaora set a clean slide beside her microscope. She glanced at Ayodele and hesitated. Every time she looked at her, there was a disorienting moment where she was not sure what she was seeing. It lasted no more than a half second, but it was there. Then she was seeing Ayodele the "woman" again.

Adaora cleared her throat and pushed these observations, along with thoughts of what she'd seen in the water, from her mind. "Come here, Ayodele," she said. "I . . . I'd like to take a skin sample." As she handed Ayodele a Q-tip, Adaora visualized the size, shape, and color of magnified cheek cells. It had always been like this. When she was afraid, nervous, or uncomfortable, all she had to do was focus on the science to feel balanced again. It was no different now.

"You don't believe I am what I said I am?" Ayodele asked, scrutinizing the Q-tip. She held it up and touched the soft, white, cottony bud.

"I . . . I do. But I . . . It's important that I see for myself," she said. *And make sure I am seeing what I know I'm seeing and know what I know I know,* she thought frantically. "Then we can get you something to eat. Do . . . do you eat?" She cringed at how silly she sounded.

"Eat?" Ayodele paused, seeming to think it over. "Okay."

Adaora took a Q-tip, opened her mouth, and rubbed the tip on the inside of her cheek. "Swab the inside of your mouth like this," she said.

As soon as Ayodele did so and handed the Q-tip to Adaora, Ayodele went to the fish tank and stood beside Anthony.

"I should be back in the club, *chale,*" Anthony said, staring at a butterfly fish as it darted by. "I only went out for some fresh air. I had a headache."

NNEDI OKORAFOR

"Too much rhythm?" Ayodele asked.

He frowned, turning to look her in the eye. She smiled back pleasantly. Always so pleasant.

"I know why the Elders like you," she said.

Anthony held her gaze a bit longer, then turned back to the aquarium. "Can you change into one of those?" Anthony asked Ayodele, pointing at a red shrimp with white stripes.

"I can," she said, pressing her face against the tank. "You know that."

Anthony nodded. "You can change yourselves but you can change the fish, too, right?"

"Precisely," Ayodele said. "We give them whatever they want."

"Damn," he said. Then he nodded with a small smile. "Respect."

Adaora slipped the slide onto the microscope's stage and took a look. It didn't take long to see what she needed to see. She switched to the lens of the greatest magnification just to make sure. She chuckled, feeling an ache of excitement deep in her belly. *"Shit!"* she whispered.

Again she pushed away crowding memories of what she'd witnessed under the sea. How she'd been floating and breathing beneath the water in whatever contraption they'd built down there on the reeflike structure. How one of them had touched her arm, and she watched as it became coated with lovely iridescent fish scales and her fingers webbed together. How the sensation of the changing felt more like rigorous vibration than pain. How they'd known that that was what she wanted so that she could horrify her husband. How easily they'd changed her back. She squeezed her eyes shut. *Focus, focus, focus,* she thought.

Agu sat on the stool beside her.

"So, what do you see?" Agu asked.

Adaora stepped aside. "You tell me," she said, motioning to the microscope.

He put his eye to the lens.

24

"Do you know what cells normally look like?" Adaora asked.

"Yes. I remember from secondary school."

As he looked, Adaora watched Ayodele gazing at the fish. She met Anthony's eyes, and she gave him a slight nod. He cocked his head and mouthed, "This is crazy."

Adaora nodded in agreement. They both shifted their gazes to Ayodele, who was still looking at the fish.

"Well, Agu?" Adaora asked, after a minute. "What do you see?"

"I'm not sure," he said, still looking.

"You . . . you see them, right?"

"Tiny balls? Moving around and sort of . . . vibrating?"

Adaora nodded vigorously. "Yes! That's her skin . . . magnified."

Agu's battered face held a deeply uncertain expression. "But . . ."

"I don't think it is *cellular* matter." She leaned against the lab table.

Agu touched his bruised nose. "Does that mean . . ."

"One thousand times!" Adaora whispered loudly, ignoring Agu. "That's how strong the magnification is. She's made of tiny, tiny, tiny, metal-like balls. It's *got to* be metal. Certain types of metal powders look like that at two hundred times. I think that's why she can . . . change shape like that. You saw how . . . how . . . when we were . . ."

Agu wouldn't meet her eyes. "Yeah. I saw."

"The balls aren't fixed together as our cells are," Adaora said.

Agu just looked at her blankly.

"I always wondered," Adaora continued. "Much of the world's most famous extraterrestrial material, mainly meteorites, has fallen right here. In *Nigeria*." She was speaking more to herself now. "Last year a big one fell in Tarkwa Bay. I was testing the water for pollution when it happened . . ." She started looking around. "I should write all this down!" She grabbed a pen and paper and started jotting down notes, focusing on each word she wrote. Not wanting to focus on Agu. If she focused on him, her world would fall apart.

She could feel him looking at her. She took a deep breath, fighting down tears as she thought about the fight with her husband. "So . . . what happened to your face?" she asked.

"It was punched."

"I see that, but by who?"

"By my *ahoa*," he said. When Adaora looked at him questioningly, he said, "My *ahoa* . . . my comrades, my fellow soldiers." He sucked his teeth. "Don't act like you didn't listen in during my phone call in the car."

She had, all of them had. Agu had used her phone to call his parents in the small town of Arondizuogu. He'd told them to leave their home immediately and hide with relatives because hired thugs were going to descend on them. "Tell Kelechi and his wife, too. Leave the yams! You can grow those back but you cannot grow your life back, o!"

Adaora had felt embarrassed and sorry for Agu when he handed back her phone. And for minutes, no one in the car said a word, not even Ayodele.

"But what did you do?" Adaora asked now. "Why are they coming after your family?"

Agu looked at her with his fully open eye and squinted with his swollen right one. "I tried to stop one of my own *ahoa* from raping a woman." He paused, a disgusted look on his face as he remembered. "We'd pulled her over on the Lagos–Benin Expressway. This fine woman; she was drunk. Lance Corporal Benson, my superior, he got out of hand with her. I . . . I punched him in the gut." He paused, frowning. Then he looked into Adaora's eyes. "He went flying like a sack of feathers!"

Adaora went cold. "What? What do you mean?"

Agu nodded. "Exactly! I'm not a weak man. I exercise, keep myself in shape. And I've had my share of fights. But . . . he went *flying*. Because I *hit* him. Then for a while, he didn't move. The rest of my *ahoa* descended on me for that. They beat me like a dog and left me unconscious on the side of the road. I must have lost my mobile phone then, so—"

The sound of the television interrupted their conversation. Anthony had switched it on for Ayodele, who had moved to the sofa. She sighed softly when the picture appeared.

On the TV, as a breaking-news banner scrolled across the bottom of the screen, a newscaster in fashionable dress pants and a white blouse stood on what could only have been Bar Beach. The wind was blowing, and military personnel behind her were setting up barriers.

"Witnesses on Bar Beach are saying that just after nine p.m. they heard an earth-shaking explosion that seemed to roll up from the water like a tidal wave," the newscaster was saying. "People are reporting broken windows in cars and buildings. A few people say they're even experiencing hearing loss. There's no sign of terrorist activity yet, but here to discuss the issue is Lance Corporal Benson Shehu, who is on the scene."

Beside her stood a stern-looking Hausa man in sharp military dress, his green beret perched on his head like a fixture. He rested a hand on his hip, as if he were working hard to stand up straight.

Agu pointed at the television. "That's him! That's my—"

"Shhh shhh shhh," Anthony hissed, frowning.

"You also happen to be the president's nephew," the newscaster on TV added.

"Yes, but that is mere coincidence and irrelevant to the issue," Benson snapped. He winced visibly, pressing below his ribs.

The newscaster nodded as Benson looked into the camera and squinted as if he were looking into the sun. "There is no destruction or, or anything like that. It was *not* a bomb. It seems to be some sort of sonic blast. Erm . . . noise from the breaking of the sound barrier. Something like that. This is not a suicide bomber. We have never had that nonsense in Lagos. But we are treating this as an *attack*," he said.

"An attack? Against Nigeria?"

"Yes," he said, turning to the newscaster.

"By who?"

"We don't know," he said. "We don't know anything. But did the Americans know who destroyed their World Trade Towers when it first happened?"

The newscaster nodded. "Good point. But that brings me back to my question about the president. Where is he? Will he be giving—"

"By morning, we hope to know more," Benson interrupted. "Where there's smoke, there's fire." He shifted uncomfortably from one foot to the other. "In this case, where there is noise, there is a source. For now, we are advising people to continue going about their business. Act normal, no need for *wahala* . . ."

"They don't know anything," Adaora said with a wave of her hand, returning to her microscope.

"I agree," Agu said, following her back to the counter. "And if Benson did, he's too dumb to process it. The president needs to come back. The last person they want in charge of what's happening on Bar Beach is Benson, trust me. Why is *he* the one they're interviewing?"

Adaora shrugged. "Looks like you did his body some damage, though."

"The man earned it."

"At least you know you didn't kill him."

Agu looked into Adaora's microscope as she scribbled more notes in her notebook.

"They can be anything and are nothing," she said as she wrote. "Basically, she's a shape-shifter." She smiled. "I wish my grandmother were alive to see this."

"Why's that?"

"She was always sure the markets were full of them, witches, shape-shifters, warlocks, things like that. This would blow her mind, *sha.*" She suddenly snapped her fingers, making Agu jump. "Ah-ah, what kind of technology must they *have?*"

"Do they even *need* it?" Agu asked. "I mean, in a way, they *are* technology. They can cha—"

Someone came running down the stairs.

"What is . . . Adaora, who are these people?" Adaora's husband, Chris, demanded. He still wore the jeans and wrinkled dress shirt he'd been wearing when they'd fought. As he moved down the stairs, he cut an intimidating figure, despite the fact that he'd been eating nothing but bread and water for the last two weeks. He slipped on the bottom step, cursing as he grabbed the banister and caught himself. Adaora groaned, mortified and feeling ill. Anthony didn't bother hiding his amusement as he laughed aloud and muttered, "*Kwasiasem.* Nonsense."

Chris glared at Agu, who was standing beside Adaora. Agu stepped away from her and Adaora flinched.

"While I'm *asleep?*" Chris said, striding up to Adaora. "In my own house? With our *children* right upstairs?!"

Adaora spotted her five-year-old son, Fred, and eight-year-old daughter, Kola, peeking down from the top of the stairs. "Jesus," Adaora whispered. She wanted to bring their presence to Chris's attention, but he was in too much of a rage. Adaora had managed to hide their physical altercation hours ago from the kids; she didn't want to push her luck. Even if he didn't hit her in front of them, he might bring the children into the argument. He'd done it a year ago, calling Kola into the room to ask her opinion about Adaora's refusal to stop listening to "filthy types of music." Poor Kola, who didn't want to speak against her father or her mother, had begun to cry. *No,* Adaora thought now. *Better he not notice the children.*

Behind her children crouched Philomena, the house girl, who should have been keeping them upstairs. A soft-spoken, chubby girl in her twenties, Philo had less and less control over

Fred and Kola these days. Adaora shelved this fact for another time.

"Chris," Adaora pled. "It's not . . ." She flinched as Chris raised his hand to slap her for the second time in three hours.

"You . . . you don't want to do that," Agu said, stepping in front of her. He sounded very unsure of himself.

Chris blinked, sizing Agu up. Agu may have had a raw face, but he was wearing a military uniform, he was taller, and he looked stronger. But Agu's demeanor clearly said that he didn't want to fight Chris at all. Chris lunged at Agu.

"CHRIS! STOP IT!" Adaora shouted, jumping back.

Agu easily threw Chris aside. He raised his hands. "Please," he begged. "Just listen. I don't—" But Chris got up and went for Agu again, throwing a punch and missing completely. Agu stepped to the side and clocked him one in the back of the head. Chris stumbled to the lab table, knocking test tubes into the sink and onto the floor.

"Shit," Agu hissed, distraught. "Not again, please not again!"

"Come on," Philo said, grabbing the children's hands and pulling them away.

"Na wetin dis?" Anthony said, stepping forward and hauling Chris to his feet. "Let it go, *chale*. Are you mad?!"

When Agu saw that Chris was still conscious, he sighed loudly with relief, bending forward to rest his hands on his knees.

Chris snatched his arm from Anthony and stood up on shaky legs, his nose bleeding. He glared at Adaora with that same hatred she'd seen hours ago just before he leaped on her. He opened his mouth to say something but instead cringed at the sound of metal balls on glass. "Eeeee!" he screeched. Adaora dug her nails into her thighs. Agu squeezed his face, pressing his hand to his mouth as he resisted the urge to grind his teeth. "Oooooh," Anthony moaned, feeling nauseous. If any of them had turned to look at Adaora's giant aquarium, they'd have seen the cowfish dart forward and smash into the glass, the shrimp fall to the aquarium floor, and several other fish swim in confused circles. It was a sound never heard on earth until this night.

When Chris turned around, he was staring at himself.

Adaora opened her mouth in utter astonishment, nearly forgetting to breathe.

"CHRIS!" Ayodele said. Her voice was identical to Chris's, as was her physique. Not only did she look like him, she was even wearing the same wrinkled dress shirt and jeans.

"Jesus," Adaora whispered. She stepped forward and grabbed Agu's arm and pulled him away. Anthony sucked his teeth at the ridiculousness of it all.

Chris's mouth hung open. He shook his head and blinked his eyes.

"Blame me," Ayodele said. "Your wife is just trying to help. Calm yourself. *Think.*"

There was a long pause as Chris stared at Ayodele. Then deep in his chest, he moaned and touched his own face with a shaky hand. He stepped back, then snapped around, turning a wild gaze on Adaora. He jabbed a finger at her. "You've poisoned me! Witch! I knew it! I am hallucinating because you've poisoned my body, o!" He took more steps back. "I shower my wife with everything she wants, only to realize I've fed the devil!" He stumbled toward the stairs. "Marine witch, o!" he wailed, pointing and pointing at her. "*Amusu!* I knew it! I knew it! Jesus Christ will send you back to hell, o! God will punish you! In the name of Jesus and the Holy Spirit!" He turned and fled up the stairs.

Adaora squeezed her eyes shut as she heard Ayodele change back. She'd heard the sound several times now, first in the water and now in her own home. In both places it somehow sounded the same. Absolutely foreign. So foreign, that hearing it made her feel like falling to the floor. She plopped down in the chair beside her computer.

"Your husband?" Agu asked as he dabbed the cut on his forehead with his fingers. It had started bleeding again.

"He works too hard and he's been fasting," she said. "It makes him a little . . ."

"That man does not love you," Anthony muttered.

Silence.

"You people are very interesting," Ayodele said, smiling.

CHAPTER 6

RED RED WINE

Chris shut his eyes and took a deep breath, inhaling the warm night air. Dirty Lagos air. So different from the air he'd breathed during his three-year stay in Germany for his MBA. He coughed. Since he'd begun fasting, he had to admit, he just hadn't felt right. He knew it was the witchcraft his wife had worked on him rebelling against his cleansing efforts. He *had* to keep fasting. Eventually it would all get better, he'd be free of her grasp and he'd be back in control of his life and his wife. Maybe.

He sat staring at the wrought-iron black gate that surrounded Father Oke's home, waiting. It was a solid gate built into a solid thick white wall that surrounded a magnificent compound. The fence around Chris's home was only wrought iron, so passers-by could see into the compound if they were nosy. He and his conniving wife Adaora did very well, but even they could not afford to build and maintain this kind of wall, not while building and maintaining the house itself.

On both sides of the wall were tiny houses where most likely ten times as many people lived. Poor people. These homes were surrounded by walls too, though the walls were really just the walls of the much larger home boxing them in. *Lagos is like a big zoo,* Chris thought. *Everyone is contained by lots of walls and lots of gates, whether you like it or not. It's secure but there is no security.*

He rubbed his red eyes as Father Oke slowly opened the gate. The man looked tired, but this was urgent. Such things warranted waking even a holy man in the middle of the night. Still, Chris was apologetic. "I'm so, so sorry to wake you, but . . ." He couldn't hold it in anymore. He wheezed and sobbed, leaning heavily on Father Oke's shoulder. He was too taken by his own emotions to notice the look of deep that annoyance passed over Father Oke's face.

"My wife . . . my . . . my . . . I don't know where else to go," Chris moaned into Father Oke's nightshirt.

Father Oke patted Chris's back and firmly pushed him backward. "What has happened?" he asked. He glanced with disgust at his shoulder, which was damp with Chris's tears. "You . . . you haven't done anything, have you?"

"No, no. Not me. I . . ."

Father Oke sighed with relief. "Come in, come in," he said. "Let us talk inside."

"Thank you, Father," Chris said as they walked between Father Oke's Mercedes and his BMW. Father Oke frowned as Chris passed a little too close to the BMW. He'd managed to keep the vehicle in perfect shape despite the Lagos roads, and he was not about to let this desperate idiot scratch it.

Chris and Father Oke sat across from each other on leather chairs. A bleary-eyed young woman in sleepwear came into the room with a bottle of red wine. Chris eyed the glass she poured for him, wondering if this would interfere with his fasting/purging of his wife's witchcraft.

"Relax, Chris," Father Oke said, seeming to read his thoughts. They watched the woman leave the room. "It will affect nothing. Wine is the beverage of Jesus. It can only do good."

Chris nodded, bringing the glass to his lips. His hand shook as he sipped.

"Well, Chris," Father Oke said. "What did you expect when you married a woman ocean biologist?"

"But she and I have known each other since we were small *children*," Chris said. "Our fathers were best *friends*. . . ."

Father Oke shook his head, putting his wine down and leaning forward. He had a pained look on his face, as if he carried a great burden on his shoulders. "Look, Brother Chris, women are . . . weak vessels. It is identified in the Bible. Your Adaora is a highly educated biologist but she's no different from the others. She could not change herself if she tried." He chuckled and sipped his wine. Then he laughed loudly. "*Kai!* But your wife is a tough one, o!"

"You really think she's a witch?" Chris asked.

"I do, Brother Chris," he said. "A *marine* witch, the worst kind. Look at her knowledge of the water. But don't worry, no shaking, o," he said, chuckling. "My church is powerful. It is my job to handle such things."

Chris sipped his wine, his hand still shaking. It left his mouth sour. "Good, because tonight she did something to me. I was trying to subdue her and suddenly I could not move! I was pinned to the floor like a goat for sacrifice!"

Father Oke frowned, but said nothing.

"Eh heh," Chris said, nodding and taking Father Oke's silence to mean he believed him. "And let me tell you what else. Only an hour ago, I came downstairs to her witch's den and found my wife with two strange men!" he said. "TWO! And there was . . . there was another. Another witch! She *changed* right before my eyes!"

"Eh, Brother Chris, slow down," Father Oke said, trying hard not to laugh at this sorry lamb of his flock. "It is imperative to fast, to purge your wife's witchcraft from your body. But you've been fasting so much, of late, and . . . perhaps you are not seeing what you think you're seeing?"

"I *know* what I saw, Father," Chris insisted. "This woman changed into ME! I can take you there right now! I can—"

"Relax, Brother Chris." Father Oke chuckled. "It's late." He sighed. "Okay, if your wife has brought another witch into your household, best to wait for daylight. I will come tomorrow."

"But . . ."

Father Oke made the sign of the cross. This always calmed his parishioners down. Now was no exception. Chris instantly quieted and relaxed. "Trust in the Lord, Brother Chris," Father Oke said soothingly. "All will be well in due time, eh? Meantime, pursue peace with your wife. Avoid the appearance of contention; women thrive on that. Do not fall for her antics. Look to Jesu Christi who asked us to turn the other cheek. Go home. Go to bed. I will see you tomorrow."

Sufficiently opiated by the words of his beloved priest, Chris felt better. He even gave a shaky smile. "I will, Father. Thank you. Oh, thank you."

CHAPTER 7

INTERVIEW

The digital video camera Adaora used when she went diving was old, and its battery was dead. But it still worked when plugged in. She put the camera on a tripod and set a folding chair in front of the fish tank. "Sit here," she told Ayodele. Adaora felt thick and groggy. While Agu and Anthony had stayed up watching TV with Ayodele and talking, she'd curled up on the sofa and gotten a few hours of sleep.

Adaora peered into the camera's window and was relieved when she could see Ayodele clearly. "Okay, good," she said. "Look this way." She pointed at the camera's lens. "Now, just talk, Ayodele, tell me about yourself."

Ayodele smiled and nodded, gazing into the camera. Adaora shivered. If there was any strong hint of the alien in Ayodele's appearance, it was in her eyes. When Adaora looked into them, she felt unsure . . . of everything. A college friend of hers used to say that everything human beings perceived as real was only a matter of the information their bodies recorded. "And that information isn't always correct or complete," he said. Back then, Adaora had dismissively rolled her eyes. Now, she understood.

"You have named me Ayodele. You people will call me an alien because I am from space, your outer heavens, beyond. I am what you all call an ambassador, the first to come and communicate with you people. I was sent. We landed in your waters and have been communicating with other people there and they've been good to us. Now we want *your* help."

"What do you eat?" Adaora asked.

"We take in matter," she said. "What we can find. Dust, stone, metal, elements. We alter whatever substance we find to suit us."

Adaora smiled. "But you are most fond of my jollof rice and fried plantain." Ayodele had eaten every scrap of food Adaora placed before her, and then several more platefuls, commenting the entire time about how enjoyable it all was. The only thing she hadn't really liked was bread.

Ayodele smiled. "In this form, consuming your jollof rice and fried plantain gave me great pleasure. And what was it? . . . Garden eggs and yam."

"You liked both of them raw . . . uncooked?" Adaora pressed.

"Yes, especially the garden eggs. The yam was nice too, though. It heightened my senses."

Adaora considered asking her for details of this but decided to move on instead. "Do you drink water?"

"In this form, yes."

"Do you enjoy taking human form?"

Ayodele smiled. "Yes."

"It's easy?"

"After the first time, yes."

"But it's hard the first time?"

"It's not easy."

"How do you change?"

"We have control of all our parts, great and small, and the forces influencing them."

"Can you die?" Adaora carefully asked.

Ayodele narrowed her eyes and looked at Adaora instead of at the camera. "Why do you ask that?"

"Because I'm a scientist," Adaora said. "I just want to know, to understand."

Ayodele turned back to the camera. "I prefer not to answer that."

"Why?"

But Ayodele just looked at the camera and said nothing.

"Okay, fine," Adaora said, after a moment. "Did you bring me, Agu, and Anthony together? Was that a coincidence? Why do all our names start with *A*?"

Across the room, Agu perked up.

"It was not a coincidence," Ayodele said. "I am an ambassador. I know—"

"Wait a minute!" Agu jumped up and rushed over. "Did you make all that happen so we'd all be there at the same time? Did you make my superior and the others attack that girl? Did you make me—"

"We are change," Ayodele calmly responded "The sentiments were already there. I know nothing about those other things."

"But *you* pushed them over the edge!" Agu said, stepping into the camera's view. "You hurt people! Do you understand *that*? You . . . I've seen what you can do, what you all are! You . . ."

"Agu," Adaora said. "I'm filming."

He shot Adaora a look that was way too similar to the one she'd seen in her husband's eyes. "Let me do this," she added quietly. "Please."

"Your husband *slapped* you!" he shouted. "Has he ever done that before?"

"No. But my husband and I have some . . . serious problems that I wouldn't blame Ayodele for in a million years. Would you really hold her responsible for your fellow soldiers, your *ahoa*, behaving that way? Think hard about it. They acted on impulses already present in their minds. And the other thing that happened . . . Was it her fault? Maybe it was yours."

Still breathing heavily, Agu shut his eyes, his shoulders slumping.

Adaora breathed a sigh of relief and turned back to Ayodele.

"So there are more of you?"

"Yes," she said.

"How many?"

"I don't know. We don't count ourselves."

"Many?"

"You would think so."

"And what do your people need?"

"Nothing. We have chosen to live here."

"Here on . . . earth?"

"Here."

"The land?"

"Your land."

"Africa?"

"Yes."

"So you are all over the continent?"

"No."

"Part of it? Like West Africa? Nigeria?"

"The city, Lagos?" Anthony asked, walking over.

Ayodele looked at him and grinned. "And the waters."

"Why Lagos? Why the water?" Adaora asked.

Ayodele shrugged. "These seemed good places for us."

Agu and Adaora both frowned deeply, but neither said a word.

Anthony laughed. "You bring in what you put out. Lagos . . ." He patted Agu and Adaora on the shoulders and dropped into Pidgin English. "'Lasgidi' you dey call am, right? Eko? Isn't that what you people call Lagos? Place of belle-sweet, *gidi gidi*, *kata kata*, *isu*, and *wahala*. Lagos is energy. It never stops. That's why I like coming here too."

"We can work with you people," Ayodele said. "And we will. We're coming."

Adaora stepped around and stood before the camera, looking into its eye. "Nine January, six thirty-nine a.m. You heard it directly from the horse's mouth. One is here, the rest are coming." She switched the camera off.

CHAPTER 8
MAMA?

The gateman opened the gate in the back of the house to let in the shiny silver Mercedes. He watched admiringly as it pulled into the side driveway. The vehicle gleamed like a diamond. The gateman had dreamed of owning such a car since he was a boy. Now that he was thirty-five, it was a fading dream, but one that still made him smile.

When the bishop got out, the gateman frowned and blinked. He always experienced the same mild surprise when this man came over. His brain simply couldn't hold the fact that a holy man could and wanted to afford such a vehicle. Ahmed Ubangiji was a Muslim and lived ten minutes away with his two wives and five children. He had nothing against Christians or any other people of the world. But a bishop displaying such extravagance seemed wrong. Then again, a lot of things seemed odd lately. He closed the gate and went back to his station to continue listening to the news of the flooding and strangeness on Bar Beach. If worse came to worst, he'd pack his family up and head north for a few days. Surely his boss would understand.

Father Oke stretched his arms and shut the car door. He'd been coming here too often, of late. Brother Chris was too needy. But he was one of Father Oke's biggest supporters, donating an ever-increasing amount of money from year to year. Brother Chris had been blessed by God, who'd made him a wealthy accountant. Even though his wife was a problem, she too brought in good money as

41

a professor and a scientist. Yes, they were good people to have in his congregation, so dealing with Chris more than he wanted to was worth it.

Father Oke dusted off his black suit and adjusted his immaculate white collar. His shiny shoes were spotless, which was just the way he liked them. He walked to the door where Chris was already standing. He must have been waiting for the last fifteen minutes.

"Good morning," Chris said, smiling a bit too widely.

They shook hands and went inside.

Adaora was scribbling frantically in her journal. She'd gone upstairs to make breakfast for her husband, the children, and Philomena. After assuring them that everything was okay, she'd run back to get her churning thoughts out of her mind. She had to remember every detail of the night's events. Of Ayodele's reactions, how they'd all met up, the sights, sounds, scents of the beach, everything. She was the scientist; the world would expect her to have the facts. Plus, it kept her from dwelling on the memory of her husband squirming on the ground as though held by invisible restraints. Ayodele and Agu were watching the news as Anthony paced the room.

"The mystery deepens hours after a sonic boom sounded somewhere off the waters of Bar Beach," the newscaster said. "The military cannot locate a source for the noise. Since the incident, however, and equally as mysterious, the sea level continues to rise. So far, it has risen over seven feet above its normal level. Lagos's lagoon is filling up, and people's homes, roads, and the beaches have flooded. Neither the military nor scientists have any answers at the moment."

Adaora rolled her eyes. *Of course they don't have any answers,* she thought. *And if they do, they're not going to share them.*

"What's happening?" Agu asked Ayodele, who was happily munching on a raw garden egg.

She bit, chewed, and swallowed the crunchy green-and-white tomatolike fruit for several moments before responding. "It's the ship," she said. "The size of it. The waters actually rose last night, not this morning, remember?"

"Yes, it was a big ship," Adaora said vaguely.

"It's not just the size," Ayodele said. "It is communicating with the water and the creatures in the water. We are communicative people."

Anthony continued to pace. He wrung his hands and wished he had a big fat joint, the finest *jamba*. "I don't know why I'm still here," he muttered to no one. "I should have left early this morning."

"It's because you can't," Agu said.

Anthony stopped pacing, annoyed that Agu was paying any attention to him. He'd been talking to himself.

"You can go home but nothing will change," Agu continued. "Who knows, they may have already overrun Accra."

Anthony flared his nostrils at the mention of his country's biggest city. "Don't say that."

Father Oke swept ceremoniously down the stairs followed by Adaora's husband and Philomena, the house girl. Father Oke was all smiles and pleasantries. "Good gracious morning, everyone," he said.

Chris said nothing, making a wide berth around Agu as he moved toward Adaora.

"This man again," Anthony muttered, glaring at Chris.

Agu and Chris glared at each other, and Adaora felt more than nervous. However, it wasn't Agu she suddenly wanted to protect. She placed herself between Ayodele and Father Oke. If there was one thing she knew about Father Oke, it was that he was a smooth-talking predator. She couldn't keep him from her husband, but she would keep him from her children . . . and Ayodele.

Philo sat on the stairs, took out her mobile phone, and discreetly started recording with the phone's camera.

"Adaora," Father Oke said. "Please introduce me to your . . . new friends."

"Good morning, Oke. What do you want?" Adaora asked. The man was a bishop, yet he insisted that people call him "*Father* Oke." This deeply annoyed Adaora, even before he'd sunken his claws into Chris.

"Greetings, my child," he said. "I—"

"How can I be your 'child'? You're only a few years my senior," Adaora snapped.

Father Oke didn't miss a beat. "You're a child of God."

"And you are God?" she asked.

He chuckled. "God speaks *through* me."

Adaora snorted, crossing her arms over her chest.

"I am not here to fight," he said. "You need to make peace with your husband."

Adaora felt rage heat her face. She clenched her fists, aware that everyone in the room was watching her. Slowly and deliberately, she said, "And how can we make peace when you are constantly meddling? You instruct him to starve himself like someone who does not have food! You convince him of your twisted nonsense." She stepped closer and Father Oke stepped back. "How does him *slapping* me in the *face* bring peace, *Father*? Eh? How can a man slap his wife 'in the name of Jesus'? *You* instructed him to do so! You think I didn't see your e-mail to him a week ago? 'Break her with your hands, then soften her with flowers.'"

Behind her, she saw Anthony shake his head in disgust. Agu glowered at Chris. Father Oke looked utterly flabbergasted. Chris looked shamefaced.

"You have little trust in your husband if you're reading his e-mails," Father Oke said coldly.

"Get OUT of my house!" Adaora screamed.

"*My* house, Adaora," Chris said.

"Oh my God, I'm going to kill someone this day, o," Adaora proclaimed. "Your house? Says who?"

"*Seke, seke, seke,*" Anthony muttered, still shaking his head.

Chris waved a dismissive hand at Adaora. "Father Oke is not here to speak with you, anyway," he said.

As if on cue, Father Oke slipped around Adaora. "What is your name, child?" he asked Ayodele, who'd been watching with quiet interest.

"I don't need a name," she said. "My people know me. But you may call me Ayodele."

"Are you a witch?" he asked.

"Will you slap her if she says yes?" Adaora snapped. She inhaled deeply, put her hands on her hips, and walked to the other side of the room. If she didn't step away, she knew she'd do something she'd regret.

"Why does this matter so much to you?" Ayodele asked Oke.

"Because I can *help* you." Father Oke stepped closer. "I'm trained to help you control your evil, to find grace and salvation and goodness."

"See?" Chris insisted. "She doesn't deny it. I saw her change. She—"

"You didn't come here to ask me about witchcraft," Ayodele said to Father Oke, ignoring Chris. "You have other things on your mind."

"What do you *want*?" Adaora loudly asked Father Oke from across the room. "People like you always *want* something."

"I want to *help*," he said to Ayodele. "Can . . . can you show me?"

Ayodele cocked her head as though considering Oke's offer.

"Don't!" Adaora said, rushing back over. But everyone heard the sound of metal balls on glass. Ayodele's skin was already rearranging itself. On the stairs, Philo gasped, still holding up her recording phone.

Ayodele had turned into an old woman with dark papery skin and runny blind eyes. Chris scrambled backward, whimpering.

Father Oke's face melted into something like grief and joy all at once. "Mama?" he whispered. He made the sign of the cross.

"I am not a witch; I am alien to your planet; I am an alien," Ayodele said in the voice of Father Oke's recently deceased mother. "We change. With our bodies, and we change everything around us."

"Ewo!" Father Oke exclaimed. He made the sign of the cross again. Philomena clapped her phone shut, and everyone turned to look up at her. "Sorry," she said, shooting to her feet. She ran up the stairs.

Father Oke smiled shakily, trying to look serene and pious when he felt like tearing out of that basement screaming. He didn't know if he believed in aliens or not. He'd never considered the question. If there *were* aliens, they certainly wouldn't come to Nigeria. Or maybe they would. He spread his hands and addressed the creature who was and was not his mother. "I have seen the news," he said. "I believe all that was caused by you, when . . . when you landed here; you coming here, it is all an act of God. I know you love God. Even if you are, *ahem*, from another place." As he spoke, his confidence grew. Speaking publicly always had this effect on him. It was why he had become a preacher.

"See it as . . . a personal race," he said, now truly smiling. "All of us have sinned! Human and . . . alien. No one on earth or in the cosmos is good or righteous. Hence God gave his only son to die for us!"

Adaora wanted to tell him to shove his nonsense up his ass. The man was the worst kind of charlatan. But Agu, now standing beside her, elbowed her to stay quiet.

"What?" Chris asked, perplexed. He'd come for a witch hunt, not a baptism. "But that doesn't—"

"Chris, can't you see?" Father Oke said, now completely enthralled by the sound of his own voice. He was on a roll. "I have been chosen to bring this creature and all of her kind into the *light!*"

Ayodele watched him blankly. Father Oke took her silence as affirmation. He was getting through to her. He had the gift of the gab. He could get through to *anyone*, even an extraterrestrial, such was the power of his faith. "Do you understand what I am saying?" he asked, certain that she did. His mission was clear; divine. "God, the Almighty, he is in control. Give yourself up to the Lord and any help you need to survive will be given to you. My church. My church is a *good* church. Come join my flock and we will be truly great." He held his hands out to Ayodele. When she didn't take them, he just kept talking. She was scared. Understandable. She was a blank slate, untilled alien soil. "You can shape-shift. That is a God-given ability," he said. "Maybe you can become one of my sisters in God. Join me on the pulpit and you and I will pull in a flock to be reckoned with!"

"See this man," Adaora said quietly to Anthony, "he's just trying to use her. So one-track minded. Even in the face of an extra-terrestrial, *sha*."

"That was obvious to me from the start," Anthony replied.

"If you join us, we can best *protect* you from the evil forces of these lands," Father Oke continued. He smirked knowingly. "In this house, anyone can come for you. It is not safe."

Ayodele opened her mouth to speak, but Father Oke held up a hand. "Don't," he said. "Just think about it for now. We will come back to hear your answer later today."

Ayodele shrugged and said, "Okay."

Father Oke nodded, slowly backing toward the stairs, grinning. He motioned for Chris to follow.

"Oh," Chris said softly, as if waking from a dream. "Okay." He scurried past Father Oke, up the stairs.

"It was wonderful to meet with you, Ayodele," Father Oke said. Then with a wave, he whirled around and followed Chris up the stairs.

Adaora let out a breath of relief. "Can you imagine?"

Ayodele was smiling. "This place is fascinating, o," she said. "*Na wao*. That man, I could see all his ideas!"

Adaora noted how Ayodele was even picking up slang. She frowned as she said, "You're not seriously—"

"We need to get her out of here," Agu interrupted. "Soon."

Anthony nodded vigorously. "My father was a preacher," he said. "I know that man's kind. He'll return with his entire congregation. Oh *chale*, of all the people your husband could have brought . . ."

"I know," Adaora replied darkly. "Once word gets out, the kidnappers will start arriving too."

CHAPTER 9

MOZIZ

"Mama?" they watched Father Oke slowly ask.

Despite what he had just seen, Moziz snickered. He knew Father Oke. The man sponged plenty of naira from his grand-mother every Sunday, leaving her with barely enough to buy gari and bags of "pure water." When the footage ended, Moziz clicked replay on Philo's mobile phone to watch it again.

Philo smiled. Back at her employers' house the children were still asleep, and she'd chanced leaving for a half hour to come to see her boyfriend, Moziz. It was worth the risk; she loved to see Moziz happy. She loved Moziz. She looked around his sparse one-bedroom flat. Nothing but a computer on a desk, a chair, and the mattress they sat on. He didn't have much, but he kept his flat spotless. Damn near sterile, from the smell of disinfectant it always carried. Moziz hated roaches, and this "face me, I face you" building was full of them.

A struggling medical student forced to take the year off due to strikes, Moziz was the most educated guy she knew. He was quite dark-skinned and short (neither of which suited Philo's tastes), but he was articulate, ambitious, and crafty. At the moment, he was making most of his money from 419 scams on his computer, but Philo knew this was only temporary. She was certain that Moziz was meant to be somebody, just like his name implied. The actual spelling of his name was "Moses," but he'd changed it because he thought it sounded cooler.

"Eyyy!" Moziz exclaimed as he watched Ayodele change again. He laughed hard. "Look at Father Oke! De man wey dey do *gragra* before see as he dey shake like waterleaf! He don nearly shit for him pant!"

Philo smiled. She'd bagged an educated man *and* he spoke like a man of the streets.

"Baby, dis ting na real? Abi na film tricks?" he asked.

"I say I take my two naked eyes see de thing as e happen, just like two hours ago," she assured him, dropping into Pidgin English too.

He pinched his smooth chin pensively with his fingers. Philo could practically hear his brilliant mind working. He really was the sharpest man she knew. She'd chosen well. With him, she'd surely have a good, easy life.

"True true, you say dis woman na from space? You say she come from space?"

"Na so she talk. She say no be only her come, she come with many others wey still dey for inside dem ship wey land inside Bar Beach."

"Okay, o," Moziz said. "Well, if dem get flying ship, wetin again dem get wey we no sabi?" He narrowed his eyes. "Maybe we fit tell am to print original naira notes for us, o. Yes na, if she fit change herself, na him be say she fit do other things, too! Miracle! Heiyaaa! Na so na! Na so universe law be, o, no be mek de law."

"Maybe," Philo said.

"In fact sef, no be even naira we go ask am to make for us," he said. "American dollars! Or even euro. Euro cost pass dollar, so na euro we go tell am to make for us!"

Philo shrugged and laughed. "If she fit do am na, dat one no be problem. But I no sabi if she fit do am, o."

"*Kai*, dis one na something, o," he said, now grinning with all his teeth. "Baby, dis one na something. You do well show me dis video."

Philo giggled as he caressed her cheek. His hand slowly made its way to her left breast. "You fit get me inside dere?" he asked, his voice lusty in her ear.

"I go try, baby," she whispered. She lay back and as he climbed on top of her, his computer beeped the arrival of a new e-mail. He paused, looking at the monitor.

"Mek una wait! Mek una wait! Eh? All of una wey be e-mail fit wait for now!" he said, turning back to Philo.

CHAPTER 10

THE PLAN

"Please, all of you, come," Ayodele said, sitting beside Adaora on the right side of the sofa.

They couldn't leave now. There would be checkpoints. And checkpoints were potential trouble; Agu knew this best. Ayodele didn't seem bothered.

"Kola, Fred, out," Adaora snapped, noticing them peeking into the room from the top of the stairs.

Philomena came rushing down, out of breath. "Sorry, Madame," she said. She took Kola's and Fred's hands. "I was . . . I was in the bathroom. Kola, come. It's time for lunch."

"Mommy, we want to see the alien," Kola demanded.

"How do you . . . ugh, Kola, go!" Adaora snapped. "Upstairs, now!"

The startled children snatched their hands from Philo's and ran up the stairs. Philo followed.

Adaora shut her eyes and sighed, tired. Agu plopped on the left side of the sofa, looking equally as exhausted and far more physically battered. It was around two p.m. and none of them had gotten even an hour of sleep. The television news droned on about the rising water, how the government still did not know who was attacking Nigeria, and how government offices and facilities were closed for the day.

"You three were chosen," Ayodele said. "You made sense. I know we've made the right choice."

"Wharreva," Anthony drawled. He was sitting on the coffee table, his long legs stretched before him. He seemed more interested in the chaos on the news than in Ayodele.

"Adaora, you understand water," Ayodele said. "You'll soon also understand something about yourself, and what's to come. You can explain."

"Myself? Meaning? And will you people affect the water?" Adaora asked. She remembered what she'd seen when they were under the sea. In the surrounding glowing water had been a riot of bright yellow butterfly fish, clown fish, sea bass, eels, shrimps, urchins, starfish, sharks, stingrays, swordfish, barracuda, a bit of everything local; some from the deep, some from the shallows. She'd never seen such a thriving coral community in any of her dives off the coast of Lagos. Would they come *out* of the water?

Ayodele took her hand and Adaora instantly stiffened. Ayodele's hand felt warm and remarkably . . . human. "Agu, soldier," Ayodele continued, looking into Agu's eyes. "You come from a family of yam farmers, they are the salt of the earth to you. They represent the heart of Nigeria. You joined the army to protect them. Now you understand your army is corrupt. You need a people to join."

The clear truth of her words warmed every part of his body and left him speechless.

She smiled. "*And* you have a direct connection to your country's leader, your president. Your superior is his relation and can reach him quickly."

Agu and Adaora looked at each other, uncomfortable. Agu wiped his eyes and began to explain. "Yes . . . but our president is . . ."

Adaora shook her head and Agu shut up. Ayodele didn't seem to notice. "Anthony," she said.

"What?" he snapped. "*Haba*, what about me?" He turned away.

Adaora almost chuckled, marveling at the fact that he was nothing like his public persona. He was actually rather reserved. He certainly hadn't bulged his eyes and randomly screamed, "Anthony DEY CRAZE!" once since she'd met him.

"You are a communicator, like us," Ayodele told Anthony. "You spent the most time with the Elders. You've heard their song. Even *I* can't imagine what you've learned."

Adaora and Agu both looked at Anthony, who backed away. Tears started to roll from his eyes. Helplessly, he held up his hands. "I . . . I don't want any part of this," he said, his voice quivering. "Okay? I just want to leave." His lower lip trembled. "But I can't stop *hearing* it." He took a deep breath, steadying himself. "*Chale*, it . . . it is beautiful. I was hearing it during my concert, too. That's why I needed to go out for some air afterward." His wet eyes grew wide. "I was seeing *trees* grow between the crowds. . . ."

He sat down hard on the sofa, breathing heavily. He wasn't going anywhere.

"This house is a good location. You will draw a crowd here," Ayodele said, smiling.

Anthony untied the veil from around his neck and wiped his face with it. Agu stood very stiff, gazing at the fish tank. And Adaora looked at Agu's hands, wondering if they'd changed size when he'd punched his superior into unconsciousness.

"Anthony, you understand, correct? You must call the people to you," Ayodele told him. "The way my people operate, we need a gathering, first." She turned to Agu before Anthony could ask why. "Agu," she said. "Go to your *ahoa* superior. Explain things to him. Take Adaora as your expert. You know what you must convince him to do." And both Adaora and Agu knew very well.

It was time to find the president.

CHAPTER 11

WAHALA

Moziz took a deep hit from the joint Troy handed to him. "Pass am give de others, e still plenty," he croaked as he held in the smoke. Troy, Tolu, and Jacobs, also students forced to "take time off" because of university strikes, had just arrived, and he wanted them to be relaxed when they watched the footage on Philo's phone. He let them smoke.

They were outside at the old table under the tree behind his apartment, a nice quiet spot. He squinted at them through dry red eyes, knowing that they were waiting for him to speak. He'd sent urgent texts to each of them saying it was a matter of lots of money. Still, right now, they knew not to rush him.

Philo looked at her watch. She could make it back to the house in about five minutes if she ran. And today Sir and Mistress were so preoccupied that they didn't even notice when she was gone, and the children didn't mind her absence. For now, she leaned against the tree, her arms around her chest. She was nicely sore from the early afternoon with Moziz. He'd made her a thousand and one promises in the dark, including marriage and a big, big house. All would come true once he got the creature to do what he knew it could do. She felt a tingle of arousal between her legs as she watched him eye his friends.

After they'd seen the footage, Tolu, Troy, and Jacobs stared at the phone. None of them knew what the fuck to think. Moziz's girl Philo wasn't smart enough to make up something so extraordinary, and Moziz had no reason to. And that meant what they saw could only be real.

"E get anybody here wey no still believe wetin e don see with him own eye?" Moziz asked, after Tolu, Troy, and Jacobs had watched the film another three times.

Tolu handed the phone back to Moziz. He held it out using only his thumb and index finger, as if it were contaminated.

"Lagos don scatter for confusion sake of say dem no fit know wetin dis kine *wahala* come mean," Moziz said, getting up. Like Father Oke, Moziz knew when he had people wrapped around his finger, and he reveled in it. He sat on the table before Troy, Tolu, and Jacobs. "*We* know wetin e be. And one of them dey my girlfriend *oga* house. Una don see am unaself. Na from space dem come. Dem get ability to change dem shape and dem body as dem like. Now, na only imagine person fit imagine all de many many other things dem fit do." He leaned forward. "Una know wetin we fit do if we kidnap them? Tink am well well!" He held up a fist for emphasis. He leaned back. "Ol' boy! If we no act and move fast now, na our chance we don miss be dat, o."

When none of them said a word, Moziz continued, "De first thing we go ask am to do na to print money for us. Naira, notes, American dollar notes, euro, even sef, pound sterling! My people, nobody go rich like us! We fit even tell am to enter online people bank accounts too. Fuck all de 419 rubbish, we go bypass dem middleman dem and go direct to the money."

Troy asked, in a small but worried voice, "If danger come dey all this plan, *nko*?"

Jacobs and Tolu murmured agreement. Moziz gave Troy a very foul look. "No worry," he said. "Na woman de ting be, o. Look am."

Troy frowned at this. Something wasn't right about what Moziz was saying, but he wasn't sure what it was. But he felt Moziz was right, what he'd seen in the video was just a woman. She looked like a slightly older version of his sister, even. She had to be harmless. She'd be easy to kidnap.

Tolu liked the idea of kidnapping the alien well enough, but more importantly, he didn't want to cross Moziz when he was in one of his moods.

Jacobs didn't like the idea at all. If the woman was an alien who could shape-shift, she wasn't *just* a woman. And maybe that made her dangerous. However, Jacobs *did* like the idea of getting rich. It was about time. He'd been a struggling university student long enough. He took the phone from Moziz and watched the footage again. He glanced at Troy and Tolu. Both were looking intently at Moziz, and Moziz was enjoying their attention. Discreetly, Jacobs sent the footage to his own phone.

"See," Moziz said. "We catch am, carry am, come my place. We go rich before sun go down. Na who no 'gree? She just woman; she no dey harm."

They were all in. Moziz glanced at Philomena, blew a kiss, and then flicked his tongue at her. Philomena smiled shyly, glad that no one could see the ache between her legs and the hopeful dreams in her head.

CHAPTER 12

MAY THE LORD CONTINUE TO FAVOR YOU

That afternoon, the church was packed, thanks to the television, newspaper, and radio, though not so much the Internet. According to the media, the water along all the beaches was "rising at an alarming rate!" and pushing into the lagoon. Government buildings and independent businesses were all "closed until further notice!" There had been an "excruciatingly loud racket tumbling off the ocean." Something was amiss, and everyone was getting ready for whatever would come next.

Some packed up and fled for the rural villages where they had built homes that they normally only stayed in during holidays. The wealthy and influential tried unsuccessfully to procure plane tickets to the United Kingdom, Germany, and the United States. Some even tried to fly to Ghana and Cameroon. But all planes everywhere were grounded indefinitely due to the unidentified sonic boom. Many flocked to mosques. And, in Lagos, hundreds flocked to the church of Father Oke. For many, Father Oke's church was exactly the refuge they sought.

Father Oke smiled grandly as he moved away from his wooden pulpit toward the three kneeling women. Behind him stood his bodyguards, just to keep an eye on things, keep everyone safe. As he stepped before the women, he glanced down at his expensive gold-tipped white loafers. They peeked out from beneath his spotless white robe. He was looking sharp.

He moved his eyes from his shoes to the first kneeling woman.

He had to work hard to keep his disgust from showing. He could almost smell her. *Peasant,* he thought. *Rubbish. Filth.* But he would take her money.

"What do you want?" he asked.

"I'm a winch."

The audience gasped.

He blinked, shocked. Her words pricked him like a needle. "*What* did you say?"

"I'm not a winch. I'm a winch . . . for Jesus," she said.

Her voice was flat, her face slack as she looked up at him with stupid eyes. She wore an old white blouse and a long blue skirt. From what he could see, she was flat-chested and her coarse hair was untouched by refining chemicals. She might have been about twenty. *This idiot must be one of those empty-headed girls who was dropped as a baby,* he thought. A waste of a woman.

"What is 'winch'? Do you know what that is? Can't you speak English? Are you uneducated?"

"I'm sorry," the woman said in her flat voice. "My English no be good, o."

"Witch. You are a witch?"

"Yes, for Jesus."

He felt the rage rise in him before he could control it. This . . . this common piece of female trash in his glorious church had the nerve to admit to the greatest sin! To his face! In front of his swollen congregation!

"You are a FOUL DEVIL! Do you know who you are speaking to? Foul *devil!*" He brought his hand back and slapped her across the face as hard as he could. The women beside her screeched.

"Praise Jesus," several of the audience members shouted. Others applauded.

Still, as his hand connected to her face, he regretted his action. He'd gone too far, he knew it. He glanced to the side of the stage where the camera was recording everything today. And did he also spot a young man in the audience with his mobile phone open? *Shit,* he thought. But the woman had just made him so goddamn angry. *How dare she?* He started walking away from her but then walked back. He couldn't leave it at that. He didn't know what he would do, but he couldn't leave it at that. He had to remain in control of the situation. Make it work for him.

"Where are you from?" he demanded. He couldn't get the anger out of his voice.

"I'm from Imo State," she said, tears in her eyes. But she stayed kneeling. *Good,* he thought.

"Where did you learn witchcraft from?"

"I'm not a winch. . . ."

"Who are you?"

". . . but I am a winch for Jesus."

GODDAMMIT! he thought, the rage flaring up in him again. *Again, she says it! What is wrong with this bitch of the devil? And look how she speaks so defiantly! Maybe she IS a witch!* He stood up straight and looked out at his captivated audience. He smiled, taking a deep breath. Then he nodded to them, taking several more. *Calm,* he thought, his heart rate slowing. Steady.

"Jesus has no witches! You are a demon!" he roared. But he spoke with controlled passion now. Confident power. His audience jumped up and shouted and applauded. He looked at the kneeling woman and again felt his heart rate try to surge. He stifled the urge to slap her a second time as she mumbled something. He put his hand in her face, refusing to hear another word. "All of you, know this! Whoever speaks a lie shall be *struck down!* Now, foul devil, get out of here before God kills you right on my stage." The other two women got up, and quickly dragged the woman he'd slapped off-stage. He hoped that the audience beat up every single one of them. In the name of Jesus.

He dabbed his face with his handkerchief. He was riled up. He needed to calm down. Today was about something special, not about idiot peasant women. Before this stupidity, for three hours, spittle flying from his lips and sweat dripping from his face, he'd preached about *change* and *opposites* and *progress*. He'd hedged around the *real* matter at hand, building to the climax that would bring it home. He knew exactly how he'd broach the topic with his loyal followers. The energy was high already. His confrontation with the witch meant he had their undivided attention. *This* was the moment. He called on Chris to stand in his front pew and speak to Father Oke's flock. The other man stumbled to the pulpit, looking ragged.

"My wife . . . She is troubled," Chris said. He wrung his hands, desperate and stressed. He was so glad that Father Oke had finally let him say his piece. He needed help. Salvation.

The congregation murmured encouragement.

"Something has taken her," he said, wrapping his arms around himself. There were sweat marks around the collar and the armpits of his white cotton shirt. He'd worn this same shirt two days in a row to work. "I don't know how to say this. . . ."

People shouted and clapped encouragingly.

"I'm sorry to say, my wife has become a marine witch, o!" he announced grandly.

The church exploded with indignation, and Chris's heart swelled. Tears gathered in his eyes. "I need help!" he shouted, clenching his fists.

"You will get *am!*" a man shouted back.

"*Kai!* God will help you, o!" a woman shouted.

"The Lord will favor you, o!" a child shouted.

Some condemned the heathens who did not go to church. Some shouted about how it was all coming to pass. Whatever "it" was, only they knew. They announced that the ocean would soon swallow them all up for the sins of these marine witches and warlocks, nonbelievers in Christ who'd taken over the country. Some blamed the Muslims of the north. Others blamed the Americans.

Al-Qaeda. Sickness. The British. Bad luck. Devils. Poverty. Women. Fate. 419. Biafra. The bad roads. The military. Corruption.

Father Oke raised his hands to quiet his flock of sheep. He had the answers for them. He was holy. They grew silent, including Chris, who looked at Father Oke in earnest. As much as he could love a man, in this moment, he loved Father Oke very much.

"Have no fear!" Father Oke told Chris. "*I* will save your wife."

His sheep sighed with relief.

"Tell everyone about your wife's friend, Brother Chris," he said.

Chris nodded, but frowned. What did his wife's cure have to do with that one? But he trusted Father Oke. "Last night," Chris said, "my wife brought something home with her. A . . . a visitor. A true visitor. I saw—"

Father Oke quickly spoke up. "A visitor from outer *space*! An alien! An extraterrestrial!" he said, dramatically rolling his *r*'s. The entire church went silent. This was the shock Father Oke had hoped to cause. Perfect. "It is in Brother Chris's home! It is only the first of many!" he continued. "You see the news, all these strange things happening. We are being *visited*, my friends."

He paused as people started talking among themselves.

"*Kai!* I knew it!" a man exclaimed to the woman beside him. "Didn't I tell you? There is no smoke without fire!"

"Why here? Why here?"

"I didn't see a damn thing last night."

"We all go die, o!"

When the chatter began to swell into panic, Father Oke shouted, "Calm down! Calm down! Listen!"

Near instant silence. He had these people eating out of his hand. It was beautiful. *Thanks be to God*, he thought. "You have seen today how I handle witches and their devilry. Have faith in my power to heal! Now, these visitors, my friends, they mean us no harm," he said. He laughed confidently and leaned against the pulpit, holding his microphone to his lips. "I have *seen* the one at Brother Chris's house. These are *people* who need to be saved! We will welcome them, enfold them into our flock. Wash them in the Blood of Christ! Make them immaculate." He paused, smiling at their frightened faces.

"Who will join me? Who will come with me to Brother Chris's home to enfold this intelligent creature into our flock? Who will make our church the first in all of Lagos, in the WORLD, to do such a thing? Who will come with me and do God's will?"

There was only silence. Father Oke looked into the crowd of faces, and what he saw made him feel a pinch of doubt. Cowards. All of them. Frail. Afraid. *The Lord has given me weak vessels,* he thought with despair. Then someone in the back started singing. The voice was shaky and panicked. Father Oke knew who it was: Memory Fulami, one of his craziest parishioners. She'd joined his flock four years ago and came to church twice a day. She sang too loudly, smelled like dirty sweat, and was known for shouting at girls who wore tight jeans. She drove him crazy. She had a voice that would kill every cockroach in that filthy "face me, I face you" compound she lived in down the road. But at this moment, of his entire congregation, he loved her the most. Father Oke dug his nails into his leg as he fought to hold the pleasant smile on his face.

"Count your blessings, see what God has done,
Count your blessings, name them one by one,
And it will surprise you what the Lord has done."

The others began to join her. Maybe it was to drown out her awful voice or maybe it was a show of true solidarity. It didn't matter. Soon the entire church was singing their support for Father Oke.

Everyone except Chris.

CHAPTER 13

CHIN CHIN

They stood in Adaora's living room, uneasy. The afternoon sun streamed in, bouncing off the white leather couches and chairs and the white carpet on the floor. The fans were on, and Philo had set out a bowl of chin chin on the coffee table. It was a room for relaxing. Not for thinking about the end of the world as one knew it.

Adaora was beginning to see why Ayodele's people had chosen the city of Lagos. If they'd landed in New York, Tokyo, or London, the governments of these places would have quickly swooped in to hide, isolate, and study the aliens. Here in Lagos, there was no such order.

Yet and still, the country had vigorous life. Her best friend, Yemi, had put it perfectly one night after they'd finished taking final exams and were talking about where they'd go when they graduated. Yemi had had too much to drink, yet her words and thoughts were clear and eloquent that Adaora still remembered her words well. *Everybody wants to leave Lagos. But nobody goes, she said. Lagos is in the blood. We run back to Lagos the moment we step out, even though we may have vowed never to come back. Lagos is Lagos. No city like it. Lagos is sweet.* Even Adaora's husband, Chris, knew this. He'd returned from Germany as soon as he had his MBA in his hand, even though a German company had offered him a job.

It was the reason why, despite the fact that she was a highly sought-after marine biologist who'd taught for some years at the University of California, Santa Barbara, she'd opted to return home.

Lagos was riddled with corruption, but she couldn't imagine living anywhere else. And its ocean life was fascinating. And problematic. It needed her. Lagos needed her. And Adaora had to go where she was needed.

There were aliens in the ocean, and they were going to come out soon.

"Text me if there's trouble," Anthony said.

"I've memorized your phone number," Agu said, tapping the side of his head. "Better up here than on a piece of paper." Still, he'd written it down, folded the paper, and placed it deep in his pocket, just in case something made him forget.

Adaora looked at Agu. "Will there be trouble?"

"Look at my face, o," Agu said. "My commander might make some *wahala*. But I think he'll be smart enough to focus on the crisis at hand."

Adaora wasn't so sure, but she didn't press the issue. It was worth a try. If they could reach the president, then things would go far more smoothly than if they did not. "Anthony, Philomena is upstairs with the children," she said. When she was teaching and Chris was working, Philomena stayed with the children, but today she didn't like the idea of being away from them. She'd get back as soon as possible and she hoped Chris would too. "Stay close to Ayodele, okay?" Ayodele was downstairs in the lab reading an issue of *National Geographic*.

"Of course I will," Anthony said.

"Call if Adaora's husband comes home with more *wahala*," Agu said.

"I sent him a text, warning him to leave you alone," Adaora added. "But he didn't respond."

"I can handle the man," Anthony said.

"And if you can't, Ayodele can, eh?" Agu said, winking.

"Ibi so," Anthony assured her, slapping hands with Agu and giving Adaora a brief hug.

As soon as they left, Anthony took out his mobile phone and dialed. "Festus," he said, smiling. He could always reach Festus, the one person in the entire Ghanaian music industry that he trusted.

"Where the hell are you?" Festus yelled.

"Relax. I'm fine."

"You should have called to let me know that," Festus growled. "You disappeared from your own after-party!"

"Sorry, o. Trust me, I have a good excuse."

"I thought you'd been kidnapped."

"I wasn't," Anthony said. "Listen, Festus, I have a job for you and the boys."

As he told Festus an abbreviated version of all that had happened since he'd left the club where he'd performed, he strolled to the window. The gate in front was high, but flimsy. People could see the entire house, but someone would have to open the gate to get to the front door. A good space for a crowd. As long as it stayed polite.

Festus reacted just the way Anthony had hoped. He exclaimed with surprise and asked a thousand questions. Then Festus came up with the perfect way to alert Anthony's fans about the "Mad mad Anthony Dey Craze free concert" that would take place on the lawn of a small Victoria Island home. "Through radio, social networks, and word of mouth," he said. "Everybody go know!" Anthony could hear Festus grin his toothy grin. At heart, Festus was an instigator, so he didn't feel guilty about the fact that it was all a ruse to bring people together for something outlandish.

"I just hope you know what you're doing," Festus said.

Anthony pulled at his short beard and bit his lip. He did . . . sort of. "I do."

While Anthony planned with Festus, Adaora's children, Kola and Fred, peeked into the room from the hallway. When Anthony didn't notice them, they oh-so-quietly tiptoed across the room to the stairs leading down to their mother's lab.

★ ★ ★ ★

Kola had to work hard not to burst out laughing. Fred wasn't help-ing. He always started giggling uncontrollably whenever they sneaked past adults. Kola had to stop for a moment; her belly was cramping from holding in all her laughter. It was funny but also really annoying. Somehow, they made it to the lab entrance.

Bellies aching, they descended the stairs and peeked in on the alien. Preoccupied with a *National Geographic* magazine, Ayodele didn't seem to notice as the two cautiously crept into the lab and hid behind the fish tank. All was silent except the tank's bubbling filter. Kola softly tapped on the glass to get a yellow butterfly fish to swim out of her line of vision. She was about to sneak closer when Fred grabbed her arm.

"What?" she hissed.

"Scared!" Fred whispered.

"Don't you want to speak to a real live *alien*?" Kola asked. "Like the ones in the movies?"

Fred vigorously shook his head. "I've changed my mind."

"Well, I do," Kola said. She stood up straight and nervously grabbed a handful of her long braids. "Hello."

Ayodele smiled, though her eyes didn't leave her magazine. "Greetings, children."

"I'm . . . Kola and that's my little brother, Fred."

Still cowering behind the fish tank, Fred waved a feeble hello.

"Are you *really* an alien?" Kola asked.

Ayodele closed her magazine and looked at Kola. "By your defi-nition, yes."

"Well, how come you look human?"

"Would you rather I didn't?"

"Why not appear as yourself?"

"Human beings have a hard time relating to that which does not resemble them. It's your greatest flaw."

Kola liked this answer very much because it made sense. In

cartoons, even the animals who could talk also had to *look* human. That had always annoyed her brother. She stepped closer.

"How come you speak English?" Kola asked.

"So you will understand me."

"Can you speak Hausa?"

"*Ii*," she said, with a nod.

"Igbo?"

"*E-eh*," Ayodele said, nodding again.

"Russian?"

"I can if I get close to someone who can, yes. You cannot, so I cannot."

Kola had to agree. She could indeed speak Igbo and Hausa and not Russian. "Do you like it here?"

"I do."

"You might have liked the United States more," she said. "They've got more stuff. And if your spaceship is broken, they can probably fix it better."

"Our ship is not broken."

"My mother says the waters are all dirty and dead because of the oil companies," Kola said. "Will you all be all right in there?"

Ayodele laughed in a knowing way that made a thousand more questions germinate in Kola's head. "Yes," Ayodele said.

"Can you die?"

"Maybe. Probably not."

"*Na wao*," Kola whispered with awe. She leaned against the sofa, now only a foot from Ayodele. This was the most interesting person/thing/whatever she'd ever met. "So, how *old* are you?"

Philomena came running down the stairs. "Kola! Get away from her! . . . Get up here! Fred!"

His fear for his sister, and of the strange woman who looked like his aunt in Asaba, finally exploded, and Fred went running to Philomena, the only person other than his parents who could get his sister Kola to behave. Kola reluctantly left Ayodele's side. "We just wanted to ask some questions," Kola said, when she reached Philo.

"I'd never hurt them," Ayodele said.

Philomena pushed Kola up the stairs. "Why would I believe *anything* you say? I don't even know what you *look* like, let alone what you will do to us." She rudely sucked her teeth and over her shoulder muttered, "Nonsense."

"Maybe you should try asking me, then," Ayodele said flatly.

Philomena was halfway up the stairs. "Stay away from the children."

"School will bring you more success than marriage," Ayodele said, raising her voice.

Philomena turned and glared at Ayodele.

"I know what your boyfriend is planning and I know why you told him about me," Ayodele said. "In the end, only you can make yourself happy. Finish school. Forget him."

Philomena dug her nails into the wooden banister. Then she ran up the stairs.

CHAPTER 14

THE BLACK NEXUS

No matter how carefully Jacobs walked, his heels made too much noise. *Click, click, click.* The hallway of the abandoned secondary school amplified the sound. It was afternoon and the sun shone brightly outside, and he was wearing his favorite long black dress and high heels. They'd parked right beside the building and quickly run inside. Right now was a terrible time to draw attention to himself, but he couldn't show up to this meeting speaking the Pidgin English he spoke with the guys, nor could he arrive *dressed* like a "guy." He needed to present this new development to his friends as *himself.* He needed to show he was serious and unafraid.

"Walk faster," Jacobs instructed, wincing at the sound of his footsteps as they picked up speed.

"It's been such a weird day," said Fisayo, her heels clicking just as loudly. "Everything being closed, all the checkpoints . . . the *wahala* at Bar Beach. My God, Jacobs, I don't know what I saw last night, but whatever's going on is *not* over."

"Trust me, I know," he said, putting a strong arm around his sister's shoulder and giving her a squeeze of reassurance. He was glad she was okay. He'd hated leaving her to walk Bar Beach looking for work alone. Usually he stayed around to at least make sure she was okay, but last night he had eaten some bad soup and thus had a bad case of indigestion. And look what had happened to her.

Worse yet, she'd probably want to return to Bar Beach when they finished here. She'd go home, change, and get herself ready and arrive at Bar Beach in the evening. Right now was the best time to pick up the safest johns. Late-afternoon johns were looking for a girl to spend an evening with, and this usually included fine treatment and a meal. Evening johns were crueler and looking for something less companionable.

Jacobs needed to spend more time with his younger sister. In the last month, he hadn't even had the time to stop by her apartment. Not that she'd have been home. Fisayo was rarely home. After all the crazy events in Lagos, today was the first chance he'd gotten to see her.

He'd met with Moziz, Tolu, and Troy earlier, so he'd only briefly heard Fisayo's bizarre story about what she'd seen on Bar Beach when the boom hit. And that conversation was via mobile phone. He'd said nothing about the footage Moziz had shown him and the others, or the plan to kidnap the alien. Not yet.

"Yes, I think things are going to get weirder, too," he said. "That's why I don't want you on the streets."

"Bar Beach is closed anyway," she shrugged. "My regular guys won't even know where to find me."

The executive members of the Black Nexus, Rome and Seven, stood up when Jacobs and his sister entered the empty classroom. Rome was immaculate, as always. Tall, lean, and as statuesque as a runway model, he wore dark blue skinny jeans and a loose white blouse. His tiny gold hoop earrings perfectly accented his closely cut hair. Even without makeup, he passed as a beautiful woman. Though he never outright said he was one, most people on campus just assumed. Seven was only an inch shorter than Rome. She had the curves of Osun the Yoruba goddess, a shiny bald head, and eyes so expressive she barely had to speak.

The two were the presidents of one of the only LGBT student organizations in Nigeria, the Black Nexus. Though most of its members were out or semi-out, the group still only met secretly once a month, in the dead of night. This was not one of those meetings. It was the afternoon, and this meeting's purpose was more specific.

"Hi there," Rome said, giving them each a hug.

"It's good to see you," Seven added, her voice low and husky. The hug she gave Fisayo lasted much longer than the one she gave Jacobs. Fisayo shyly stepped back. She was in no way attracted to women, yet Seven always made her want to giggle like a schoolgirl.

Seven didn't have to invite Jacobs and Fisayo to have a seat. They could read it in her eyes. Seven and Rome sat on desks across from them.

"Okay, man, what's so important that you dragged us out when Lagos is on lockdown?" Seven said, leaning forward. Her eyes added, *And it better be a* good *reason.*

"It's a good reason," Jacobs said, bringing out his mobile phone. "Come close. It's better if we all see it at the same time."

Jacobs had a nice phone, so the footage was even clearer than it had been on Moziz's cheap disposable one. Jacobs had watched it at least fifty times, and it still blew his mind. She was a young woman, then she seemed to turn inside herself to become a smoky, metallic-looking cloud, then she turned inside out again to become a completely different woman who was old and bent. She'd even spoken with an ancient-sounding voice. And Jacobs knew the man the shape-shifting thing was talking to; he was the bishop of his mother's diocese. His mother had gotten Jacobs to attend service with her once, three years earlier.

That day, Father Oke happened to be giving a sermon on the "evils and filth of homosexuality." Jacobs had had to sit there beside his mother in his suit and tie, itchy and miserable with embarrassment and sweat as the bishop equated homosexual activity with bestiality. Afterward, the bishop had come up to him and said that Jacobs's mother had told him all about Jacobs's . . . habits. Jacobs experienced a moment of complete panic.

He had seen Father Oke slapping the hell out of those he

disapproved of and calling them "the foulest *devil*." And when the bishop slapped, he slapped you hard. The receivers of the front or back of his hand were usually women but, once in a while, he slapped a man, too. Jacobs knew that if the bishop "slap delivered" him, he'd punch the bishop in the face. But he also knew that, if he did, the bishop would never forgive him; he would out Jacobs and run him out of the city, or worse.

To his relief, the bishop only shook his hand and congratulated Jacobs for taking the first step toward "healing his soul in the name of Jesus." But Jacobs felt so humiliated that he couldn't bring himself to tell the bishop (or his mother) that he wasn't gay at all. He just liked wearing women's clothes.

He loved the colors, the feel, the material, the creativity, and, oooh, the fit. A year later, he joined the Black Nexus because they were the only people who accepted his ways. If anyone needed the help of the Lord, it was his sister Fisayo, who was too smart and sweet to be out hustling her body.

"Whaaaat?" Rome whispered, bringing his face close to the high-definition images on Jacobs's mobile phone.

"Play it again," Seven said, grinning. "Is this for real? Even if it's not, that's a person changing into another person! Would've been better if it changed from a woman to a man but this will do. We could have some fun sending this around."

Fisayo was quiet, biting her nails.

Jacobs replayed it. "My boy Moziz got this from his girlfriend Philo," he said. "It's real. No Photoshop or anything." He turned off his phone. "Philo says that this woman . . . man . . . whatever is an *alien* who is at the house of the people she works for." He thought about mentioning the kidnapping plan but held off. He needed to get out of his parents' house, and he needed money for tuition when the university reopened. Kidnapping an alien would solve all of that. Yet . . .

"Hey! We should go see her. Get her on our side," Rome said.

"The Black Nexus can come out of secrecy for *this*. Who better to understand than a shape-shifter?"

"My exact thought!" Seven agreed, breathless with excitement. "This is what we've been waiting for, o."

Fisayo raised an index finger and frowned. "Wait . . . wait just a minute," she whispered. "Last night, I saw . . ." She looked at Jacobs. "Did you tell them?"

Jacobs shook his head. "Thought it would be better if you did."

Fisayo got up. "I was on the beach talking to a guy when I heard the loud booming noise."

"The one they are all talking about on the news?" Rome asked. "You were there?"

Fisayo nodded. "Everyone was looking around, all scared. The guy I was with ran off to check his car. A lot of windows shattered from the noise."

"That man left you alone?" Seven said, looking disgusted. *"Anuofia!"*

"He wasn't gone for long," Fisayo replied uncomfortably. "Anyway, before he returned, I was just standing there looking at the water. It looked . . . It was moving strangely. The waves had kind of lost their rhythm and the water was rising. I saw what I am sure was one of the creatures come out of the water! It looked like smoke at first, like smoke that bubbled out of the sea." She paused, bothered by her own recollection. "Then it was a woman. *That* same woman in the video. She dove back in the water and seconds later I saw a huge wave go after these three people on the beach, one woman and two men, I think. I couldn't see them that well. They ran, but the water . . ."

Fisayo frowned and pressed her lips together. When she spoke again, it was in a whisper. "There . . . there weren't any other waves, just that one. It splashed over them and pulled back into the sea . . . *with* them. They were gone! Stolen. If you're saying this woman-thing is an alien, then that must have been what took them! They're taking people! Maybe eating them or something!" Tears squeezed from her eyes. "Like in that old American movie . . . I forget the name. When are aliens ever *not* evil?"

"*E. T.*?" Rome said.

Jacobs put his arm around Fisayo. "Relax. It's—"

"No," she said, throwing his arm off. She sat down on one of the desks and began to sob. Jacobs put his arm back around her and looked at Seven and Rome.

"She's just upset and tired," he said.

"No I'm *not*; I know what I saw."

"Well, how do you know they didn't bring them back?" Seven said carefully.

"I heard that noise and I saw those people get taken. That's all I needed to see."

"Maybe some of the people in that room were the taken people," Jacobs said.

"I don't think so," Fisayo said. "I saw them get snatched; you don't just return from something like that, o. That video is just . . ."

"Let me see it again," said Rome, waving Fisayo's words away.

All of them watched the footage, even Fisayo. After it finished, none of them said a word, yet in their minds, they saw plenty. Jacobs saw an end to living with parents who refused to accept him. His sister Fisayo saw all of Lagos in flames. Seven saw infinite possibilities and a people from outer space that could make the world embrace and love everyone. Rome saw the rise of Rome.

"Let's get the Black Nexus together tomorrow," Rome said. "We've been hiding for too long. Tell me you don't feel it. This is it. This is *revolution*."

Jacobs *did* feel it. And if there were more of these aliens, then the Black Nexus could definitely come out of hiding, whether they came out to meet the one at the girl's house or some other one. Jacobs could see it clearly. He could be a part of the money-making kidnapping scheme *and* the Black Nexus revolution. He'd have his cake and eat it, too.

CHAPTER 15

ALCOHOL, MY NYASH

The drive to Agu's barracks should have taken a mere half hour, but extreme Lagos traffic stretched it to two. Agu couldn't believe it was already four o'clock. Everyone was trying to get somewhere, be it a church, a bar, home, or out of Lagos. Then there was the exodus of people from Lagos Island, Ikoyi, and Victoria Island to the parts of the city that had the least chance of flooding if the water rose too high. Almost all the lanes in both directions were packed with people moving inland, which was in the opposite direction to the one in which Adaora and Agu were going. In the one lane they had, they were forced to constantly swerve around people using it to bypass the traffic heading out of the city. By the time they arrived at the building for Lagos military personnel, they were exhausted, sweaty, hungry, and nervous.

Adaora turned the engine off and sat back.

"You don't have to go in with me," Agu said.

"Oh, I'm going," Adaora told him. She smiled and held up her notebook. "I brought my notes, too."

Agu sighed and shut his eyes. "How will I face the man after punching him into unconsciousness?"

Adaora frowned. "He was going to *rape* someone."

"You don't know the army." He rubbed the side of his forehead that didn't have a Band-Aid on it. "Adaora, is this really happening?"

Adaora slowly took his hand from his forehead. It was rough, and there were tan scars on two of his knuckles. She wondered if they were from fighting. He did say he'd been in a lot of fights. "You don't want to start that cut bleeding again," she said quietly. She looked into his dark brown eyes. "Thank you for stepping in front of my husband."

Agu smiled tiredly. "I was already beaten up. I had nothing to lose."

Adaora laughed, still holding his hand. "Is that the only reason?"

He grasped hers now. "Thank you for cleaning the cut on my face," he said. He leaned forward and she did not lean away. It was a sweet kiss. So sweet that neither of them noticed the car that slowly drove by on Agu's side.

Chris's window was open as he passed. He'd been following them on a hunch since they'd left the house, and now his suspicions had been proven. He gazed at his wife as she proved to him what he'd suspected for over two years. Somehow he managed to stay quiet and keep driving instead of jumping from the car, dragging his wife out, and beating her senseless right there in the street. This time, his rage would certainly have overpowered any black magic she might have practiced on him. But instead, he decided to wait, to tell Father Oke about what he had seen. Chris was sure Father Oke would agree—Adaora needed harsh punishment. Witches needed to be vanquished and cheating wives needed to be beaten down. So Chris drove on. And when Adaora pulled away from Agu, the road beside them was empty.

"Oh my God, what have I done?" Adaora gasped. She grabbed the handle and opened the door.

"I'm sorry," Agu said quickly. "I shouldn't have done that."

Adaora paused, the door half open, as dread washed over her. "I'm a married woman." She was crying now. She hated how the tears came but she couldn't help it. She wasn't an adulterer. Even during the worst moments, it had *never* crossed her mind to cheat on Chris.

Agu reached out and touched her face. She slapped his hand

away and sniffed. "Don't." She pushed the door wider but didn't leave. "In less than twenty-four hours my life has fallen apart," she whispered.

"It's the alien's fault," Agu said softly.

Adaora tried but couldn't keep the smile from her lips. She shut the door again. "Maybe my husband is right," she said. "Maybe I am a witch."

When Agu took her hand, she didn't snatch her arm away.

"Your husband is a fool," he said. "You're stronger than this. Got your notes?"

"Yes."

"Then come on," he said, opening his door.

Lance Corporal Benson was a large, middle-aged hulk of a man in need of a vacation. He wanted time away from his wife, away from his three young children, and away from his job. And then there was the madness yesterday. He didn't know why smoking weed always made him get crazy, but it did. The first time he'd tried it, he'd run wild in the streets for five hours, harassing women and talking shit to anyone who'd listen. Then he'd passed out and wound up in the hospital with an IV in his arm. Yesterday, he'd smoked with some of the younger privates. He'd been bored and annoyed with his life. He needed excitement. He hadn't meant to attack that girl. He felt horrible about it . . . and not just because the left side of his head was swollen and his belly felt like it had been crushed with a hundred-pound weight. Thankfully, the medics said his ribs were merely bruised, praise Allah.

The last thing he wanted to see right now was the self-righteous mug of Private Agu. Benson watched intensely as Agu entered his office. He glanced at Agu's hands. They looked normal enough. A curvy woman with a notepad followed behind him. Agu saluted Benson. Benson didn't salute back.

The moment she entered the office, Adaora knew they'd made

a mistake. She and Agu stood in awkward silence as Benson stared them down. Angry energy radiated from the burly, swollen-faced man behind the desk. He looked ready to wring Agu's neck. Despite the large fan blowing right behind him, he was glistening with sweat.

Benson sat back in his leather chair, twiddling a pencil in his hands. The silence stretched out between them.

"I didn't come here to talk about yesterday, sir," Agu finally said.

Benson chuckled deep in his throat. "Are you sure?"

"This is Adaora," Agu said. Adaora gave him a quick nod. "She is a professor of marine biology I met last night after the . . . I met her on Bar Beach."

Benson's eyes grew wide before he gained control of himself. "You were there? When it happened?"

"Yes, sir."

"Sit."

Agu and Adaora sat.

"Sir, we know what caused the sonic boom and what is causing the water to rise. We . . . we met one and . . ."

Benson frowned. "One what?"

Silence. Adaora looked at Agu after no one said anything for several seconds. Agu and Benson were staring at each other.

"Why don't you start from the beginning, Agu?" Adaora ventured. But Benson and Agu just glared at one another.

"Um . . . Please, sir," Adaora tried again. "Just listen to him, sir. Please. Sir?"

Silence. Adaora could practically hear the anger that flowed between Agu and Benson.

"Look," Adaora said, desperate. "I met Agu last night. We were both walking on Bar Beach. We and one other man were in the same place when we heard the boom. It was *painfully* loud. Then . . . something . . ." She bit her lip. No, she didn't think this was a good person to tell about them being taken. "This woman came . . . from the water."

Slowly, Benson dragged his eyes from Agu and set them on Adaora. Adaora spoke louder and faster. "She . . . she told us she was from outer space," she said. "She can *change*. Into many things! The three of us have seen her do it twice now.

"We took her to my home. I've examined her skin cells under a microscope. Again, sir, I am a marine biologist. I have a lab in my house." Adaora leaned forward, excited despite herself. "I've never seen anything like it. She isn't made of cellular matter. And she's not the only one. There are more of them . . . in the water. That's why the water is rising."

Finally Agu spoke. "Sir, your uncle, the *president*, needs to take control of what's happening. I know no one knows where he is but you can reach him, can't you? It's an opportunity for Nigeria to—"

"My uncle is very ill."

"But he is still the *president*, sir," Agu said, trying to control himself. "He has not relinquished even one presidential responsibility, isn't that true? Absurd as the idea of aliens in Lagos, in any part of Nigeria is, it's real. It's happened. He *must* get involved." Peripherally, Agu could see Adaora, nodding.

"So you have one contained, Private?" Benson asked.

"Yes, sir," Agu said. "She's not violent or—"

"Is it green?"

Agu frowned. "Well, sir, she's—"

"Slimy? Does it have antennae and those big *yanfuyanfu* eyes?" Benson asked, a smirk on his face.

"They're not evil like the ones in all the movies," Adaora added.

Benson grunted, twirling his pencil in his hand. "You know, it was just alcohol."

"What?" Agu snapped.

"At the checkpoint last night," Benson said. "We were all drunk and tired. And you can't tell me she didn't want it."

Agu and Adaora looked at each other. Agu's face went dark.

Alcohol, my nyash, he thought. He'd seen Benson with his own eyes smoking *igbo* last night. How stupid did this man think he was?

"I didn't come here to discuss that, sir," Agu said evenly.

"No one could argue that she was drunk and practically spreading her legs for me," Benson said.

Agu clasped the arms of his chair, digging his fingers deep into the upholstery. Adaora grabbed Agu's hand. He didn't notice at all. "That's it, I can't do this! I'm going to make sure all the newspapers and all your superiors know what you did!" He jumped up out of his chair. "Women don't scream, cry, and fight if they *'want'* it!" he shouted.

Adaora smacked her forehead, exasperated. "Can't you two deal with this later?" she said to Benson. "This is an emergency! A national crisis! Call the damn president *now*! Tell him we need to see him! Tell—"

"I'll do what's necessary, miss!" Benson bellowed, standing up. He pointed at Agu. "I'll see you tried for this insubordination, Private Agu! Private Julius, Private Akunna, get in here!"

The office door swung open as two beefy soldiers burst in. Adaora flinched at the smug expressions on their faces.

"I've been waiting for this," the taller one said. He pointed at Agu. "I will *kparoof* you."

"I guess he didn't get enough last night," the other one added.

Agu raised his fists, his unhurt eye bulging. He looked from one soldier to the other. "Come on then," he said. "I will bring you both down." He didn't want to punch anyone. He didn't want to kill anyone. But he could feel the potential in his fists. Without looking down at them, he quickly put his hands behind his back.

The two men hesitated. Then they moved forward and grabbed him.

"What the hell are you doing?" Adaora shouted, pressing away from the soldiers, her back against the wall.

They cuffed Agu. Then the short one held him, and Benson

nodded. The taller one smashed a fist into Agu's belly, causing him to cough and gag.

"STOP IT!" Adaora screamed, tears in her eyes.

They punched Agu in the belly again and then in the face, opening up the cut on his forehead. Blood dribbled into his swollen eye.

Adaora launched herself away from the wall and toward the fight when Benson grabbed her arm. She gave him a vicious look and tried to snatch it away. She considered biting him but couldn't bring herself to do it.

"Get him out of my sight," Benson instructed his lackeys. "Put him somewhere where he can't cause trouble." As they dragged Agu out the door, Benson followed, pulling Adaora with him. "Come on, woman. After I make an important phone call, I'd like you to introduce me to your friend."

Adaora finally tore her arm away, freeing herself from his grip. Benson looked amused.

"You can't do this," she said, shaking as she fought to control her outrage. "I won't cooperate!"

Benson smirked. "This is a question of national security, prof. It's not a good idea to get in the way of a military operation. People get thrown in jail for that kind of thing. And our jails are not so nice, especially for a woman like you."

Adaora frowned, her mind racing. "What if we're *not* telling the truth? What if this isn't really an alien invasion? You'll look like a fool in front of everyone."

Benson smiled as he took her arm again. "Agu never lies. That's his biggest problem."

CHAPTER 16
HEADLESS STATE

The president of Nigeria had been in the same place for over fifteen hours since waking from his heart surgery, staring and staring at the news on television. He still couldn't believe his eyes. His nurse and his wife had assured him that his head was clear. They insisted that his pain medications were non-hallucinogenic. And because he could speak, though doing so was rather taxing, he knew he wasn't in hell. Not yet. For the first time in months, he forgot about his pericarditis. He was free of the nightmarish images that haunted him, the images of his heart encased in a sack of vile yellow diseased fluid.

But this was worse.

Oh Allah, what am I going to do all the way from Saudi Arabia? he wondered. He wasn't about to call on his VP. Handing things over to Wishwell Williams, indeed! There was no way he was delegating something so serious to a power-hungry, money-grubbing Christian blockhead with such a stupid name. Who would name their child "Wishwell"? The very idea of handing over the country to a man named Wishwell Williams made him want to spit. The man's master's degree was in *zoology*, for Allah's sake! Williams knew more about governing lizards and birds than human beings.

"What are you going to do?" his first wife, Zena, asked. She was sitting on the edge of his bed watching the news with him. He wished she'd leave. Her cloying perfume was giving him a headache, and her clicking porcelain bangles were making too much noise. He needed his advisors. He wouldn't have minded his second wife Hawra's presence, either. She had a better feel for policy, being a lawyer herself. The only good thing about Zena was that she preferred to speak to him in Hausa instead of English.

He shut his eyes and took a deep breath, feeling his heart skip a bit in his chest. This situation was going to kill him. He wished he were at his home in Abuja with a glass of cool Guinness, watching *Star Wars* on his high-definition wide-screen television. He loved *Star Wars*, especially the more recent installments. There was such honor in *Star Wars*. In another life, he'd have made a great Jedi knight. Being a vigilante loyal only to justice was always better than being any kind of head of state. "I don't know what I'll do," he said in his dry voice. "We need to do proper research."

Zena looked at him but did not speak her thoughts. His illness made her presence more important. She was his senior wife; she'd known him longest. Thus, when he had fallen sick, she was the one he wanted around to care for him. Still, sometimes the sight of him made her want to spit. He looked so thin, so frail, so impotent in his white hospital gown. His skin was a blotchy mess. His eyes were rheumy and yellow. He was nothing like the lion of a man she'd married decades ago. And he wasn't even thinking straight. How could he do "research" when he was a continent away? The slightest amount of stress made his heart do a death dance. Nevertheless, if he didn't return to Nigeria soon, there would surely be a coup d'état.

The president wanted to shut the television off. He knew more than his wife, for he'd had a phone call that he'd sent her out of the room to take. It was from his good-for-nothing nephew, Benson. Of all people, why did *he* have to be the one handling this? Benson said he believed Lagos had been invaded by extraterrestrials. He'd sent a group of soldiers and two local oceanographers to patrol Bar Beach, and those men reported that the waters were teeming with ocean life that had not been seen there in over thirty years, and some that had *never* been seen—whatever that meant. And they couldn't explain the copious amount of seaweed washing ashore, either.

Most troublesome was the report of the woman in someone's house in Lagos believed to be one of the space creatures. Benson said he'd been told that she could shape-shift and was potentially dangerous. And right now Benson was on his way to the house to either capture or kill her. Benson, his most foolish nephew.

I have to get back to Nigeria, the president thought, rubbing his stubbly chin.

CHAPTER 17

CASHEWS, PURE WATER, AND CHIN CHIN

Anthony looked out the window at the crowd of fans gathering in the narrow residential street outside the house. Most were young people, and they brought a festive air. Local hawkers had picked up the scent and were selling bottled soft drinks, bags of "pure water," cashews, peanuts and chin chin, and packs of cigarettes. Many had probably been at last night's concert. And all of them seemed to have some kind of mobile phone in their hands. They talked, texted, took photos and footage of Adaora's house. His friend Festus said that the social networking sites were buzzing with news of the Ghanaian rapper's whereabouts and that he would give a free concert if enough people showed up. Word was traveling fast.

Behind him, Ayodele sat on the sofa. Adaora's children sat across from her, staring in fascination. Philo stood sulking on the other side of the room. She was preoccupied with looking at her silent phone.

"Your audience gathers," Anthony said.

Ayodele smiled. "You're well liked."

"I'm loved," Anthony said, turning back to the window. He hoped they'd still love him after they learned that he wouldn't be giving a concert.

Impatient, Philo opened her phone, flipped it shut, then opened it again. She couldn't stand being in the same room as this woman, thing, whatever she was. Philo was positive that the woman-thing was evil, with her pleasant demeanor and long, too tightly braided hair and wicked ways. *God will punish her,* Philo thought darkly.

CHAPTER 18
SMOKING IGBO

Moziz was trying not to speed. With all the military and police out, he knew it was best to be as inconspicuous as possible. Especially since it was still late afternoon. But he had the feeling that time was short. He turned up his music—Anthony Dey Craze—and let the bass shake his well-traveled tan '94 Nissan.

Troy was in the passenger seat, quieter than usual. Jacobs and Tolu were in the back, also quiet, as they smoked *igbo*. The smoke smelled especially sweet, and Moziz inhaled deeply. All of them wore black masks and were dressed in black clothes as Moziz had instructed. It was broad daylight, but Moziz didn't care about being seen as much as putting fear into everyone in that house.

"We go be rich, oooo!" Jacobs shouted over the music, feeling very *irie*. He'd pushed thoughts of the Black Nexus out of his mind. Both Seven and Rome had been calling him all day. They could wait. Everything in his life was about to come together. He was sure of it. Once he had the money, he'd bring them in on things. He did wonder about Fisayo, who was supposed to have called him hours ago. But he was sure she was fine. And when he brought money to her, she'd be even finer.

Jacobs slapped hands with Tolu, who took a deep pull on the joint and handed it to Moziz. As Tolu spoke, he exhaled smoke: "Small time now, dem go trap all of them and we no go see chance take dem make money again. Moziz, na pot of gold your girl hand us so, o."

Moziz took a pull on the joint and nodded. "We never begin eat cake yet. Mek we first pray say mek checkpoints no dey this road today."

It was only Troy who was not caught up in the moment. "Nigerian police dey jump on top people motors and *okada* like say dem American ninja dem, and like say dem be Bruce Willis for *Die Hard*, abi?" Troy said. "Dem dey even chop women like groundnut." He sucked his teeth with anger and muttered, "Nonsense."

Moziz, Jacobs, and Tolu burst out laughing, but Troy only looked out the window, a dark expression on his face. He was thinking about the phone call he'd gotten a few hours earlier from his cousin Inno, saying his sweet pretty cousin Oregbemi had been raped last night by some soldiers or police, one of whom had had the nerve to be on television last night. Making appearances so soon after trying to kill Oregbemi. He, his cousins, and friends would get all the details and handle that soon, after he did what he had to do here. Once he had some money, he could take down even the authorities.

"Listen, if we reach dere, we enter and we comot fast," Moziz said.

They all agreed.

Anthony had his phone to his ear as he watched the festive crowd swell larger and larger outside of Adaora's house. He frowned. "Why won't either of them answer?" he muttered. He looked at his phone, pressed end, and redialed.

Ayodele was showing Kola how to use Adaora's old but reliable digital camera. Kola's brother, Fred, looked on with great interest.

"So I just press this button, then?" Kola asked, holding it with both hands and extending her index finger to the red record button.

"Yes."

"It's so easy!" Kola proclaimed, looking down at the screen. "Mommy never lets me touch this." She giggled. "Wait until she sees that I can use it better than she can." She lowered it and fiddled with some of the buttons.

Philomena stood on the other side of the room, looking out the window anxiously. She hadn't mentioned the growing crowd to Moziz, afraid that he might not come if he knew. She no longer cared if the damn kids wanted to play with the alien. Even she sensed the urgency in the air. Something was about to change, and somehow this knowledge gave her the strength to take charge of her life. The first thing she'd do was not feel an ounce of guilt for what she was about to help happen.

Adaora was fuming. Why *did we think the man would behave rationally?* When had the Nigerian government and military done *anything* for its people? They were all about covering their asses and stuffing their own pockets. She wanted to slap her other cheek. She'd been an idiot. She and Agu, rare patriotic Nigerians trying to do the right thing. Stupid members of the populace. Insignificant, powerless civilians. She should have known better.

She leaned her head against the car window. Lance Corporal Benson was in the passenger seat, the shiny silver SUV driven by yet another of his stupid lackeys. Poor Agu. What would they do to him? She nearly jumped when her mobile phone went off.

Benson held the phone up, looking at the caller ID. He turned around and scowled at her. "Who is Anthony Dey Craze?"

Adaora gritted her teeth. Her phone was *her* personal property. And when had he even snatched it from her pocket? "He is the other man who was with Agu and me when we first met the woman on the beach."

He grunted, looking at the phone. "Sounds like that *mumu* rapper my niece listens to who is always screaming that he is crazy," he said, putting it in his pocket. "If it is, maybe we should arrest him, too." Both he and the soldier driving the SUV laughed.

Adaora sullenly crossed her arms over her chest and looked out the window as they passed the tall buildings of downtown Lagos, weaving madly through the dusty traffic. Two orange-yellow *danfo* so overstuffed with people that both had passengers hanging on to the outside swerved in front of them. Adaora pushed her hands against the back of Benson's seat as they came to an abrupt stop. As they maneuvered around and passed one of the *danfo*, the solider driving the SUV leaned out the window, spat at it, and smacked its side, shouting, "Damn your mother! *Mumu!* Idiot! Go and die!"

Moziz parked the car on the far side of the busy street. He had to squeeze between a beat-up old Honda and a dusty Ford SUV. There were no other spaces. There had to be over two hundred people milling about. Most seemed to be around his age. They all removed their masks.

"Which kine fucking nonsense come be dis one, na?" Moziz said yet again, turning the engine off. The four of them just sat there. Philo had said nothing about a damn mob. "Jacobs, find out wetin dis people sabi."

Jacobs nodded, got out, stood beside Moziz's open window, shoved his hands in the pockets of his baggy jeans, and looked around. Moziz frowned as he watched people. Everyone seemed excited. "Na craze be dis," he said.

"Maybe na people wey dey come from big party from person house," Tolu said.

Moziz rolled his eyes, annoyed. "You no dey see," was all he said, wishing Tolu would just shut up. Tolu never saw anything until it was explained to him in full. "Mek you no waste time, o," Moziz said to Jacobs.

"I no go waste time," Jacobs said. He walked into the crowd.

A few minutes later, he spotted several familiar faces from back when he had been in school. He was about to approach a guy he knew from his biology class when he saw bright flashes of color a few yards away. It took him several minutes to shove his way close enough. Then, he just stared. People were so taken aback that they gave the group enough space to wiggle through. The slow-moving procession brought music, confetti, and a great big rainbow-colored sign with a giant BLACK NEXUS painted in the center. Jacobs's entire body went cold.

There were nine of them, the whole organization. Eze, Yinka, and Michelle wore matching black suits and red lipstick. They walked slowly, aware of all the attention. Royal wore red platform thigh boots, red spandex pants, and a tight pink T-shirt. He carried the boom box and was jumping about, shaking his backside for anyone who would watch. Royal would dance for his grandmother in the village, the man was so free. Okechukwu wore jeans and a white T-shirt, but he was the same, dancing to the music and even joining in with a group of laughing women at the perimeter of the crowd. Chioma and Yemi held the Black Nexus sign. Both looked like they wanted to creep right back into their closets, but they held their chins up. Seven was wearing tight jeans and an even tighter top as she smoked a cigar, ignored the leers of the men, and blew kisses at the women.

And who better to lead the group than the greatest queen of them all? Rome was decked out in a breathtaking *rapa* and matching top that fit his body as if such clothes were indeed made for men, too. He looked like a Yoruba queen. All of them were wearing headbands with alien antennae bobbing from them. All Jacobs could think as he approached them was that they were going to get themselves killed.

Jacobs raised a hand. "Rome!"

Rome caught his eye, smiled confidently, came up to Jacobs, and said, "The Black Nexus has come down to earth."

Jacobs's mouth was hanging open. Everyone was watching, too thrown off by the sight of the student organization to react. Yet.

Jacobs was having trouble finding words. "What . . . you guys . . . didn't . . ."

"We've been calling you for hours."

"Well . . . I . . ." He could feel a hundred eyes boring into him.

"Anyway," Rome said, waving a dismissive hand, "we heard there was some commotion on this street and we assumed it had to do with what you showed us."

Jacobs was having trouble deciding between doing what he had to do for Moziz and the others, and seeing the Black Nexus out in the open. He wanted to join them, but he didn't want Moziz, Troy, and Tolu, who knew nothing about his cross-dressing, to see. For the first time in his entire life, he was immensely proud and intensely ashamed at the same time.

"But we were wrong. These people are here because of a damn celebrity!" Rome said. He snapped into a practiced pose as some women stopped to take his picture with a mobile phone. "Enjoy it," Rome said to them, smirking. "That's the closest you'll come to looking this good." The women laughed and scurried away.

"Celebrity?" Jacobs asked.

"That Ghanaian rapper Anthony Dey Craze is in there." He pointed at the house.

Jacobs blinked and frowned, trying to mask his confusion. What did a rapper have to do with aliens? "I'll . . . I'll be right back," was all he could think to say. He turned and pushed into the crowd. A few had begun to grumble about "*adofuroo*," "fags," and "bottom power." "*Kai!* Wetin dey do you?" Jacobs heard a guy ask. "Are you man or woman?" He moved faster toward the car, feeling like a deserter. The Black Nexus had to be *crazy* to come out in a place so public. Yet they were so brave to do so. They'd been hiding for such a long time. Not so much out of shame, but out of a need to stay safe. Now an alien had come to Lagos. It wasn't just the Black Nexus who were unsafe or at least vulnerable now. It was everyone. In his heart, he knew that if that alien was in the house, it was time. It was time for a change.

"Jacobs don return!" Troy exclaimed. Jacobs jogged back to the car, a smile plastered on his face. With each step he took toward the car, the need for revolution left him like air from a leaky balloon. *Not yet, but soon,* he told himself, to stave off the guilt that replaced his hope for change. He resisted the urge to turn around when he heard people shout in surprise as something happened. He joined his other group of friends.

"Whoo!" Jacobs said, getting in the car. "You no go believe dis one, I swear."

"Wetin?" Moziz snapped. "How people hear about her if na only Philo sabi about am?!"

"No be de winch 'tory I wan nack you," Jacobs said, feigning excitement. "Na Anthony Dey Craze! Dem say e dey for here!"

"Eeey," Tolu and Troy exclaimed, sitting straight up and looking out the window.

Jacobs took the moment to glance back into the crowd, but he couldn't see Rome or any of the Black Nexus. Moziz just sat there scowling, arms crossed. Things had suddenly become far more complicated. Moziz sucked his teeth. "God forbid dis kine situation, o."

CHAPTER 19

OFFSHORE

For the third time in his life, Agu was somewhere that didn't quite make sense. The first had been when he was ten years old, walking home with his fifteen-year-old brother. That evening, they stood out there on the road leading to their house, staring at the newspaper-wrapped bundle. Instead of going to the market, he and his brother had bought the meat a half hour before from a man selling it cheaply on the roadside. It was late in the evening and the sun had already set. They'd brought it home, given it to their mother, and secretly kept the leftover money.

Agu would never forget the moment when their mother unwrapped the meat, expecting a slab of beef or haunches of goat. An arm with a tiny, humanlike hand flopped from the package as if asking for a handout. The monkey was dead, its pink tongue lolled out, its tiny forehead smashed in, and its dried eyes wide open. Agu nearly vomited. His mother beat them both and sent them out to get rid of it.

Then there was the time when he was twenty-seven and woke up in the Sahara Desert. He'd been visiting his brother up north in Katsina and boarded a bush taxi he thought would take him home. The driver spoke terrible English, and Agu spoke terrible Hausa. Agu thought the driver said the destination was Lagos, but the driver had meant Agadez. Exhausted from a night of partying, Agu had fallen asleep as soon as the bush taxi full of people started moving. He woke up two hours later to serious desert in a part of the world he never thought he'd see. They had stopped in a tiny town called Maradi, and the driver was refueling for the drive across the Sahara!

Now he was on a goddamn speedboat in handcuffs. If something happened and they capsized, he would sink to his death; Private Akunna and Private Julius were too stupid to realize this, or maybe they did not care. Aside from the two idiots who'd beaten the hell out of him in Benson's office, there was a worried-looking oil worker and an irritated engineer.

They were heading for an offshore oil field where, he gathered, something had gone wrong with the hose attached to the supply vessel FPSO *Mystras*. The report had come that thousands of gallons of crude oil were spilling into the sea. Because of everything going on in Lagos, many oil workers, military personnel, and police were abandoning their responsibilities and fleeing the city with their families to villages and towns east and north. Those who had stayed were dealing with the flooding, traffic, and general panic of the city. There was no one except Akunna and Julius available to check out the malfunctioning hose, nor was there anyone to keep an eye on Agu. So Private Julius and Private Akunna had had to bring him along. Thankfully, the water was smooth, so the risk of Agu bouncing off the boat into it was relatively low. Still, it was not long until sunset. With all that was happening, Agu didn't want to be on the water at night.

"Are you sure we should be out here?" Agu shouted.

"Shut up!" Private Akunna snapped over his shoulder.

Fifteen minutes later, they arrived at the offshore oil rig and vessel, and Akunna cut the engine. The rig was a spidery structure made of concrete and rusty steel. Anchored firmly to the seabed by steel beams, it was a decades-old monster, a hulking, unnatural contraption of production facilities, drilling rigs, and crew quarters. Agu had circled it on boat patrols plenty of times. It was usually a place of noise and activity. Now it was deserted and quiet. The large vessel seemed unnaturally silent, too. Agu noticed that there was no pungent stench of crude oil from the reported spill. And there was an odd sweetness.

"Where is the oil?" Akunna asked, grabbing the shoulder of one of the oil workers. "I don't see it. I don't even *smell* it!"

"Ah-ah, we were all there," the oil worker said, flinching away from Akunna's grasp. His name was Biko, in homage to the South African anti-apartheid activist Steve Biko. However, Biko the oil worker was not South African, he was Igbo, and in the Igbo language the word *biko* meant "please." He hated his father for giving him such a stupid name. It seemed all his life he was stuck begging people to listen to him. "You don't mistake spillage, o. Please, you have to believe us. Call the *Mystras*. People will still be there. They will tell you!"

"He's right. We had to evacuate the place because of the boom but there *was* leakage here," Rafiu the engineer said. His stomach lurched. He would never be able to dislodge the guilt he felt for abandoning the oil rig when the hose was spewing oil into the water. He'd become an engineer to *save* the environment. He swabbed his sweaty face with his handkerchief. "We flashed the light on the water. You could see it bubbling up. I was going to—"

Private Akunna held up a hand. "Shh, shh!"

They all listened, bobbing on the water about a hundred meters from the oil rig.

Silence.

"I think we should turn back," Agu ventured again.

"Shut up!" all of them shouted.

"Take these cuffs off me, at least!" Agu insisted. "Where am I going to run?"

Akunna looked at Agu with disgust. Still, he reached for his pocket and Agu's heart lifted.

Private Julius's voice stilled Private Akunna's hand. "You hear that?" he whispered.

Agu felt chills crawling up his spine. Of all of them on that boat, only he recognized it. The sound of metal on glass. The noise came from the water just over the side of the boat.

"Uncuff him," Akunna said, giving the key to Biko. Akunna went to look over the edge with Julius.

"You see that?" Julius said, pointing at something in the water. Rafiu joined them to see. As soon as Biko got the cuffs off, Agu moved closer to the center of the boat. Biko stepped to the edge with the others.

Fwit!

It flew right past the four of them and grazed Agu's arm before plunking into the water on the other side of the boat. Agu felt a wet sting, and looked down at his arm. It was dribbling blood from a cut three inches long near his elbow. It only took Agu a moment to realize what had happened. He threw himself down and managed to crane his neck around to see fifty more flying fish zip from the water like poison darts.

He shut his eyes and closed his ears. But he could still hear the meaty sound of fish slicing human flesh and the agonized screams of the others.

BUMP!

The entire speedboat shuddered, and the floor cracked beneath Agu's body. Something very big was ramming the boat. When it was hit again, the boat capsized, and they were all dumped into the waters roiling with monstrous and alien ocean life. Opening his eyes, Agu found himself trapped in the water beneath the boat. He saw a huge swordfishlike creature stabbing the boat with its spear almost playfully. Then he saw something terrible. A shark was tearing Biko's arm from his body. Then Private Agu ran out of breath, and saw no more.

CHAPTER 20

SIEGE

"When you arrive, wait for me," Benson said.

They were still on their way to Adaora's house. Benson was using her phone to speak with some of his men who were already there. Adaora's hatred for the man had reached an all-time high. "What?" he shouted into the phone. Adaora imagined his spit spattering her phone's mouthpiece. He turned in his seat and glared at her. "What did you people do?" he yelled. "Tell the whole goddamn world?"

She felt more than a pinch of pleasure at his anger. So Anthony had succeeded. "If you'd have listened to us instead of—"

Benson ignored her and continued to growl into the phone. "Won't be a problem," he said. "There's only one. How hard can it be? Just be on standby. The president will be landing at Lagos Airport around six a.m." He paused and looked at his watch. Adaora glanced at hers too. It was 5:19 p.m. "We capture it, lock it down, and transport it to Kirikiri Prison. No fuckups." He slapped her mobile phone shut and said, with a malicious glint in his eye, "Private Agu's going to be looking at some jail time for this."

Ten minutes had passed, and Moziz and the others were still in the car. Without the air conditioning, the car was becoming a sauna. Moziz wanted to bang his head on the steering wheel. He had a headache, and his high was making him paranoid. Philo had texted him that indeed Anthony *was* in the house, but so was the goddamn money-making alien. How were they going to kidnap the alien with all these people around? With each minute, the crowd grew bigger. He even thought he saw a group of circus performers a few yards away.

Tolu wanted to forget the plan and go scope out women, but he didn't want to cross Moziz.

Jacobs wanted his money. The Black Nexus could wait.

Troy was this close to getting out of the car, finding an *okada* motorbike, and heading to his cousin's house. He had things to do: a cousin's honor to avenge, a military man to exterminate. His phone buzzed again with a text from his cousin's brother, ready to join the hunt for her attacker.

"Focus!" Moziz said. "*Forget* Anthony Dey Craze. Na bigger fish!"

Outside the noise of the crowd increased. "Fuck. What *now?*" Moziz groaned. They turned to see about thirty people coming up the other end of the road. The newcomers were all dressed in white and singing a Christian hymn. A bishop carrying a giant metal cross led the way. Moziz shut his eyes and took a deep breath. Then he opened them, and started the car.

Jacobs felt nauseated as he watched. The Christian procession was moving right toward the Black Nexus. Rome, he knew, hated Christians and often got into violent arguments with anyone who wanted a piece of him. And Seven wasn't any better. She would insult any priest, reverend, pastor, imam, rabbi who looked her way. As the Christian procession approached, members of the Black Nexus didn't even notice because they were focused on arguing with a group of husky guys. Jacobs knew he should have gone to them, supported them. Still, he didn't move, and he felt awful for it.

"We're going to go around," Moziz said as they slowly drove out. "We'll sneak in from the back." The bishop leading the pack looked a little crazy. Moziz noted that some of the people with him looked angry. He rolled his eyes. These kinds of people always showed up whenever the masses stopped "suffering and smiling."

CHAPTER 21

THE SEA'S COW

Agu held on for dear life to the fattest animal he'd ever seen. The manatee smelled like ocean-soaked cedar wood. Its thick wet skin was wrinkly like an elephant's, hard like the corky material of a bulletin board, and rough like sandpaper. It swam at a leisurely pace, close enough to the surface of the water that Agu was able to keep his head above it. Around and below him the clear ocean waters roiled with strange, impossible sea life. What looked like a giant, bright-red-and-white flat snake undulated by not three feet below.

"What have you done to the ocean?" Agu asked the manatee. Were the monsters attacking the oil rig and the supply vessel, too? These were Ayodele's people and earthly allies? Ayodele was not only a shape-shifter, she was a liar. She hadn't come in peace at all.

He heard the sea cow's response in his head, like a child's voice through a mobile phone.

"*You will see,*" it said.

CHAPTER 22

RELAX

Moziz parked the car in the narrow road that ran behind the house. Philomena was there waiting at the door.

"Put your masks back on!" Moziz instructed. All but Troy piled out of the car and ran inside. Troy climbed into the driver's seat and waited for the others to come out with the alien. His mobile phone buzzed, but, for the moment, he was not thinking about the rape of his cousin.

Kola was filming Ayodele as she stood by the window watching the crowd. Holding the camera as steadily as possible, Kola adjusted the contrast, faded out the scene, then tilted the camera up so she could clean the lens with the hem of her shirt. She was having a wonderful time. She turned the camera back on to film the crowd outside, zooming in on the man in white standing before the gate with his arms spread.

"That's Father Oke," Kola whispered. She snickered. He looked silly and really sweaty. He was surrounded by other people who were also in white. Two of them were arguing with a tall tall woman who looked like a fashion model and a woman who was dressed like a man but still looked like a woman. One of the men in white slapped the tall woman, and she responded by punching him in the face so hard that he fell into the crowd. Kola grinned and zoomed in on them. High drama, like in the Nollywood movies her mother loved so much and her father hated.

A car slowly pushed through the crowd, annoying the people around it. The car's doors opened, and five people, one well-dressed woman, and four men in suits, got out. They had pads of paper in their hands and immediately started talking to people and snapping pictures of the people fighting. "Newspaper people!" Kola exclaimed. She zoomed in on one of the male journalists, who walked up to one of the people in white who was not fighting. The journalist said something, and several people in white instantly started shouting at him until he stumbled away, shocked. "Oh, this is great!" Kola said, giggling.

Ayodele paid Kola no mind as she stood watching the crowd, a satisfied look on her face.

Anthony sat on the chair with Fred, calling and calling Adaora's and Agu's phone numbers. "Shit shit shit! What is going on? This is bullshit!" he hissed when he got no answer for what seemed like the twentieth time. He glanced at Fred. "Sorry, o," he said, patting the boy on his head.

Fred smiled. "It is okay," he said. "I've heard my mother and father say those words. Usually when they say it, there is a good reason."

Anthony smiled back, patting the boy on the head. He looked up, his eyes falling on Philo. She was staring at the kitchen entrance with wide eyes. He slowly got up, his hand sliding off Fred's head and pushing the boy behind him. "What are you—?"

The men in black burst in from the kitchen.

"A beg, mek everybody relax," Philo said in a high-pitched voice, moving aside to let Moziz and the others forward.

"We no wan injure person!" Moziz and Troy were wielding guns. Philo pointed to Ayodele. "Na she!"

"Everybody lie down, now!" Moziz shouted, aiming at Ayodele.

Ayodele stared blankly at him and didn't move. But Kola and Fred dropped to the floor as if their lives depended on it. Anthony held his hands up and asked as calmly as he could, "What is this?"

"Lie down!" Moziz commanded.

"Eii! Na Anthony Dey Craze, o!" Tolu exclaimed, lowering his gun and grinning.

Distracted, Moziz blinked and looked at Anthony again. "Shit," he said, lowering his gun.

"I get all your album!" Tolu exclaimed.

Moziz smacked Tolu upside the head. "Ee remain mek you kukuma ask am for him autograph!" He looked at Anthony. "Sorry, Anthony. But you sef, you need to lie down for floor, too. We no mean any harm. We just want dat woman." He pointed at Ayodele, who still hadn't moved.

"Please," Moziz said to her. "Mek you just follow us quietly."

"What do you want with me?" Ayodele asked. She cocked her head and switched to Pidgin English. "Wetin una want with me?"

"We go talk dat one when we comot outside. Just—"

"I no dey go anywhere with una," she snapped.

Moziz looked at Tolu and Jacobs, then gave a small nod. All three of them lunged at her. Then they immediately froze. To Moziz it sounded like the house was full of those noisy bugs in the trees, all screeching in terrible harmony. He clapped his hands over his ears, dropping his gun. His mouth hung open and his hearing was muffled as, right before his goddamn eyes, she . . . she . . . melted? Melted! Imploded? Disintegrated? Right before his eyes. Evaporated into something small on the floor. A green . . . He squinted. A green lizard.

Tolu stood there, gun in hand, ears uncovered, and shrieked like a little girl.

"You see dat?!" Jacobs shouted. He'd pulled off his mask, and his face was wet with sweat.

"Catch am!" Moziz shouted.

Chaos ensued as all three went after the lizard. Moziz's mind was blank, his world shrinking down to focus on the impossible thing before him, the lizard-that-was-once-a-woman. Retrieve her and get out. First she had been a woman. Now she was a lizard; he would catch the lizard.

Philomena just stood there watching Moziz scrambling around, chasing a lizard. Like a child. His legs looked so short and skinny, and she realized how stocky he was, how graceless, how he had a bit of a gut that bounced when he ran. She sighed, her shoulders slouching and her stomach dropping. Moziz was just another young area boy.

They knocked over vases and threw aside the coffee table. They stepped on pillows and cushions. And they cursed the entire time. Anthony grabbed the children's hands and ran to the front door. He threw it open only to be met with the excited cheers of his fans.

BLAM!

Kola screeched and Fred crouched at her feet. Anthony shoved the children behind him. "Stay low," he said, frantically looking for the gunman. Near the sofa, Tolu was shooting at the scampering lizard.

"*Biko!* No shoot am! We want am alive!" Moziz shouted.

Tolu's eyes were wild. "Na evil she be, o!" he babbled, waving the gun wildly as he tried to follow the lizard's path with the barrel. "We suppose kill am! *Kai!* Kill am!" He pulled the trigger again. *BLAM!*

"What are you doing?!" Jacobs shouted. "Stop it!"

Anthony, Kola, and Fred were still trying to figure out which way was safest to flee when the lizard ran out the door between Anthony's legs.

The first thing Adaora thought as she got out of Benson's car was that the street outside her house had turned into a carnival. The very air smelled deliciously festive. There were vendors selling suya, fried plantain, boiled eggs, Fanta, beer. One woman had even set up right across the street from her house. She was selling fufu and what looked like egusi soup, jollof rice, and other hot food items. And she was making a killing, from the looks of it. She had no less than ten people waiting to be served.

There were young people milling about, laughing, conversing, smoking, drinking. Two clean-shaven men wearing white native clothes and matching caps stood side by side in the middle of the street, frowning in disgust. "We should return to the mosque," one said. The other nodded, but neither of them moved.

Most everyone in the crowd kept one eye on her house. "Anthony DEY CRAAAZE! Anthony DEY CRAAAZE!" some people chanted, then they started laughing. But, despite the festive atmosphere, not all was well. On the far side of the gate was a colorful group of people who seemed to be in distress. A tall woman had a bloody nose. Had there been a fight? Adaora squinted. Some from the group were nervously holding up rainbow-colored signs with a large spinning black sphere drawn in the center. She remembered similar flags when she'd visited San Francisco, California, once. A gay pride group? In Lagos? There were women in suits, and a man standing beside them was wearing a pink shirt and . . . leather thigh boots? *Well, that's both bold and stupid,* Adaora thought, frowning. They were going to get their asses kicked, or worse. She considered asking Benson to send some of his people to help them, but then realized that was an equally stupid idea. Better *not* to alert the military.

Father Oke and his parishioners were monopolizing the area directly in front of her house. They were singing, praying, swaying, and clapping. Some were jeering at the group carrying the gay pride signs. More were pleading for "Ayodele the Extraterrestrial" to come out so that they could embrace her and welcome her into their church. But Adaora could have sworn she also heard a few of them calling for "the abomination" to "show its heathen face." A bad sign.

Also a bad sign were the ten army trucks and cars parked nearby. And the soldiers walking toward Benson carrying AK-47s. Benson motioned for them to wait. He clutched Adaora's arm. "Walk," he said, dragging her toward her house.

"You don't have to be so rough," she snapped.

They were yards from the fence when the entire crowd suddenly sprang to life and started surging toward the gate.

"Anthony Dey Craaaaaaze! Anthony Dey Craaaaaaze!" people shouted.

"Hang on to me!" Benson yelled, pulling her toward the wrought-iron fence but away from the house's front door. Thankfully, the gate was still closed or the front yard would have been overrun. They made it out of the crunch, yet still had a good view of her yard. They watched as a tall, lanky, dark-skinned man, a little girl with braids, and a small boy in pajamas stepped out of the house. Anthony, Kola, and Fred. Kola was carrying Adaora's camera, filming the chaos in spite of the danger. Anthony kept anxiously glancing behind him into the house.

"Fred! Kola!" Adaora shouted, trying to rush forward, but Benson kept hold of her arm.

"Those are my *children*," Adaora yelled at him.

"Get us the creature and then you can get your children."

"We love you, Anthony!" a woman yelled.

"Let me go to them!" Adaora snapped, trying to tug away from him. "I've brought you here, haven't I?"

"*I* brought *you* here," he said. But he let go of her arm. "I have soldiers surrounding this place. Don't try to run; they all know what you look like."

Adaora took a step toward the gate when somebody grabbed her arm yet again. She turned, prepared to dig her nails into Benson's hand if she had to. It wasn't Benson.

"Chris?"

His eyes were wild, staring. She noted that he wasn't wearing white. He was wearing the same jeans and dress shirt he'd been wearing yesterday when he'd slapped her. "Fred and Kola are in danger! Let me go!"

"I've been following you," he snarled. "Who is *this* man? Another of your boyfriends? How many of them do you have?"

Adaora glanced toward Fred and Kola. "Don't you see the children in— Let *go* of me!" She threw a look at Benson, pleading for help. He smirked at her before moving to intercept Chris.

"Excuse me, sir, I need your wife to come with me," Benson told her husband. "This is important business. *Military* business."

Benson might as well have not spoken. "Nothing but a whoring witch!" her husband spat at her. "I saw you with him in the car, that other man . . ."

As Adaora braced herself for another slap across the face, she heard the sound of metal balls on glass coming from inside her front yard. Even from afar, the sound made her want to vomit. A few people around her actually did turn to the side and vomit. At the same time, Adaora felt relief. She knew exactly what was happening. The way things were going at the moment, *something* had to give. Something had to *intervene*. And something was about to.

"Ayodele," she whispered. "Thank God."

All around, people began to scream and press their hands to their ears as they stared into Adaora's yard. There were the clicking sounds of guns being raised and aimed. But all Adaora saw was the creased, starved, unshaven, raging face of her husband as he swung her by the arm and slammed her against the fence.

Moziz looked out the open door at the surging crowd. "We need comot for here, *jo*!" he shouted. "Now!" At his words, Ayodele the lizard became Ayodele the woman. Tolu whimpered, still clutching his gun, and backed into the house. They all followed, including Philo, fleeing into the house and out the back door to Troy, who waited in Moziz's car.

"Where she dey?" Troy asked as they threw themselves into the Nissan.

"Drive!" Moziz shouted. They peeled out exactly one minute before soldiers and police flooded into the narrow road behind Adaora's house like water flooding a beach.

CHAPTER 23

GREETINGS

This time when he attacked her, nothing magical happened. He wasn't held down by some mysterious force or anything like that. Then again, this time she felt no fear, no desperation, no shock. And she wasn't alone with him in their home, as she had been last night; there were soldiers and a mob around her. But still, she realized, she'd expected the strange force to have its effect, if necessary. She could *make* it happen.

Oh God, she thought.

It took two soldiers to pull Chris off Adaora. They wrestled him to the ground. Adaora grasped the gate for balance. She stared down at the man she'd lived with for over a decade who'd never ever laid a hand on her up until last night.

"Witch!" Chris sobbed as a soldier pushed his head to the concrete.

Benson took her arm, more gently than before. "Come on," he said. "Let's move to the front. Maybe you can help."

It was easy for them to get through the captivated crowd of fans, Christians, soldiers, Black Nexus members, curious passers-by, and press people now. Even Father Oke was speechless, the metal cross in his hands forgotten.

Where a moment before there had been a tiny green lizard, a woman now stood. Ayodele, in the middle of the lawn, looking at the crowd.

★   ★   ★   ★

"Mommy!" Fred shouted when he spotted Adaora through the fence. Anthony squinted then waved. Adaora waved back. *At least she's alive,* Anthony thought. Before he could stop the child, Adaora's son ran across the lawn to his mother. Anthony didn't dare move. The crowd was bewildered, confused, frightened. Anything could set them off. They didn't need to see him do anything but stay where he was.

As Fred ran toward Adaora, Ayodele looked down at Kola, who was still filming her. "You are doing a good job, Kola," Ayodele said. Kola grinned and continued filming. "You see your mother?" She pointed and Kola looked.

"Mommy!" Kola said, waving.

Adaora waved back with her free hand. Fred had reached her and was holding her other hand through the gate.

"Keep the camera on me, Kola," Ayodele instructed. Kola nodded, holding the camera up. She had about two hours of battery time left; she'd checked.

Ayodele looked over her captivated audience. She raised her chin and smiled.

"Greetings, people of Lagos," she said.

CHAPTER 24

GREETINGS

The Lagos Internet café was full of the usual suspects. There was the owner, Nonso Daouda, who sat behind his counter doing a poor job of not seeing what his customers did with his computers and Internet connections. Then there were about twenty men between the ages of nineteen and forty—all were in the process of e-mailing, texting, chatting, researching. Some were legit, most were up to some sort of 419. There was also one woman chatting with her boyfriend overseas. There was not one person here who had not been here yesterday doing the exact same thing.

Suddenly all the screens blinked off. They came back on showing the face of a young woman who called herself Ayodele. Everyone in the café sat back, watched, and listened. One guy who'd been in the process of texting his sister was watching the beautiful woman with long braids on his mobile phone.

"We landed here in the night," the woman said, her strange voice smooth and confident. The picture moved a bit. It was obvious that someone was holding the camera and trying his best to stay still. *"From beyond Earth. From space. You all will call us aliens. We are guests who wish to become citizens . . . here. We chose here. I am the first to come and I greet you."*

The Lagos restaurant served everything from Nigerian cuisine to Chinese food. Expats and locals alike frequented the place. That's what gave the Tribe's Calabash its reputation and popularity. Today it was full. But, now, all the eating and conversation had stopped. The eyes that weren't watching the wide-screen high-definition television on the wall were glued to mobile phones, computers, an iPad prototype, even e-readers, where the same slightly shaky footage aired.

"I apologize for the noise of our arrival and your rising waters from our landing," Ayodele said. *"Nobody is attacking you. And nobody will dare now. The winds of change are blowing. We are change. You will see."*

In a busy open-air market in the central Nigerian city of Abuja, people crowded around a clunky television that was for sale in a used-electronics booth.

"In less than twenty-four hours, I have seen love, hate, greed, ambition, and obsession among you," Ayodele said. *"I have seen compassion, hope, sadness, insecurity, art, intelligence, ingenuity, corruption, curiosity, and violence. This is life. We love life."*

Unoma was driving her old but wonderfully reliable off-white Peugeot down the Lagos Expressway listening to an Anthony Dey Craze song when her mobile phone buzzed. When she flipped it open to answer, the footage Kola was filming showed on the small screen.

Unoma worked hard to keep her eye on the road. "What the—?"

"Please, listen to me," Ayodele was saying. *"Consider me, consider us. As you have much to offer, so do we."*

Unoma pulled her car over to the side of the road to watch Ayodele on her phone. There were several cars in front of her that had also pulled over. Every single one was filled with people holding their mobile phones.

In Lagos, father, mother, and boy child sat in their family room, watching the alien on their old television. The adults wondered if what they were witnessing was real. Or maybe this woman on TV claiming she was from outer space was some sort of elaborate hoax. The mother had flipped through the channels, and the alien was speaking from every single one. But how hard could it be to take over Nigeria's broadcasting networks?

The boy child soaked in every word. Why not? It was so cool, *sha!*

"We come to bring you together and refuel your future," Ayodele said. *"Your land is full of a fuel that is tearing you apart."*

In Saudi Arabia, the Nigerian president, the First Lady, and two other officials, Yuusuf and Nicholas, were in the president's hospital room watching Ayodele on Yuusuf's mobile phone. It was a cheap phone he'd bought in Lagos. He hadn't turned it on in weeks, since he'd arrived in Saudi Arabia with the president. Why would he, when his phone service didn't reach outside of Nigeria? However, minutes ago, it had turned itself on and started communicating a most peculiar message from a strange woman.

"We do not seek your oil or your other resources," she said. *"We are here to nurture your world."*

A single thought went through the president's mind: *Benson was telling the truth.*

Ayodele looked out at the people. Kola was directly in front of her with the camera, and so it seemed that when Ayodele looked at the crowd before her, she looked out at all the people watching on large and small screens in Lagos. The expression on Ayodele's face was serious, almost threatening. Intense.

"So, what will you do?" Ayodele asked.

Her captivated audience was completely silent.

Then . . . *BOOM!*

CHAPTER 25

THE BARRED BEACH

Bar Beach was deserted. There were now barricades preventing anyone from coming onto it. A minute after the second great sound eruption, military men and police who'd been guarding the place had dropped or pocketed their mobile phones and run off. The noise was enormous. It was bigger and richer than the one from the previous night. All the car and building windows within a one-mile radius were shattered; birds, insects, and bats fell to the ground; dogs barked; cats hid; lizards scurried; several forms of bacteria died, and others germinated. The noise this time was so profound that many of the weaker multicellular organisms in parts of the ocean closest to the source were obliterated. This kind of noise would awaken goddesses, gods, spirits, and ancestors.

Only Private Agu sat on the beach, yards from the water, sopping wet. The cut on his forehead had begun bleeding again, but the swelling on his face had gone down . . . some. The sea cow had left him about a fifth of a mile from the beach. As he'd started swimming to safety, a rip current nearly dragged him back out to sea to his death. Thankfully he knew to swim parallel to it and managed to make it to shore.

He'd crawled out of the water and turned to see if the sea cow was anywhere in sight. It was gone. It probably hadn't even witnessed his brief struggle in the water. And that was when he'd heard the sonic boom. It knocked him off his feet, and he fell, face-first, into the sand, where he lay for a long moment, his ears ringing. He didn't cover them. He didn't wipe the blood from his face. He forgot for the moment about finding his way back to Adaora's house to find them: Adaora, Anthony, and the possibly evil Ayodele. Instead he just sat there. For nearly twenty minutes, he sat there.

Gradually, he realized something was happening. He squinted at the sea. At first all he could see were tiny weaving lights against the darkening sky. Then he became aware that he was no longer alone on the beach. There were people with mobile phones and flashlights. He could hear voices raised in excitement.

A crash came from the street behind him, but his attention was drawn to something that was lying on the beach, huge and black against the city lights. Was it another monster? He'd seen plenty in the sea as the manatee had brought him to shore. But if it was, why would these people be here? It was black and nearly the size of a bus, and there was a crowd around it.

"A whale?" he whispered, squinting harder. It didn't help. He got up and stumbled toward the huge lump, but then his legs collapsed and he sat down hard on the sand.

There was a man running from the lump up the beach. He changed course and ran to Agu, a grin on his face. He was carrying a big whitish chunk in his arms. "Na from street you come?" he asked.

"No," Agu said.

The man laughed. "You look like say na from de street you come. Anyway, no *wahala*. People dey craze. Na only God fit provide. E get big fish for there wey from water come. De fish face look like auto-bus, but e get plenty meat for body."

"What . . . ?"

"Go get your own before other people take am finish, o!" the man said. "Na sea pork! De meat is so sweet!" He took off with his meat before Agu could say more. Agu felt as if the world had turned upside down. Everything seemed dreamlike. He looked toward the street where the flames of a burning building lit up the area. He saw and heard people milling about vigorously in the streets and cars and trucks beeping as they tried to get through. It looked like a riot. Yet here were these people carving up what could only be a whale. Even in the midst of such chaos, people were still people. Still hungry and hoping to take advantage of a good situation.

As he sat, he saw shapes in the water, illuminated by the last rays of the setting sun, moving toward the land. They grew, rising out of the waves, coalescing into recognizable shapes. Human shapes. They were people, hundreds of people, walking straight out of the ocean onto Bar Beach. First they were wet. Then they were dry. At least, that was how it looked to Agu in the waning light. Some passed by only a few steps from him. Others walked farther up and down the beach. Several walked out of the water mere feet from the dead whale. The Lagosians were so preoccupied with securing their share of the bounty that they never looked twice at the space people walking out of the sea.

Some of them were dressed in various types of traditional garb, some in military attire, some in police uniforms, others in Westernized civilian clothes. Most of them were African, a small few Asian, one white. All were completely dry, and Agu could smell roses and seaweed as they drifted past him. All of them could pass for Lagosians.

They walked up the beach as an enormous object, all shifting oily black spires and spirals and brown and yellow lights, rose out of the water. It swallowed up the darkening horizon with its girth.

Only then did the people carving up the whale pause to look up. Then they took their meat and got out of that place as quickly as possible.

ACT II
AWAKENING

THE BONE COLLECTOR

For a tarantula, he is not very big. He lost a leg battling a pepsis wasp five years ago. But he is healthy. He lives well. This patch of forest is good for him—full of plump, slow-moving, and juicy prey, and rich dark places to catch them.

Nevertheless, the tarantula believes that life is best lived by embracing the changes that come his way. So he gently places a leg on the warming pavement; the leg beside the space of the one he lost. This leg is the most sensitive, always has been. With it, he can feel the soul of the great spider artist of the land, she who weaves all things into existence.

There is no vibration on the road. No approaching human vehicles. But he knows that when they come, they come fast and hard. He has crossed this highway many times. And always in the late evening when the surface is cool. Like now.

Still, each crossing has been a close call. First he would feel the vibrations, and then a vehicle would appear on the horizon. He'd scramble for the other side, wondering if it was finally time to be reborn. But he had always made it and gone on to experience the meaty bloody bounty of the new patch of forest.

Today it is time to seek fresh pastures again. Something dynamic has happened. Last night, he felt a vibration so intense it made his entire body shudder with pleasure. Then hours ago, he felt an even more intense vibration, down to the finest hairs on his body, the spinners in his abdomen, the bottoms of each of his feet. The vibration was glorious. It was a call for change.

Now, he will answer that call.

The moment his sensitive leg touches the pavement, he starts running. Strangely, losing a leg has made him faster and more agile. This has always been to his advantage in capturing food and mating. Despite the physical pain, the blow to his identity that the loss of the leg caused, he knows that that wasp did him a favor.

He is only a third of the way across the road when the rumbling comes. The vibration. But not the delicious vibration of last night, or of hours ago. This one is average, expected, uninspiring. A human vehicle. The tarantula scrambles faster, certain that he will make it across. Certain of his extraordinary speed.

Crunch.

Once Adaora's car passes the small stretch of road flanked by forest, this portion of the Lagos–Benin Expressway stretches its old tired asphalt with ease and comfort. The crushed body of the large, seven-limbed tarantula sinks into the road's sun-warmed surface like fresh palm oil on hot bread.

Ayodele will be fascinated at this aspect of her new world. She has yet to realize that there are other things inhabiting Lagos besides carbon-based creatures. There are greater beings of the earth, soil, sea, lagoon, and land. This stretch of highway has named itself the Bone Collector. It mostly collects human bones, and the bones of human vehicles. But sometimes it likes the chitinous bones of spiders, too.

CHAPTER 26

PAPA

The boy was there. He had no mobile phone. He had never touched a computer. The cramped room he shared with seven other homeless boys had no television. He had no access to any type of screen, large or small. He hadn't even been immunized against polio. But he was there. Standing before the wrought-iron fence with the hundreds of other people.

To his left was a group of colorful, odd-looking folk who were arguing with a group of mean-looking men. And to his right, dressed in white, were people who'd been "born and born again." They were the type who would bring him into their home which was really a church to feed him pounded yam and meatless egusi soup as they talked about the magic white man who used to live in the desert.

Despite all these interesting things happening around him, his attention was on something else. The woman he knew wasn't a woman was speaking.

Papa, the man who took care of him and the other boys, had brought him and four others after hearing on the news that there was a gathering in front of this house. Such gatherings were good places to pick pockets and beg. The boy was not good at picking pockets. He was too slow, too distracted. Something always caught his eye. A woman's shiny shoes, a man's funny way of speaking, an insect on his shoulder. And next thing he knew, he'd forget what he was doing, sometimes with his hand still in someone's pocket.

Today, the distraction was the woman who was not a woman. Even before she started speaking, he noticed her. Oh, he had *seen* her. She was a lizard and then she was a woman. He saw her run out of the house as a lizard, between the tall dark-skinned man's legs. It hurt his brain to process the sight of the tiny green lizard swelling and inflating into a mysterious woman with scary eyes.

Vaguely, he remembered her from Bar Beach just before the water had taken the three people. The memory of the stolen people was stronger than most in his head, but he still could not make sense of the one who was the woman who was not a woman. He could not comprehend the fact that he was seeing her a second time. He could only feel a remote sense of recognition and curiosity.

He'd pressed his face to the fence and listened but barely comprehended a word she said. Still, he understood he was witnessing something deep, just as he had witnessed the three people taken on the beach by a grasping fist of water. One of those people had been that dark-skinned man whose legs the lizard had run between. That he remembered.

The boy grinned as the woman spoke. She had a voice like the sweetest candy. He rarely got to eat candy. He especially liked minty chewing gum; it made his thoughts clearer. And when he chewed, the motion of his mouth made him know that if he tried really, really hard, he could speak. His voice would rush up his throat like warm honey and he would produce words and they would make sense.

Yes, he liked the odd woman's voice very much. As he grinned, he felt warm wet saliva dribble from the sides of his mouth down his chin. Drooling would earn him a slap on the back of the head if his guardian noticed, but he couldn't help it. Not right now. He was imagining he could speak, and doing so was worth the punishment.

When the woman finished talking, there was silence. Everyone around him just stood there. But he liked the looks on their faces. People were dreamily staring at the woman or their mobile phones. He turned this way and that. It was as if he were the only living person

in a sea of people-trees. No one moved. They all just smiled pleasantly, as if they were imagining charming possibilities and surprising potential. As he was.

"See what the Lord has brought us?" one of the born and born
again people finally said, breaking the silence. He held up his hands,
making his bright white robes billow. He was heavyset, and his shiny
black leather shoes were the type worn by men who drove shiny
expensive cars that they would park in the driveways of those gated
houses the boy was never allowed near. The last such house he'd
walked past, the gateman had sneered at him and pointed his big
gun at the boy and said, "Boom!" as he laughed and sat back on his
stool. Yes, this man looked as though he would hire a man like that.

"These alien beings will be embraced by the Lord!" the man said.

"Enough!" someone shouted back. "This isn't the time for that!"

It was a woman's voice. The boy looked around, but he was too
small and could not see who it was.

"Enough?" the man in white responded. "The size of the Lord's
flock will never be large enough! Not until he has gathered *all* of his
sheep! Today is a *new* day. A day when—"

The boy followed the stone with his eyes as it sailed through the
air. It hit the bishop on the butt, leaving a dirty mark on his immaculate robes. He yelped and whirled around, furious. There were
squeals of protest from the people near the bishop.

"Hey!"

"O ga, o!"

"*Chineke!*"

"What the hell!"

Then something flew in the opposite direction. A bottle of
mineral, the liquid inside was brown, possibly Coca-Cola. It must
have missed its target, for it landed on the ground, shattering,
splashing a young woman with glass and liquid.

There were exclamations in three different languages, none of
which the boy could understand, except for the Pidgin English.

The man in white raised his hands, pleading, "I . . . I didn't throw—"

The boy turned around and saw his guardian a few steps away. The other boys had already pressed themselves to him. None of them looked like they had stealing on their minds. Except one boy named Oyo, who was extracting a man's wallet from his pocket. The man looked down into Oyo's eyes and slapped him across the face. Their guardian flared up and punched the man in the belly.

The mute boy laughed silently and was about to run to his guardian when he heard another hard slap. He jumped, and for a moment, because the sound was so familiar to him, felt his own cheek sting and warm up. He turned around and saw the bishop had fallen. There was a tall, sour-faced man with an open hand standing over him and another woman and man yelling at the bishop.

BAM! BAM! BAM! BAM!

The gunshots made the boy crouch low to the ground, hiding his head in his arms. He stayed there, even as people started running. Two men beside him were throwing punches and then a third jumped in. A woman was shrieking in a high-pitched voice that made the boy want to tear his hair out. Then she grunted as something smashed into the side of her head.

"Heeeeeeey!" several men beside her exclaimed. Something crashed to the ground. Two soldiers shot in the air to get people's attention. This only caused more chaos. When the boy saw a soldier's chest blow open from the impact of two bullets, he took off with everyone else. Where was the white smoke coming from? He sneezed and coughed, his eyes tearing up and his nose running. The air smelled sour, bloody, dirty. His chest burned when he inhaled. His ears felt stuffed with cotton. He didn't know where he was going. Or where his guardian had gone.

There.

His guardian. Dragging the four other boys down the street. The mute boy raised his hand and waved, before being overcome by a fit of coughs. He wished he could scream. He *needed* to scream. He glanced at the house, looking for the womanlike creature with the sweet voice. If he could only hear her speak again, he was sure he could force his voice to work. But she was gone. There were people on the lawn. Some trying to get into the house. There was a group of people embroiled in a terrible fight. Why was everyone fighting?

He could not think about that now. He tried to run toward his guardian, but the people around him were running in the opposite direction. People on the other side of the crowd must have tried to come toward his part of the crowd, because now the boy was pressed between five older boys as the crowd squeezed. He couldn't see his guardian anymore. He struggled, but his feet weren't even on the ground and the crowd was moving away.

When it released him, he ran. A woman fell right before his eyes, wisps of smoke issuing from a bullet hole in her leg. She was one of the women wearing the men's clothing. The boy ran and ran. As the sun went down, the boy would witness more than his mind could contain.

CHAPTER 27

FISAYO

It was different for Fisayo, the younger sister of Jacobs. The Yoruba woman who was the smart secretary by day and prostitute by night. Since seeing those three people taken by the fist of water the night before, she hadn't felt like herself. Seeing the footage her brother had shown to the Black Nexus only made her feel more hopeless.

She stood on the concrete walkway that ran alongside Bar Beach. Less than twenty-four hours after the creatures had invaded the water, she had returned to the beach out of habit. Since dropping out of university, this stretch of sand was where her future resided. She would walk it until the day some man wanted more than just to have sex with her. Since she'd put aside her dream of being a nurse, she'd embraced the idea of being a wife, like her mother. A woman who minded the home, the children and lay on her back for only one man. The prostitution was just to make ends meet until that time came.

The time had already come for Bunmi, her best friend, the person who had first shown her how to exchange sex with men for money. Bunmi, whom she no longer heard from. Bunmi, who lived in a mansion on Victoria Island with a rich and powerful businessman she'd met while walking along Bar Beach. The future would come for Fisayo. Bar Beach was where she knew her destiny waited for her.

Nevertheless, after the great boom last night, seeing the shapeshifting creature skulk out of the water and then the three people kidnapped, she'd started wondering if her future was somewhere else. Something else. She had started walking, and her legs took her to Bar Beach. When she got there, she barely recognized it. The waters had crept more than halfway up the sand. There were barricades set up in front of the concrete walkways, closed beachfront shops with signs up that said KEEP OUT. And in front of the barricades, every hundred feet, stood armed soldiers. The one she approached was young, probably no older than twenty. He was sweating and shifty-eyed. He clearly didn't want to be on duty.

Why are there soldiers on the beach? she wondered. *And barricades?* As she approached the young man to ask him, her phone went off. The caller ID said "unknown." When she opened it, she saw the face of an angel. A serene African woman with dark skin and perfect braids. She reminded Fisayo of an old photo of her grandmother when her grandmother was young.

"That's the girl from the beach," she whispered. *And from the footage Jacobs had,* she thought. *My God.*

This woman on her cheap mobile phone that couldn't do more than make and receive phone calls, gazed at her as if she could actually *see* her. Fisayo froze. If she had looked up, she'd have realized that people walking up and down the street had also stopped and were looking at their phones. Two cars and a truck on the road nearby had pulled over. Hawkers had stopped hawking.

Then the woman on her phone began to speak. Right there on the walkway, Fisayo sat down. Today, she was wearing jeans, a gently fitting red blouse, and gym shoes, instead of her usual tight short skirt, breast-popping top, and pumps. So she was comfortable as she heard the most horrifying thing in her life. The alien woman had hijacked her phone. She was speaking about taking over Nigeria. Fisayo shut her phone.

She got up. She closed her eyes and took a deep breath. This was the rapture, the apocalypse, the end. She opened her mouth to take in more air. She wanted to get to the beach and stand before the water. She wanted to be taken, like those three people who'd been embraced the night before. *What have I done that is so terrible?* she wondered as she stepped up to the soldier. *Selling my body? It is just a body. I have a pure heart.*

The soldier was staring at his mobile phone, his mouth hanging open, his gun leaning against his leg. His hands shook. Fisayo could hear the strange woman speaking on his phone too.

"We do not seek your oil or your other resources," the woman was saying. *"We are here to nurture your world. So, what will you do?"*

"What the hell is this?" he whispered, looking at Fisayo. "Is this a joke? Are we under attack by terrorists?" Her heart leaped. His eyes were filled with raw fear. One could not gaze into such eyes and not feel the same thing.

It was hard for her to speak but she did. "I . . . I don't know," she said. "But I know that—"

BOOM!

They grabbed each other and dropped to the ground. Fisayo screamed, clutching the soldier. Her head was vibrating. The ground was shaking. The young man, who smelled like sweat and soap, was shuddering and holding on to her, too. Everything trembled. Birds and bats fell around them. These were followed by smaller creatures—mosquitoes, flies, gnats—which fell to the ground dead. The concrete walkway cracked beneath them. Car alarms went off. Two cars on the road crashed into each other. Several people fell over. The air began to stink of fish.

And then it stopped. Fisayo thought she might have gone deaf. Her ears felt plugged, and the young man was speaking to her. All she heard were muffled sounds. He was helping her up. Her nose was bleeding, as was his.

He was asking her something. She squinted, straining to hear him. "Are you all right?" he shouted.

"Yes!" she shouted back, wiping the blood from her nose.

He grabbed his gun, looking beyond her. She turned and gasped.

Four men were fighting. There were several naira notes on the ground. Two of the men were grabbing at them. Another two were trying to stop them; one picked up a large rock.

Fisayo turned away before the man brought it down on the other man's head. The soldier started running toward them, his gun in his hand. Not bothering to remove her gym shoes, Fisayo turned and ran past the barricade onto the barred Bar Beach.

Aside from the surf being way too high and starting to flood some of the beachside restaurants, the water seemed normal enough. It wasn't boiling hot or freezing cold. It was still clear and wet. She touched the water that lapped at her shoes and brought it to her lips. Still salty. A low wind blew gentle waves on the water and the sun was setting.

"Take me!" she shouted at the ocean. The air smelled cloyingly fishy, yet the more she inhaled, the clearer her mind felt. Clean, clean air. "Take me!" She threw off her gym shoes and socks and moved into the water.

Dead fish, large and small, littered the sand and the gentle waves that moved in and out. She saw a deflated jellyfish and the lumpy red-and-white claw of a large crab. She splashed past them. "Please! Take me, o!" she screamed, crying. Her head ached, her nose was still bleeding, and the world was still muted.

She stopped, thigh deep, the waves moving around her legs, staring out at the vast, dark blue water. The sun was barely above the horizon. Soon to set. Yellow-orange like a piece of candy. She spotted an oil tanker in the distance. Then she saw . . . She didn't know what it was. In the growing darkness, the huge thing was black and undulating, pushing up and pulling in great pillars like giant phalluses. Red lights pulsed within it. A horrible vehicle; the devil's *danfo*. It stretched across the horizon. Had the oil tanker heard the great BOOM, too? Was it louder there? She couldn't see the tanker any more. Had the aliens taken all of them?

In the middle distance, something enormous and serpentine leaped out of the water and splashed back. She felt a lump in her throat. Strange ships in the distance, monsters in the deep. The end was certainly near. "TAKE ME!" she screamed. Then she dove in. *Plash!*

She swam. The salt water stung her eyes, and her arms quickly felt strained. Soon, she was far out enough to not feel the bottom. She kept swimming.

She felt her lace-front wig lift from her head, leaving only her wig cap. That wig had cost her far too many naira, but at the time she'd seen it as an investment in her future. Now it was gone. . . . She hoped she'd soon follow.

The water embraced her. Like a hand. Like a womb. *It's taking me,* she thought. She shut her eyes and stopped swimming, held out her arms, floated on the surface. She could feel her body being turned in circles. She opened her mouth and inhaled her last breath of air, fighting to stay relaxed. Then she rolled over, exhaled, and sank into the darkness.

When she was washed back onto the beach, she thought she was dead. She opened her eyes and tried to gasp. Instead, she threw up nearly a gallon of water. She vomited and vomited. Then she got up and walked to the water and shouted, "May God set you on fire!" She tore off her wig cap and rubbed her short, wet, damaged hair, freeing it. As she turned to leave Bar Beach, she noticed someone sitting on the sand. A man.

She squinted. It was a man in military uniform. She went a few steps closer and then froze. He was soaked . . . because he'd just dragged himself out of the ocean. She recognized him. He was one of the stolen people. He, too, had been rejected. Or maybe *he* was one of *them* now. She moved toward him, her bare feet kneading the sand as she walked. She would shout at him. She would slap him. She would . . . She stopped. There was something enormous lying on the beach beyond him. Enormous like . . . a whale? There were people around and on top of it too. She could see that several of them had machetes and knives. "Oh my God," she whispered.

Then movement in the water caught her attention and she gasped. *They* were coming out of it—people who were not people. Men. Women. No children. Tall. Short. Mostly African. Some Asian. They walked around her and past her without looking at her. Without seeing her. What looked like a white man dressed like an Igbo man; he even wore a red-black-and-white–striped woolen chieftaincy cap. Ridiculous! All wrong. Foreign. *Alien.*

She felt something break, deep in her mind. Last night, she had sold herself to an American man who afterward told her she was not dirtier than any other women from any other part of the world. She had watched the devil snatch people into the ocean and return them, infused with evil. She had later seen one of the evil shape-shifters in recorded footage on her brother's phone and then on the screen of her own phone. A whale had died on Bar Beach. Now she was seeing the city of her birth and upbringing invaded by the evil. And not one of the creatures turned to look at her. To them, she was nothing.

Her eye twitched and her shoeless feet ached. She shoved her wig cap into her bra and scratched at her tender scalp. She had to find her brother. But she would help others, first. She had to tell people. She had to bring Lagos the news, and it wasn't good news.

When she'd walked down to Bar Beach, she'd been looking for her future. Now she had found it. The world was ripe, on the brink of rotting, of apocalypse. She had to save it. Save it from *them.*

She'd start with him, the man they'd returned.

But when she looked where he'd been sitting, he was gone. Then she saw him. There he was, stumbling onto the walkway. She took off after him.

CHAPTER 28

THE PLANTAIN TREE

Adaora grasped her son Fred's hand as they watched Father Oke, who stood a few feet away. Someone had thrown a rock at him, and then one of the people in his flock responded by throwing a bottle of Coke toward where the rock had come from. Now the tall, sour-faced man who'd initially thrown the rock stood before Father Oke. The woman who'd been splashed with Coke and broken glass stood behind him, glaring angrily at Father Oke.

Father Oke raised his hands, pleading, "I . . . I didn't throw—"

The man slapped Father Oke hard across the face. As Father Oke went down, two of his followers surged forward, only to be yanked back by other followers.

"You may not have thrown it, Father, but you've kept my mother poor with your damned church," the man who'd slapped him sneered, looking down at the cowering bishop. "Rubbish." He glared at the stunned followers and spat to the side. "All of you are rubbish."

"Look am!" a young man in the onlooking crowd said. "Na de idiot priest who go slap woman on YouTube! Na justice!"

"See how you like it!" a woman shouted at Oke. "Who winch now?!"

Adaora would have smiled if she hadn't been in fear for Father Oke's life. She despised him, but she didn't want him beaten to death by a mob. She squeezed Fred's hand harder, and he squeezed back. "Mommy," he said, tears in his eyes. "Don't let go."

"I won't."

Near the front door in the yard, Ayodele was watching all the *wahala* in the crowd, a pleasant smile on her face. Anthony stood beside Ayodele, grasping Kola's hand as the little girl continued to film, holding the camera with her other hand.

Benson still stood outside the wrought-iron gate. "Shoot it!" Benson yelled to the soldiers on his left, spit flying from his mouth. He was standing beside Adaora, hopping from one foot to the other like a child about to have an accident, his eyes wide and wild. He was pointing at Ayodele. "Shoot it, Private Elenwoke! Shoot it *now!*"

"No!" Adaora shouted. Still holding Fred's hand, she turned to Benson. "No! Don't!"

Private Elenwoke looked confused as he raised his AK-47 and aimed through the gate at Ayodele.

Ayodele's eyes fell on him.

"Don't!" Adaora screamed.

BLAM! BLAM! BLAM! BLAM!

The smile dropped from Ayodele's face as she stumbled back and looked down at her abdomen. There were several holes through her white dress, at her belly and her chest.

"Kola!" Adaora screamed. Kola had been next to Ayodele, filming her, when the soldiers started shooting. Now she was sitting at Ayodele's feet. Her left arm was bleeding. Adaora let go of Fred's hand and pushed past Benson and Father Oke's white-robed followers, fumbling for her key ring. She shoved a key in the keyhole and opened the gate. The moment she was in, Fred ran to her and grabbed her hand. They both ran to Kola. Adaora heard people flooding into the yard behind her.

She reached her daughter as Anthony stood looking down at Ayodele, who'd begun shrieking and thrashing. Adaora picked Kola up and moved her away from the woman writhing on the ground.

Kola was whimpering as she sat, trying not to look at her left arm. "Is it bad, Mommy? Is it bad?"

"It's not bad, honey," Adaora said, looking over her daughter's arm. Blood pumped from the gunshot wound to the beat of Kola's heart. It took all Adaora had to stay calm. "Relax," she breathed. "Lie down, sweetie." As Kola did so, Adaora took her arm and held it up. Gravity would slow the blood loss. She wasn't sure if she should apply pressure with the bullet possibly still in there. Beside her, Fred began to cry.

Adaora glanced at Anthony. He was looking down at Ayodele, who screamed and undulated and . . . began to melt. The sound of marbles on glass was everywhere, filling Adaora's head, the noise making it hard to think. Adaora could feel even the tiny hairs on her face vibrating and pulling. Her stomach shuddered and her head throbbed. Benson and five soldiers stood over them, pointing guns at Ayodele, expressions uncertain.

Benson was shouting at Ayodele; he'd been shouting the whole time. "Don't move! Just, just, just stay right there, now."

A soldier knelt beside Kola with a first aid kit.

"Keep her arm up," he said, opening up the box.

"Ah!" she heard Fred cry. She turned round to see Chris wrapping his arms around the boy, and every muscle in her body tensed.

"It's okay," Chris whispered into his son's ear. "Shhh." He looked at Adaora. "Is she okay?"

"She's been shot," Adaora said.

They looked into each other's eyes for several seconds. Then Chris nodded at Adaora and she nodded back. The soldier was examining Kola's arm. The bleeding didn't appear to be slowing.

Yards away, Ayodele was still shrieking as Anthony stood over her, unsure of what to do. She had bled not a drop of blood. She wasn't just melting, she was *disintegrating*. Her skin was growing grainy, her hands and the lower part of her face losing their shape. Her dress melted away like cotton candy touched by water. She was staring at Kola, and Kola was staring at her. Then Ayodele looked up at Benson, her gaze moving wildly between him and the other soldiers. Her left eye had dissolved to nothing, but the look in her still intact right eye was one of pure hatred.

Benson fired his gun, hitting Ayodele in the leg. Anthony leaped to the side. "Shoot it!" Benson yelled. "Kill it! Kill it!" Three soldiers opened fire on Ayodele again. They shot her in the thighs, chest, face, everywhere. Her fragile, graying body was hopping and jerking on the ground. Adaora pulled Kola close as the child screamed and sobbed. She hoped Chris was doing the same for Fred.

The sound of marbles grew so loud that she hunched over Kola to protect her from the harsh noise. She struggled to keep Kola's arm up. Through it all she could hear muffled screaming. The voices of men, not Ayodele. Then she felt more than heard a wet *pop!*, and hot liquid sprayed across her face. And then . . . silence.

She opened her eyes and immediately wanted to shut them again.

Where the soldiers had stood, heaps of raw meat wriggled and then became still. Her husband was covering Fred's face. The one soldier who had been tending to Kola's arm had his hands over his ears and his eyes shut. Anthony was on the lawn, mere steps away, his head pressed to the grass, his hands over his head. All of them were wet with blood. Adaora was the only one in the group who had her eyes open. There were people from the crowd in the yard, some running into the house, others standing yards away, staring. Most were still cowering, terrified by the gunshots and alien noise. However, Adaora focused only on her children, husband, the soldier beside her, Anthony, and . . . the alien. Ayodele slowly got up and stood tall before the veiny masses of yellow-white fat, pink-red tissue and muscle, bunched brown skin, and broken bone. She was whole, spotless, and now wearing a plain brown dress. She was scowling at Adaora.

Adaora looked up at her, pleading silently. She didn't know what she was asking for but she was pleading. These aliens had come in *peace*. Had come. *Had.*

Ayodele turned to the bloody lumps, and Adaora hid her face in

Kola's neck. "It's going to be fine," she murmured into her daughter's ear. She heard the sound of marbles again. And when she looked up this time, she hoped that Ayodele would be gone. She was not. But the wet piles of meat, the scattered clothes, even the spattered blood, were gone as though they had never been there.

In their place was a plantain tree, heavy with unripe plantain. Adaora stared at it, understanding what had happened. She felt like both vomiting and sighing with relief. Ayodele had taken the elements of oxygen, carbon, hydrogen, nitrogen, calcium, phosphorus, potassium, sulfur, sodium, chlorine, and magnesium that had been Benson and the other soldiers and rearranged them into a plant. *Does the soul transform too?* Adaora wondered. She'd never believed in God, but she was a scientist and knew that matter could be neither created nor destroyed. It just changed form.

"Are you happy with *that*?" Ayodele snapped at Adaora.

Adaora nodded.

"I am not," Ayodele said. She walked toward the gate. In the emptying street, a few people were fighting, some were gawking, others crying, but most of them fleeing. Adaora's mouth fell open as she noticed this for the first time. She'd been so focused on what was happening in the yard that she hadn't realized that something worse had happened in the street! There were *bodies* lying on the road, wounded people crawling to safety, a car burning, people crying. Adaora could hear the sound of glass breaking.

"Don't," Kola whispered. She cringed at the pain in her arm. She was looking at Ayodele, now halfway across the yard. "We need you."

Adaora looked at her daughter, shocked. *No! No, leave us. Keep going,* she thought to Ayodele. *I beg you.*

Somehow, over all the noise, Ayodele heard Kola's soft words. She stopped.

"I'm sorry that you hurt," Kola said weakly. "So do I."

Ayodele came back to them. Chris got to his feet and picked up Fred, backing away from Ayodele as she knelt beside Kola. There were tears in Ayodele's eyes. Adaora put a protective arm around Kola as Ayodele looked at them. As Adaora watched, two tiny, dented metal objects fell from beneath Ayodele's brown gown; one landed in the grass beside her, and the other landed on her thigh and tumbled to the grass. It was still hot, but not enough to burn. A bullet.

Ayodele looked into Adaora's eyes. Adaora held her breath. The warm, curious, lighthearted being that Ayodele had been was gone. The eyes Adaora looked into now were those of an angry, bitter old woman. Adaora didn't move away with Kola as Ayodele leaned closer. It was instinct. Despite the look on Ayodele's face, Adaora knew this creature would not harm her child. Ayodele unwrapped the tight bandage from Kola's arm. Blood immediately began to seep out of the wound.

"Mommy," Kola moaned. Adaora took her other hand.

"It's okay," Adaora whispered.

The expression on Ayodele's face softened as she ran her hand over the blood on Kola's arm. Wherever her hand touched, it absorbed the blood like a sponge. Soon, there was only the bullet wound left. Adaora's stomach clenched at the sight of it. Ayodele lightly touched the injury, and her hand seemed to disintegrate into a colorful mist like the type one would see rising from a waterfall in the early-morning sun. Kola tensed as the mist sank into her arm.

"Does it hurt?" Adaora asked, trying to keep her voice calm.

"Feels like ants," Kola whimpered. "I hate ants. I hate ants, Mommy!"

"They are not ants, dear," Ayodele said, her voice gentle and soft, almost as it had been before. "It is me. I am *speaking* with you. Rebuild yourself, Kola."

Kola closed her eyes, and Adaora could have sworn she felt heat pulse from her daughter. She smelled smoke.

"Good," Ayodele said. "Become better."

Kola was breathing heavily now and frowning, her eyes still shut.

Now Adaora could actually see the acrid-smelling smoke lifting from her daughter's arm. It was thick and white and rose lazily into the air like incense.

When Ayodele took her hand away, the hole was gone. Kola took one look at her healed flesh and then leaned forward and vomited, coughing between heaves from the smoke.

"It is overwhelming," Ayodele said flatly. Adaora didn't think she sounded all that overwhelmed.

Something crashed, but not from the street. Adaora looked up at her house. "Oh my God!"

The smell of smoke hadn't come from her daughter's healed arm. Something in the house was on fire. Her husband, Anthony, and the soldier who'd been helping Kola ran inside. Ayodele followed at a walk. Adaora scrambled to her feet, hesitated, and then followed, dragging Kola and Fred.

While Ayodele had been transforming the soldiers, dispelling bullets from her flesh, and healing Kola's arm, looters had stolen Chris and Adaora's televisions and computers. They'd tracked in dirt and destroyed the back door. And someone had purposely turned on the gas stove and tried to set some yams from the pantry on fire. Chris put out the smoldering tubers with the fire extinguisher. The soldier, whose name was Hassam, helped too, though he had a glazed look of shock and confusion in his eyes. "That woman healed the child," he said, turning the stove off and opening a window. "She kills *and* gives life."

Adaora sat the children at the kitchen table, and Ayodele sat across from them. She made a fist and rested it on the table. To Adaora, this was worse than slamming it. She paused, glancing at her husband, who was a few steps away. Then she went to check on her lab. The lab's door was closed. A good sign.

"I hate humans," Ayodele said. Adaora could hear her clearly, even though Ayodele was in the kitchen and she was down the hall. "I want nothing to do with you," Ayodele continued. "Any of you."

Adaora frowned, about to go back to the kitchen. She trusted Ayodele to not hurt her children, but that was as far as her trust went. Ayodele had caused those men to explode and then turned them into a tree. That's what one got for trying to kill her. . . . Could she even *be* killed? Adaora didn't know. *Maybe Ayodele responded so strongly because they made her experience pain,* Adaora thought. *The way she was screaming and thrashing, she was not just in pain, she was shocked to be in it.* Whatever the reason, it clearly wasn't good to get on her bad side. Adaora brought out the key to her lab as she grasped the door's knob. Her heart was racing.

"Do you hate all of us?" she heard Kola ask Ayodele. "You just saved me."

Before inserting the key, Adaora tried the door knob. It turned. "Shit," Adaora hissed. She leaned her head against the door, tears rolling down her cheeks. She focused on the voice of her children in the kitchen.

"And just because a few humans acted stupid, it doesn't mean we're all stupid," she heard Fred add. "We learned that in school. And you're much smarter than everyone at school put together."

Adaora smiled, wiping away her tears.

"And you can't cause all that has happened and then just leave," Kola said firmly. "You said you had a mission! That you were the am . . . ambah-sidoor, remember?"

"I will think about it," Ayodele said.

Adaora went into her lab. As she descended the stairs, she could practically feel it. Yes, people had been down here. The broken lock made that clear. As soon as she'd turned on the lights, she turned them right back off again. She'd seen all she needed to see. Nothing was on fire. But the floors were wet from the smashed aquarium, the limp bodies of her beloved fish already drying. The television and computer were gone. The place was ransacked. *They did all this while we were fighting for our lives in the front yard,* she thought. *What kind of people would do that?* But she knew the answer. It didn't take much in Lagos. All it took was a semi-peaceful alien invasion to destroy everything she held dear. Well, nearly everything. Her children were alive and happy.

She went back up.

"Sit," Anthony told Chris. The children were upstairs in Kola's room, asleep, and Adaora was watching over them. Downstairs, Ayodele watched out the window with the soldier Hassam.

In the kitchen, Chris sat down at the table. Anthony placed the large bowl of cold jollof rice before Chris and dug a spoon into it. The power was out, and it would have been crazy to turn on the generator; the noise would attract more attention. Plus, the microwave had been stolen.

"Eat," he said.

"Do you think she's an angel, then?" Chris asked.

Anthony shook his head. "Not at all, *chale*. You need to start thinking outside the box, my friend."

Chris frowned at him, frowned at the rice, and frowned at the spoon in the rice. He slowly picked it up. Then he ate, and as he ate, he began to feel better. Anthony crossed his arms over his chest, watching him.

Upstairs, Adaora leaned against the wall, glad her two children were asleep before her. They were okay. Both of them. She felt emotion swell in her chest as she allowed herself to remember Kola being shot. The blood. The pain on her eight-year-old face. Adaora took a deep breath and steadied herself. When she turned to go downstairs, she realized that she was floating three inches above the ground. *My idiot husband is right,* she thought numbly. *I am a witch.*

Outside, Lagos rioted and aliens invaded.

CHAPTER 29
THE EKO HOTEL

They walked up the beach and into Lagos. All were well dressed. All were dry. There were about a hundred of them. They were solemn. Not serene like Ayodele. Though they did not shamble along, though they looked alive and well, they reminded Agu of zombies. It was something about the way they had walked out of the water and seemed so indifferent about doing so. As he sat there facing the ocean, his back to Lagos, he felt present at the death of something. The death of Lagos. The death of Nigeria. Africa. Everything?

He squinted, the salt on his drying face stinging his eyes. The surf slapped his ankles as it rushed in and out, slowly retreating to its normal level. The spacecraft in the sky (this was all Agu could think to call it), spread across the entire near-dark horizon, hovering above the water. Shifting and undulating, peaks rising and melting and rising again. It was too far out for him to tell just how high it hovered over the water. Or what sound it made, if it made sound.

Something huge and snakelike leaped out of the water. It arched in the air, twisting in a spiral and noiselessly dropping back into the depths. At least ten gray sharklike fins all in a row surfaced not far from shore. They—or it—sharply turned and headed farther out to sea. *What have they done to the ocean?* he wondered, pulling at his soaked clothes. He coughed as he inhaled a whiff of smoke. He could hear the distant crash of shattering glass, shouting, shots being fired, echoes of raucous laughter. Something had happened while he was out at sea. Wet warmth dribbled down his face, and he touched the cut on his forehead.

"Dammit," he moaned, leaning back on his elbows. His head ached, and his entire body felt as if it weighed a thousand pounds. He'd deal with the cut later. He'd deal with *himself* later. He coughed again as he pulled off his shirt. He wrung it out, the water spattering on his soaked boots, and put it back on. He was alive, and worse things had happened. He chuckled. This wasn't the first invasion of Nigeria, after all.

He trudged across the sand, then through the back roads to Adetokunbo Ademola Street. Here, the sound of many voices, honking horns, the patter of hundreds of feet increased the closer he got. He walked up an alley to the street, and for the first time, he saw what was happening.

"Shit!" he exclaimed. "What in God's name . . . ?"

He couldn't move; he became two eyes and a sinking stomach. The streets were full of people. A group of teenage girls ran by screaming, looking over their shoulders like they'd seen a ghost. There was a fight going on across the street. A group of boys was smashing car and building windows with wooden planks and hammers. They jumped on and kicked at unfortunate vehicles that had to slow down as they tried to get down the congested road.

Several buildings were on fire. Competing music blasted from multiple places. There was a sudden rush as a white man ran by, pursued by ten Area Boys all shouting, "Stranger! Kill *am*! *Kill the stranger!*" The man rounded a corner and the boys followed. After a moment, Agu heard the sounds of cheering and laughing and one voice screaming.

To step into this nightmare was to step into the unknown. He'd seen such chaos before, when he was sent north during fresh riots between Christians and Muslims. He'd learned the hard way that he could never trust people during such times. Anyone could get swept in to the mob's violent mentality at any moment.

He spotted police and soldiers trying to break up a particularly large fight between many men. He felt a stab of guilt. He was supposed to be with them, working to restore peace and order. He shook his head and stepped into the street. *No,* he thought, remembering Benson and the others assaulting the woman and then beating him up when he tried to stop it. *All that's changed.* He stepped back into the shadow of one of the beach shops and reached into his pocket, feeling for the piece of paper with Anthony's phone number on it. It was mush, soaked through from the water. Slightly panicked, he ran through the number in his head. Relief. He remembered it clearly.

"Excuse me, sir," he called to a man rushing by. "Sir, *abeg*, may I borrow your phone?"

The man stopped and turned to him with eyes so wild that Agu stepped back.

"Eh," the man said, frowning and stepping toward Agu. "My phone, you say?"

There was a loud crash. Agu and the man whipped around. There were cheers as someone smashed through a computer storefront window. The alarm went off as over thirty people rushed in, then it died. Agu could hear the people inside.

"Yes," Agu said, fighting to focus. "I just . . . I just need . . ."

"Why?" the man said, now narrowing his eyes. "Why do you want to use my phone? What for?"

"To reach my friends," Agu begged. "Please, o. Something is happening on Bar Beach, I have to—"

"Your friends? What about Bar Beach, eh? Are you one of *them?*" the man gasped, stepping farther away. He spoke in Igbo. "Do you want to communicate with *them?*"

"What?" Agu asked in English.

The man turned on his heel and ran off, as did a few others who had heard what the man said. Agu felt the air leave his lungs; something was very wrong. Looters, rioters, several of them stopped to stare at him. Some moved toward him. A group of Area Boys gathered to his left.

"This man!" a woman shouted, pointing at Agu. She had short wild hair and no shoes. She looked like she'd just walked out of the ocean herself. "He is one of them! Look *am*. Get *am*! He is one of them! I *saw* him go into the ocean last night and come out!" Her eyes bulged with madness. "He was taken by the aliens and infected with alien disease!"

Agu felt a flash of rage toward Ayodele. *What has she done?!* But he was trapped. All he could do was turn and run like hell. The Area Boys and who knew how many others gave chase. They came at Agu from all directions, but he dodged them. He ran past a burning car. He leaped over two women fighting. He crunched over the glass of a broken window in front of a burning building. Then something smashed against the side of his head and crashed to the ground. A bottle. *Coca-Cola?* he wondered. *The gods must really be crazy.*

He stumbled, his head hurting. But he had to admit, he did not feel like a man who'd just been smashed upside the head with a glass bottle. He felt . . . fine. He touched the spot where he'd been hit and pressed it. No pain. No swelling. But his hand came away bloody. The other cut was still seeping. He was okay. But the rage that was already boiling in him surged. This time toward the people who'd just tried to kill him . . . for being something he was not. He could hear his heart pounding in his ears.

A man ran up and punched him in the face. "Kill you," the man growled. He punched Agu again. Two other men joined in, kicking him in the small of his back and kneeing him in the balls. His goddamn *balls!* Yet it didn't hurt. He felt nothing but a fresh hot flare of fury, and it filled his entire being.

He grabbed the man who'd kneed him, brought his fist back, and smashed him in the belly. The man flew back, his arm denting the side of a car before he tumbled over it and fell into a group of onlookers like a meteorite crashing to earth. Everyone on the street went completely silent, staring at the pile of unmoving people, knocked over like bowling pins; the man Agu had grabbed lay among them, one of his legs twisted in a bizarre direction. Agu blinked, his mind calming, the red clearing.

So Agu, the soldier, trained to defend people during a time of need, who had instead probably just killed someone, turned and ran like hell.

Shouting, fighting, breaking, laughing, running, hiding: This was the scene on Adetokunbo Ademola Street. Agu needed a mobile phone. But something had happened while he was riding the manatee, and now asking to use one suddenly seemed like a bad, bad idea. Thankfully, Agu had a plan B.

He stumbled up a manicured driveway to the luxurious Eko Hotel, skirting around the over-maintained palm trees and past the locked-up gift shop. As it was a haven for expats, he'd expected the place to be like a fortress. The Eko Hotel was made for times like this. Instead it was surrounded by skittish armed security guards who barely said a word to him as he passed. They let him, because he knew every single one of them. He'd known them for years. Thankfully, for the moment, the rioters weren't focused on the Eko Hotel, but Agu had a feeling that the respite was only temporary. Any symbol of wealth in Lagos would eventually become a target.

What struck him most when he stepped into the lobby of the posh hotel was the shiny floor. It was so shiny he could see the terrible state he was in. His fatigues were wrinkled, wet, soiled with sand, and spattered with his own blood. His face was puffy and ashy with sea salt, his lip and forehead crusty with dried blood. At least the swelling had gone down in his right eye and he could see through it now. Here, he could find out what had happened while he was in the sea. And use a telephone.

The lobby was packed with terrified tourists and expats. The

Eko was one of the few places in Lagos where, ordinarily, you saw more than a few white faces. European and American businessmen, mainly. It was no different now. To Agu's eyes, they looked bloated and red.

"The fuck if I know," a thickset British man yelled, throwing himself onto a nearby sofa. He had a wheeled suitcase, but he didn't look like he was going anywhere. "It's a citywide 419! The whole bloody place is fucking itself!"

The businessmen around him nodded in agreement.

"I have a satellite phone. How the blazes did they hack into it?"

"That guy says they're tearing each other apart out there because everyone thinks everyone else is an alien and no one knows *what* the aliens really look like."

"Superstitious bollocks. At least this place is safe."

"For now."

"How can they just shut down the airports?"

"Fucking aliens, my arse."

Agu tucked his chin into his neck as he slipped past them. He didn't want to answer any questions. He peeked into the computer center. Every single one was in use. "Shit," he whispered.

He rubbed his forehead as he approached the reception desk. *Focus, Agu,* he thought. *First things first. Get back to Adaora's house.*

"Obi," he said, leaning on the reception desk. A smile touched his lips, his first in who knew how long. It felt good.

His little cousin Obinna's back was to Agu as he spoke with several of his colleagues. Farther down the counter, one poor desk clerk was stuck arguing with a frazzled-looking group of white women.

"Please, just calm down," the desk clerk begged, holding up her hands.

Two of the white women were leaning on each other and weeping as they glanced at the front doors. They were probably afraid that machete-wielding Area Boys were about to burst into the hotel.

On any other night, Agu would have sneered at such women. Tonight, it seemed, their fears were more than justified.

Obinna turned around. *"Agu?"* He grinned. "Brother!" He leaned over the counter to give him a hug.

Agu held up his hands. "You don't want to hug me," he said. "I smell like hell and I'm dripping with sweat."

"You came from out there?" Obi asked.

"It's bad," was all Agu said.

"What happened to you?"

Agu had always looked out for his little cousin. He'd been the one to get him this receptionist job. The son of his mother's closest sister, Obi might as well have been his brother. But that didn't change the fact that Agu had been aware of all his life: Obi lacked courage and imagination. When there was a fight, Obi fled. When challenged, he fled. When someone did wrong and it was time to stand, he fled. Best for him to stay at the Eko and know nothing about Ayodele or where Agu was headed.

"I just got caught up in it," Agu said. He glanced over his shoulder and met the eyes of the flustered, red-faced British expat. The man was staring at him as if *he* were an alien. *Not again,* Agu thought. He turned back to his cousin.

"Obi," he said. "You've got to help me."

"Na wao," Obi said, looking him up and down. "Seriously, bro, what has happened to you?"

"You will never believe me," Agu said, lowering his voice. He hesitated, reconsidering his request. But what choice did he have? "Please, *abeg*, I need . . . Internet. Let me use your laptop. I know you have it back there."

"Why not use the public ones?" Obi asked, frowning.

"I need to send a text. But all your computers are being used," he said.

"For?"

"I just need to contact someone."

Obi paused, looking at him for a moment. Agu almost laughed at the ridiculousness of his little cousin looking him over as if he were some Area Boy. Obi was still the Obi he'd always known: a coward, and more loyal to his job than the cousin who got him the job.

"How do I know you're not one of . . . one of them?" Obi blurted. He looked as if he regretted the question the moment it escaped from his lips, but he didn't take his words back. Agu snorted with disgust and sucked his teeth loudly.

Two of Obi's colleagues were walking toward them. One was a tall, intense-looking man, and the other was a short woman. Toyin and Vanessa, going by their name tags.

"Who is this?" Toyin asked.

"*Abeg*, fly," Agu snapped at Toyin, growing impatient.

"Do you know him?" Vanessa asked Obi, ignoring Agu. "We can have him thrown out. Look at him."

Obi, his own cousin, looked uncertainly between Agu and the newcomers. Images of all that had happened tried to flood Agu's mind. Being underwater. The questions. Fighting Adaora's crazed husband. And if he ever got his hands on Benson, that would be a dark day indeed. The speedboat and the men torn apart in the water by monsters. The sea cow that had brought him to shore. The dead whale. The riots. His power. He might have *killed* someone back there in the street.

Agu took another deep breath, feeling a bit steadier. He had to get to Ayodele. If he could get her to the president, all this might stop. Might.

"Look," Agu said, raising his voice. "I *know* what's going on. I am a soldier. You see my clothes? *Ehe.*" He nodded. "I have been to hell and back tonight." He paused. "I have . . . *seen* them. I *know* them. Please, *abeg*, Obinna, brother, let me just get online for a few minutes, o."

Vanessa and Toyin stared at him, open-mouthed.

"So you have seen them?" Vanessa finally asked, her voice soft with awe.

"I have."

"Are they dangerous?"

They could be, he thought. "No."

Vanessa shook her head. "I have to disagree, after what that one did to the airwaves and networks."

"And by the way *you* are looking," Toyin added.

"*They* didn't do this to me," he snapped. "Human beings did!"

"What the hell is going on out there?" Obi asked him, ducking down to get his laptop and setting it on the counter.

"Chaos," Agu said, waking the computer and clicking open Obi's Skype application. Thankfully Obi had some credit on it. "And if you let it touch you, you become part of it. Do things you'd never do." He looked up at his cousin. "Obi, I know you have a mobile phone." Obi looked away. *Mumu! Idiot!* Agu thought angrily. "Just call my parents, *sha.* Please. Make sure they are all right." He typed in Anthony's number—he hoped he remembered it correctly—and quickly tapped out a brief message.

Obi nodded, bringing the phone from his pocket and turning away.

After hitting send, Agu leaned back against the counter. He could see that a building across the street was on fire.

"They are okay," Obi said, turning back and hanging up the phone. "They said there were some men—soldiers—but they stayed inside and they're fine. Who—"

"The story is too long to tell," Agu said. He felt faint with relief. So it seemed that Benson had made good on his threat against Agu's family. Evil man.

"Do you think this is the end of days?" Obi asked, wide-eyed.

"No."

CHAPTER 30

CRUSADE

Adaora read the text message from Agu three times: "Stay put. I'm coming. Agu."

She handed the phone back to Anthony, put her elbows on the table, and let her head fall into her hands. Hassam, the soldier who had tried to administer first aid to Adaora's daughter, had left. He said he was going to try to restore peace to Victoria Island. Adaora was glad he was gone.

The windows were open to let in fresh air—hot, humid air. The house stank of smoke, regardless. She wasn't sure if it was from the fire Chris had put out or the burning house a block away. With her eyes closed, the sounds of windows being smashed, a door being kicked in, screeching tires, and people running and shouting on the roads and lawns was louder.

She peeked through her fingers at the tiny monkey sitting on the kitchen table looking sullen, and her belly cramped from suppressed giggles. The monkey was fuzzy, soft, brown, had a pinched face like a sour elder, and was so small it could comfortably sit in the palm of Adaora's hand. It looked exactly like a smaller version of the stuffed animal Kola grasped in her arms every night.

"Please," Kola said to it. "Don't be like that. Didn't you say that you came here to talk to us?"

Fred was staring at the monkey, his eyes glassy and his mouth hanging open. He needed a nap. He needed real rest. They all did. The monkey pulled the sides of its mouth down, looking even more sullen. It crossed its tiny thin arms over its furry body and turned its back to Kola. It was clenching its fists so tightly that Adaora could hear the tiny joints pop. Ayodele had changed herself into this creature an hour ago because she'd decided that she no longer wanted to be a human being.

"I don't think we should stay here long," Anthony murmured, looking out the front window.

"I know," Adaora said, joining him.

They watched Father Oke for a moment. He'd approached with about twenty-five others, and now they stood on the lawn in front of the plantain tree. Father Oke marched back and forth, speaking passionately and gesticulating wildly. His flock clapped and waved their hands in the air, rejuvenated by whatever he was stirring them up to do. On the road behind them, a band of young men set upon a parked car, smashing the windows with tire irons and bricks. Some of them laughed and pointed at Father Oke and his people.

An *okada* pulled up to the curb outside Adaora's house, and someone climbed down. Adaora squinted, trying to see what was happening. The woman and the driver exchanged words, and then the driver sped off. The woman shouted after him, looked around, and started walking. She was wearing jeans and a red blouse, and she walked with an unafraid, angry gait.

When the woman passed the group of destructive Area Boys, they pointed and laughed. One even smacked her backside. The woman glared at the boy and slapped him in the face. He only laughed as he shoved her along. She cursed at the boys but kept moving. Father Oke and his congregation were too preoccupied to notice the woman and her troubles, let alone offer her any assistance.

Bad, bad, bad, Adaora thought, shivering. *This is a bad situation about to get worse.* She got to her feet. "I'll be right back."

Adaora closed the door quietly and descended the stairs into her lab. Chris was staring at the remains of her aquarium. She didn't follow his eyes. She could smell her dead pet sea creatures and that was enough.

"Chris," she whispered.

He didn't turn around. After eating the bowl of jollof rice Anthony had placed in front of him, Chris had gone on to eat some leftover gari and egusi soup Adaora had made days ago. Then he'd eaten some biscuits, a bag of groundnuts, and three oranges, and washed it all down with a bottle of Guinness from a box the rioters had missed in the cupboard.

"I'll . . . I'll go out and talk to Father Oke," Chris said.

"No," Adaora replied. "Are you blind? The man's gone mad." She took a deep breath and made herself speak before she could lose her nerve. "Take the children to your mother's. They live in that gated community and—"

Chris whirled around, fire in his eyes. "How stupid do you think I am?"

"What? Chris, I'm just—"

"I saw you," he said.

Adaora frowned, confused.

"Witch, harlot, tramp . . . *whore!*" He whispered his words, but this didn't make them any less painful to him or Adaora. "I *saw* you with him, Adaora." He sneered. "Wife."

"You . . . saw? Saw what?"

"'Saw what?,' she asks." He stepped up to her. "Saw *you!* You and that soldier in the car, kissing. Out in public, like a common whore."

Adaora was too shocked to speak.

Chris nodded. "God shows all," he said. "In Jesus's name."

"I . . . I'm sorry," she whispered. "I didn't mean . . ."

"*Don't!*" He lowered his voice. "Don't give me that rubbish. You did something to me . . . before you left, you did something to me. You probably did it to him, too. If I could beat it out of you, I would. Because I love you, you are my wife. But you're evil. Father Oke was right about that. You're a marine witch. Tell me you are not a witch, tell me I didn't feel what I felt. Tell me it wasn't you holding me down on the floor when we were fighting." He paused, and when she didn't say anything, he added, "I don't want you near the children."

"I don't care *what* you want," she snapped. "They're *my* children too. *I* gave birth to them, not you!"

His eyes grew wide, and his face went from brown to a deep dark brown red. He clenched his hands into fists. But Adaora wasn't afraid of him. She could feel it inside her. All she had to do was let herself loose and this fight, like the last one, would be over before it began. She stared him down.

"Is everything okay down there?" Anthony called from the top of the stairs.

"Mommy?" Kola called. "Daddy?"

Chris's eyes were twitching, but he was unclenching his fists.

"Yes, we're fine," Adaora said. She didn't let her eyes leave Chris's. "Just . . . talking. Kola, we'll be up soon."

"You sure?" Anthony said.

"We're fine."

"Okay."

Adaora didn't hear the door shut, and she was glad. She swallowed and repeated the hardest words of her life. "Take them to your mother's. It's safer there."

"And you'll stay here? To wait for him?"

"To finish this thing with Ayodele," she said. "We need to get her to the president."

"Let the soldier do it. That's *his* job, not yours."

"It needs to be the three of us."

"Why?"

"It's . . . it's God's will." Adaora held her breath.

Chris laughed hard, and she was relieved when he stepped away. "You know nothing of God's will."

Neither do you, she thought.

"You'll leave your children to go with *him?*" he asked.

"Oh my God," she said, rolling her eyes. "Didn't you see what Ayodele . . ." She took a deep breath, gathering herself. "Listen to what's going on out there! Did you not hear what she said? This isn't about our relationship, or whether I'm a bad mother!"

"You're leaving me."

Adaora sighed and looked away. "This is not the time for this conversation, Chris."

"You decided to allow him to touch you." His eyes glistened as he traced his fingers over her face. Every part of her wanted to flinch, but she didn't. "God is always in control," he said. Then he strode past her and up the stairs. Adaora sat down on the bottom step and looked at her feet, smelling the destruction.

Later, upstairs, she found Kola and Fred slipping on their shoes and arguing over who got to tell Grandma everything. Chris was packing biscuits, groundnuts, and bananas into a briefcase. Anthony leaned against the counter, his arms across his chest, silent. Chris glared at Adaora but said nothing. Ayodele, still in her tiny monkey form, sat on the dinner table, her furry back to everyone.

"We called Grandma," Kola said. "She said if we could get there, we will be safe!"

Adaora nodded. "She's right."

"Yet you'll stay here where it isn't safe at all," Chris said.

Silence. Something outside crunched loudly.

"Correct. I'll stay," she finally said.

"Why?" Fred asked, breathing heavily. His nostrils were flaring. Adaora knew the look; he was trying not to cry. Kola hugged him to her.

"We need to wait for Agu," Adaora said, trying not to cringe at the anticipation of Chris's reaction.

"Why?" Chris snapped. "Is *he* your husband?"

Anthony chuckled to himself and looked at his feet, muttering, "Nonsense."

"Kola, Fred, go upstairs and grab some of your school books."

"Mommy, you should save the world," Fred said. "If you have a chance to—"

"Shut up and go upstairs," Chris shouted. "What kind of child enters adult conversation? Abomination!"

Kola and Fred ran upstairs.

"I'm not having this discussion, Chris," she said when they were gone. Unconsciously her hand went to her cheek. "We've talked enough."

"I . . . I'm sorry," he said, his shoulders slumping. "I should never have laid a hand on you."

"I don't care."

Pause.

"Adaora," he said. "What . . . I . . . What was it that you did? When . . . when we were fighting?"

She felt her belly flip but said nothing.

He stepped closer and she didn't move away. "Does it have to do with how you were born? You—"

"Chris, didn't you dismiss me as a marine witch or whatever the hell you and those people fear so much?" Her eyes stung but she continued. "Just go with that for now, if that sets your mind at ease. Three things need to happen. One, our children need to be safe. Two, Anthony, Ayodele, and I need to find Agu. You won't understand and I'm not going to explain. Three, we need to get Ayodele to the president. And guess what, Chris, I happen to know where the president is going to be at six a.m. If Agu comes soon, we've got all night to get there. But we have to *get* there. With what's going on outside, that's going to be difficult."

Pause. "Why the three of you?" Chris asked.

"I don't . . . No, that's not true." She blinked as it dawned on her. She took his shoulder, gripping it. "Chris?"

"What?" He looked afraid.

Her heart was pounding. Her hands were shaking. She'd never been religious. She'd never believed in the mysterious as her husband did. She was a scientist. Her world was founded upon empirical evidence, on rigorous experimentation, on data. She was the thinker, and he was the one willing to simply have faith. That had been what kept them balanced. Chris was a genius when it came to securing and growing contracts. He had stocks in America and in the UK. He followed hunches when he did business. He consulted dibias, witch doctors, and babawelos when he felt he was at a crossroads. And this had always worked. It had made them rich.

For Adaora, however, logic determined her actions. She went to church because she was expected to go, not because she believed. She studied the ocean and its creatures. She calculated, documented, observed. She wrote articles for academic journals and was respected in her field. She was a well-regarded professor, and, though she made far less than Chris, her income had made them that much richer.

They had known each other all their lives. There was history. And there was mystery in that history that they had silently agreed never to discuss. Neither of them had ever called the other evil or illogical . . . until the last year after Chris had had the scare on the airplane from Lagos to Owerri and became born again. Since then, things had unraveled.

"You're right," she whispered.

"About what?"

"The world."

His eyebrows went up. Then he smiled.

"No, no, not all the Christian stuff," she said. "But the *mystery*." She paused. "Ayodele spoke of her people being catalysts of change. Wherever they go, they bring change."

"You are part of the change," he said.

"Maybe." She took his hand. "Will you get the children to your mother's place? Please. They are all we have."

After a long pause, he said, "Yes." He raised her hand to his lips and kissed it.

They both turned to go upstairs. Anthony, who'd been leaning against the door, listening, took a deep gulp from the bottle of water he held. He sighed as he walked back to the living room and said, "Finally, some progress."

Chris took Adaora's Mercedes, leaving her his smaller, faster BMW. Fred and Kola cried and cried. Aside from wanting to stay with Adaora, they didn't want to leave Ayodele, who remained in her monkey form and still refused to speak. As soon as they were gone, Adaora sank into the sofa with the beginnings of a headache that could only come from deep conflict, the internal battle between relief and anxiety. And then a brick smashed through the window followed by a Molotov cocktail, setting the sofa on fire.

CHAPTER 31

THE RHYTHM

"Come out!" Father Oke shouted.

Anthony was beginning to lose his temper. It had been draining from him since those idiots had tried to shoot Ayodele. The drainage had increased tenfold when the soldiers wounded Kola. Normally, a deep breath and a glance at the sky could settle him. Not now. And the worst thing about it was that the Elders would see whatever he did.

The Elders. That's what Ayodele called *them*. Not *the* Elders who were his ancestors, the Elders from the stars. Those . . . creatures that Anthony was having a hard time separating from himself. He could still hear their song, still hear the beat of their drums; yes, he could still feel them. They were deep in the ocean, just off the coast of this great megacity called Lagos. He felt them in a way he'd never felt anything before. Because they were still with him. They were listening through him. They were hearing, seeing, and feeling with him. Nevertheless, he was still himself and when he got angry, he got . . . mad. When he was mad, he would take from everyone around him. He would take from the earth. From the very ground beneath his feet. And then he'd wield what he had taken, and the damage would be great.

He'd done it once when he was ten years old, when he still went by the name his parents had given him, Edgar. Just after his father had died and left his mother to shoulder the blame for his heart attack. For a month, Edgar had stayed in that house with his mother and siblings. They survived on leftovers from the funeral and supplies his mother had managed to buy the day before the ceremony. Nevertheless, when their water supply grew too low, his mother had finally given in.

On that fateful day, she was at the market while Edgar stayed home watching his younger brothers and sisters. His mother had thought the in-laws had given up. She'd been in the house for a month. But he knew they'd come. And a half hour after she left, they came to the small white house in the village with the satellite dish perched on the roof and the brown water stains on the walls. His relatives. His uncles, aunts, older cousins. All from his father's side. They came to take what they felt was theirs. Back then, there were no mobile phones, but the bush radio, the village grapevine, worked better than any digital form of communication. It was probably Auntie Osei who lived across the dirt road who had notified everyone that his mother had finally gone out.

Edgar had sat on the small porch, watching them come. Their cars and SUVs pulled up and they waited. Gathering like ants preparing to haul away a dead spider. Ants never sleep. Ants are relentless. And ants know the scent of opportunity and do not hesitate to follow its trail.

His father's relatives—about twenty of them—gathered beneath the large mango tree in front of the house. It was heavy with ripe fruit. Several in the group picked the largest mangoes. As if the mangoes were theirs to take. The day was warm and Edgar started sweating. After several minutes, as one big group, they walked toward Edgar's home. His youngest sibling, Helen, was only seven months old. His brother Bamfo was nine. There were five of them in all, and ten-year-old Edgar was in charge.

"Get inside," he told Bamfo. His little brother looked at him with such worry that Edgar felt like crying. His brother's love, all his siblings' love was so strong. They would die for each other. And they knew what death was. They had all been there when their father died of a heart attack, right in front of them all at the dinner table. They'd been in the middle of a wonderful Sunday feast—fufu and peanut soup with goat meat. A rare hearty meal. Edgar couldn't remember what they had been celebrating. All he remembered was the look on his father's face. From happy to pained to shocked. The expression remained as he took his last breath.

Edgar's father had been the family's Great Son. He was the oldest. He was the most successful. He was the loudest. And he'd been blessed by God to spread God's Word. Edgar's father's family accused his mother of being a witch. They believed she had caused his death so that she could take all his money and build an empire with the children she had robbed from him. They were determined not to let her. They wanted their Great Son's wife to be destitute for what she'd done. They wanted the children to starve. Those children were evil if they'd let their mother kill the family's Great Son.

Edgar was an outspoken, compassionate child. He could never stand to see anything suffer. So he was known for helping tortoises across the road and ushering lizards out of the house. He'd once even caught a bird in the living room with his bare hands and set it free outside. He was tall for his age, though very lean no matter how much he ate. And when he spoke, because he had the gift of gab, he seemed even taller. His mother beat him often for his silver tongue and hugged him even more often for his praise songs. His father nearly burst with pride whenever Edgar sang a praise song to him. Edgar knew how to make his parents happy, most of the time. And Edgar had plenty of friends and never had to fight. Words were his weapons. He knew how to crack his tongue like a whip. But that was only when he got angry.

And this day, as Edgar watched his father's people, who blamed his mother for his father's death—this fateful day, Edgar got angry.

Uncle Kuffour was leading the way, flanked by Auntie Boteng and Uncle Mensah. They looked heated and self-righteous. These were three people who had spread the worst rumors about his mother. Just as he was good with words, Edgar was a sharp listener. He could hear a conversation from far across the room, catch every word, every syllable. He'd heard these three talk about his mother as if she were a dog.

According to them, in her village, before she married his father, she was known to commune with the devil. Since his father's death, his mother not only cooked for but slept with all of his father's friends. And even before his father had died, she'd aborted several children. So they said. According to them, his mother's nails were always dirty, her soup was always sour, and she'd used charms to get his father to marry her.

His mother knew of the rumors, even while forced to stay home and guard the house for the past month. And she cried every night because of them. Edgar could hear her through the thin walls. His mother was a pediatrician, and his father had been a well-loved and well-known preacher. They'd done well. Together. And now that his father was dead, the relatives wanted it all. Edgar knew family was supposed to take you in when things were bad. But this family wanted his mother, his brothers, his sisters, and him out of the way.

Edgar stood as they approached, and blocked the open doorway to his parents' house. His house. His siblings' house. His bare feet pressed firmly to the ground. He wore an old T-shirt and black shorts. He was dark-skinned like his father, and he looked them all in the eye like his mother. "What do you want?"

"Get out of the way," Uncle Kuffour said. The others assented.

"Move."

"Make this easy."

"No one will blame you."

"No," Edgar said. "This is my parents' house."

"You won't invite your own relations into your home, then?" Auntie Boteng asked, narrowing her eyes.

"Do you behave like my relations?" he asked. He took a brave step forward, feeling the rage bloom in him. In his mind's eye, he saw his middle sister sobbing in the kitchen as she peeked around the entrance and watched Auntie Boteng act like a stranger. Auntie Boteng was her favorite auntie.

"Have any of you come to wish my mother well?" Edgar asked. "To see how your brother's children are doing? Do any of you have hearts that aren't frozen? Do any of you have any shame?"

He could feel it. In his chest, first, but then it radiated out to his entire body. He curled his shoulders to hold it in. But it was so hot, so powerful.

"Old man." His uncle chuckled. He stepped closer to Edgar.

Edgar didn't move. These people were here to take everything. He would never move.

As soon as his father's oldest brother grabbed his arm, Edgar heard the music—sweet and pure and electric. It hummed up through the earth. And it sang to him in a clear voice, *"Defend them."*

Then that which was building up within him, humming to the rhythm of the earth, burst. His uncles, aunts, cousins were all blown back. Two of the cars closest to them were blown onto their sides, before slamming back down onto the road. The homes across the street, including his aunt's, were bombarded with red dirt, and they rocked on their foundations.

Those relatives never came back.

Edgar never explained the incident to his mother, though she later learned from the neighbors what had happened. Edgar never used the rhythm to do violence again. But when he got on stage, when he rapped and let the words flow from his tongue like warmed honey, he could feel it. It would be there when he needed it. So far, he hadn't needed it.

But he needed it now.

Father Oke's people were crowding the lawn, and Anthony could sense they were about to do something terrible. They'd just thrown a Molotov cocktail into the house, and some of them held more. He stepped toward the front door.

When he performed, he spun words as a spider spins its web. He drew it from within himself and worked with it. Then he threw it back at his audience enhanced and laced with energy and images. No one left his concerts unchanged. He was a positive force. But only because he *chose* to be one. That day, in the doorway of his mother's house, he'd been something else. He'd had to be.

Now, he slipped his shoes off as he stepped out of the house to face Father Oke and his diocese. He stepped onto the soil of the flowerbed beside the path to Adaora's house. It was cool beneath his feet.

"What are you people doing?" he asked evenly.

He set his eyes squarely on Father Oke. The man was bewitching and charismatic, so much like Anthony's father. Anthony frowned. Father Oke's actions were not so unlike what he did himself when he was performing as Anthony Dey Craze. *But I don't use people,* he thought. *I free them, I open them up to God.*

Father Oke's garments were smudged with dirt, and the side of his face was swollen like Agu's and Adaora's. His eyes were rimmed with red and glistened with unshed tears. But his voice was firm: "We would like to speak with the extraterrestrial."

"No," Anthony said. "Speak to me."

Now Father Oke laid his eyes squarely on Anthony. The two stood tall, proud, and powerful. Both were adored by the people around them. Both knew it and could feed it. Anthony was calm as an underground river. Father Oke was a volcano ready to erupt.

"Bring it *out!*" Father Oke shouted, his eyes wide. "Bring it out *now!*"

Several of his followers threw stones at the house. Others shouted and shook their fists. Two men walked up to Anthony, hunched forward, fists clenched. At the door, however, they stopped, looking past him. Anthony turned around. Adaora stood behind him. She was holding Ayodele, who was still a tiny monkey.

"This is she," Adaora said, her smile an angry smirk. She stepped past Anthony, eyeing the two men. "And she has nothing to say to you."

She could hear the crackle of flames, feel the heat, and see light reflected in the broken glass on the ground. The top floor of the house must now be completely on fire.

"I don't believe you," Father Oke said.

"Where the hell would I get a monkey at this time of night?" Adaora snapped, but she knew his response before he spoke it.

"You're a witch. I'm sure you have your ways."

Several of his followers muttered agreement.

"Father Oke, or whatever your name is," Anthony said. He stepped forward, placing himself between Ayodele and the two men. "Remove yourself and your people from Adaora's property. There is nothing for you here."

Father Oke flashed a menacing look at Anthony, then turned to his followers. He lifted his injured left arm, wincing theatrically. "Please say it with me, 'This is my Bible. . . .'" He pulled a Bible from his pocket and held it up with his right hand.

"This is my Bible," his followers repeated, their faces earnest.

"It is the Word of God!" he shouted.

"It is the Word of God!"

"Yes! Good, my sheep, good! I believe I am who I am. I believe I can do what it says I can do. Do you believe in me?"

"We do!"

"Yes, o!"

"Speak the truth!"

Father Oke, buoyed by the trust of his flock, did an excited hop, grinned, and shouted, "Amen!" But when he turned back to Anthony, his grin was gone and his face was angry. He snapped his fingers and flung his right arm toward Adaora and Ayodele. "Grab *am*, grab *am*!" he yelled. The two burly men stepped forward.

"Adaora, get inside!" Anthony growled.

The moment the two men lunged at Adaora and Ayodele,

Anthony let it loose. For the first time since he was ten years old, he unleashed the raw power of what he called the rhythm. It was a vibration that swelled up inside him and allowed him to touch all things. It rolled warmly over Father Oke, the two men, his followers, and everyone on the streets. It put out the Molotov cocktail–ignited fire that had been eating Adaora and Chris's home, and the one across the street that had ravaged most of the house. Weaver birds that had taken refuge in a nearby tree fell to the ground. Car alarms went off. The few unbroken windows around the block shattered.

And as the sonic wave rolled, Anthony stood still, eyes closed, and received information about all the things that the wave touched. His ability had grown stronger since he was a kid. Back then, when he'd handled his bitter relatives, he'd blown himself backward into the house, hit the wall, and been unconscious for ten minutes. Now he stumbled back only a single step. It was the rhythm. Ayodele's people knew it well, too. They'd used it twice to read the city of Lagos.

Anthony took a deep breath and opened his eyes. There was smashed glass all around him. More glass fell from a broken window, tinkling as it broke against the sidewalk. Then everything was silent. And there were bodies on the lawn. *Bodies.* But he knew they were not dead, just unconscious. And yet he felt the same rush of power and stunned terror that he had felt when he was ten. *He'd* done this.

He couldn't help comparing what he'd done to footage he'd seen of pastors in churches using their so-called power of God to knock down whole groups of church members at the same time. He shook his head. This wasn't that; this was something true and real. His father would have been proud. Anthony had controlled the vibration, the energy. He controlled it during his concerts to the point where the women felt ecstasy and the men felt exhilarated. Now he controlled it here, to read everything, to stop everything. To make order from chaos.

He knew so much. "Ayodele," he said. "We're not all bad, *chale.*"

Ayodele stood in the doorway, staring at him. She'd returned to her human form, except now she'd made herself taller, taller than him. She was at least seven feet. She was wearing a long, thick white dress.

"We will see," she said.

"There's more to this city than you imagined," he said. He'd seen all that was happening in a three-mile radius.

He stepped inside and shut the door behind them, leaving Oke and his followers unconscious around the foot of the plantain tree. "We should get the car ready," he said. "Agu is almost here."

CHAPTER 32
STYLISH, EXPENSIVE, AND UNIQUE

"Who I be?" Jacobs whispered as they slowly drove down the near-empty street. He could barely hear himself think. Moziz and Tolu were arguing in the front seat about which way to go. They'd dropped Troy on the side of the road minutes before, where his machete-wielding cousins waited for him. Jacobs wondered how they planned to find the soldier who'd assaulted their cousin.

"Dis night na him be de night wey I go bombard am," was the last thing Troy had said, before joining his relatives. As they drove away, Jacobs saw Troy snatch a machete and thrust it into the air. Those around him shouted and did the same. Two women walking toward them immediately turned and hurried the other way.

Jacobs leaned his forehead against the cool car window, trying to tune out Moziz and Tolu. He didn't care which way they went. They passed a group of market women carrying obviously looted goods on their heads. Chairs, bundles of textiles, baskets of tomatoes, desktop computer towers, all of the women were laughing and singing as they passed a burning office building. A slack-jawed Philomena sat beside Jacobs, watching the women. At least she'd stopped crying.

As they navigated the side road, Jacobs focused on the trees. If he shut his eyes, he'd only see Rome, Seven, and the other members of the Black Nexus getting beaten to the ground. He'd left them so that he could go capture some sort of being from space for the sake of making money. Was this what he'd come to? He was no better than Moziz or Father Oke.

"Mek we comot for Lag!" Tolu was bellowing. He had tears in his eyes. They'd been shouting back and forth for the last five minutes. "Na de last place wey anybody go wan dey if true true alien wan take over, *sha*. Remember, dem no human person!"

"Tolu close ya mouth. Mek I concentrate, drive," Moziz said as he swerved dangerously close to the side of the road. "When we reach my place, we go decide."

"I don tell you now, mek we act fast," Tolu said. "If we no do am now, we fit no do am again, o."

"Look ya front!" Philomena screamed.

Moziz's eyes grew wide as he tried to stop the car from hitting the woman in the road. Jacobs pushed at the seat in front of him as they screeched to a stop, his seat belt biting into his chest and neck. There was a sickening *thump*, and he looked up just in time to see the woman's body thrown onto the hood. Then she slid to the ground.

For a moment they were silent. Moziz just sat there, staring blankly at the woman lying in the street like a discarded doll. The headlights glinted off her skin. She didn't move. Philo numbly got out of the car. Tolu reached under Moziz's wrist and turned off the engine.

"Oh, men!" Jacobs screamed, throwing himself out. He shoved Philo aside and ran to the woman. The road was empty and it was pitch dark, except for the headlights. In the silence, Jacobs could hear crickets singing. The woman was tall and maybe in her thirties. She wore dark blue pants and a matching top with silver and red embroidery. *Stylish, expensive, and unique,* he thought. One of her black high-heeled shoes had flown off. Her nose was caved in, as was her forehead. She wasn't bleeding, but Jacobs could see the white of bone and something squishy coming out of her forehead.

"Oh God! She don *peme*," Philo said, standing beside Jacobs, as if he didn't have eyes.

From far off, something grumbled like an enormous empty stomach, and he looked around. "Wetin be dat?" he whispered.

"I no know," she whispered back, moving closer to him.

When they heard it again, this time louder, Moziz started the car.

Philo looked up at Moziz through the windshield. "Wetin you dey do? We no fit just leave am! De woman—"

"Enter the ride!" Moziz shouted.

The concrete beneath Jacobs's feet shifted. No, not *shifted*; *softened*. He looked down. It was squashy like a pillow. From down the road came a deep guttural growl that intensified into a roar. Every hair on his body stood up. His grandmother always used to yell at him for playing soccer with his friends in the road at dusk. She said one day the road would swallow him right up the minute the sun went down.

"Grab *am*!" he said. He had done enough shameful things tonight. "Help me!"

But Philomena had already run into the car. Jacobs ran to the woman, stumbling on the soft concrete, which now shuddered with every step he took. It reminded him of the way a bull's skin twitched when a fly landed on it. And it was warm beneath his feet. He could feel the heat right through his gym shoes. He locked his arms under the woman's armpits. The first thing he noticed was that she was warm too . . . and light. The second thing he noticed was that she was sinking. The road was trying to swallow her.

"Ah-ah! She no *peme*, o!" Jacobs shouted at the road, hysterical. "She no *peme*!"

With all his might, he pulled her body from the softening asphalt and, ignoring the angry roar of a creature denied a meal, slung her over his shoulder and carried her to the car. Moziz was accelerating before Jacobs even shut the door.

Philo, who was looking out the window as they turned and drove back toward downtown Lagos, started screaming and pointing. Jacobs wanted to slap her, until he glanced back and saw for himself. The road behind them was rearing up like a serpent of asphalt. It swayed this way and that, the two sets of yellow stripes clear in the darkness. It slapped at the trees beside the road as it rolled after them.

"She no *peme!*" Jacobs shouted back at it. "She no die, o!"

Moziz pushed the car's speed up to eighty. It shuddered and shook but sped away from the road-monster. Breathless with relief, Jacobs plopped down in his seat and looked at the woman beside him, who should have been dead but wasn't. She was staring back.

Tears were flowing from her eyes, and her crushed face was pinched with pain. He quickly looked away, disgusted and disturbed. He bit his fist to keep himself from vomiting. "Papa God," he gasped. He dragged his eyes to the back of Moziz's head and then Tolu's. None of them had noticed the woman was alive. Even Philomena, beside him in the back seat, was still looking out the window.

Because Jacobs was looking away from the damaged woman, he didn't see it happen. None of them saw it happen, which was just as well. Jacobs, Philo, Moziz, and Tolu had already seen more than they could handle. Any more strangeness and all their minds would snap. The woman's crushed nose and forehead began to rebuild from bone to sinew to skin.

"Wetin be dat tin in de road?" she whispered.

Jacobs turned to the woman, and his eyes grew wide at the sight of her undamaged face. For a moment his mouth simply hung open. Then he said, "I . . . I no get any idea, at all, at all."

CHAPTER 33

STICK BOY

Agu was hiding in the shadows.

In the street was a parade of Area Boys and a few Area Girls with machetes, sticks, and probably guns; looters, police and soldiers who'd deserted their duties, and several other kinds of riffraff. Agu could handle all of them; he just didn't want to. Better to sneak behind buildings and through back roads than be forced to hurt or kill people.

His nose was bleeding again after a fight with a group of guys who'd just finished destroying someone's Mercedes SUV. Agu understood that they were angry at Lagos, angry at Nigeria, angry at the world. The alien invasion was just an excuse to let it all out. A beat-up-looking soldier in uniform was a treat for them . . . until they learned Agu wasn't a normal soldier.

Agu had known he was abnormal since he was twelve, when four boys had cornered him and Stick Boy behind the church. Stick Boy was a poor skinny kid with a big mouth and a nose for mischief. Agu had a soft spot for Stick Boy, so he stood up for him often. This day, Stick Boy had won a large sum of money playing cards against some older boys. The card he'd been using to cheat had fallen from his pocket just as he was getting up to leave. Agu had been coming out of the church where he was an altar boy when Stick Boy ran and stood behind him crying, "They are trying to beat me, o! Help!"

Agu grabbed Stick Boy and they ran behind the church. When Agu refused to give Stick Boy up to the angry boys, two of them shoved Agu against the wall, and one of them stepped up and slapped him hard across the face. That slap . . . It was unnecessary. They'd already gotten Agu out of the way, but that boy wanted to make Agu hurt for having the nerve to try to defend Stick Boy. And that was when Agu tore his arm from the other boy who held him against the wall. He punched the boy who'd slapped him. The force of the blow was so powerful that the boy hit the ground hard and didn't get up.

Everything stopped as the boy lay motionless. Agu was sure he'd killed him. His father had been a great wrestler in his day and, just like Okonkwo in the book *Things Fall Apart*, his father was nicknamed Agu, which means leopard. His mother had happily given the name to her son. Now it looked like more than just his father's name had been passed to him.

One of the boys ran to get his mother. Agu stayed. No matter the punishment, it was Agu's duty to stay with the boy he'd hurt. Two minutes passed before the boy finally sat up, shaking his head and moaning. Those were the worst two minutes of Agu's entire life. In those two minutes, Agu saw the future. He would be sent to jail. His brain would rot, and his body would grow malnourished from a poor diet. His soul would deteriorate from exposure to other murderers. In those two minutes, he became a useless man who, when released from prison years and years later, would go on to rob people along the road instead of going to school. He would never become a somebody, someone who protected and preserved his family. His family was his heart.

When the boy finally stirred, Agu had decided two things: that he would become a soldier to protect the innocent and that though he might get into fights, he would never punch anyone hard again.

But he could feel the potential inside him. It left him feeling heavy and rock solid, despite the fact that he wasn't that big at all. It lived in him like the roots of a thousand-year-old tree in its plot of land. So because he could not be rid of it, he locked it away deep.

Until Benson and his other *ahoa* attacked that woman two nights ago. Outrage had prompted him to unbury his ability, and he found it even more potent than when he'd been a child.

Agu was nearly at Adaora's house. He smelled smoke and realized the roof of the house beside him was on fire. It was one of those gated houses with a wrought-iron-topped concrete fence. How had anyone managed to set it alight?

"Sssss!" someone hissed.

Agu turned around. The two men were about his age and height. One of them wore a military uniform like his and the other a police uniform.

Agu realized immediately that the police officer was badly injured. The soldier was holding him up with difficulty.

"He's been shot," the soldier said.

As he spoke, the police officer's legs buckled. Agu could smell blood and sweat from both. He moved to help.

There was laughter behind Agu. He groaned. A group of Area Boys. Young and armed.

"Shit," both he and the soldier said at the same time.

The Area Boys swaggered into the alley, swinging their machetes and bats. There were smiles on their young brown faces, their teeth glowing white in the dark. They addressed Agu and the soldier in Yoruba, which Agu didn't speak. But the soldier beside him did. The tone of his voice was firm, and he motioned to the injured police officer.

Before Agu could say or do anything, one of the boys swung his machete at the soldier. *Thock!* The blade chopped through the soldier's shoulder, and blood spattered onto Agu's face. The soldier screamed. Shocked and guttural. Then the scream became high-pitched and inhuman. Like glass balls whirled around in a glass jar. Agu was running before he knew he was running. Behind him he heard the Area Boys start screaming. Then there was a wet slurping sound. He didn't look back.

Ayodele, he thought. *That thing was like Ayodele.* They were not helpless. They could feel pain. And they did not like it.

He ran across a street clogged with women linking arms—he didn't hear what they were chanting, but walking in front of the linked women were three women who looked as if they'd been severely beaten. He ran through two groups of people smashing and looting. He ran through a main road congested with a go-slow so tightly packed that no one was moving and the air was nearly unbreathable. He stuck to as many alleys and side roads as he could. He did not speak to anyone. He did not fight with anyone. He did not help anyone . . . unless he couldn't avoid it. Though the night was cool and the sky was clear, Lagos was broiling.

It had only been five hours since he'd seen Ayodele's people walk out of the sea. Now, the gate in front of Adaora's house had been torn down. The lawn looked as if it had been trampled by giants. Only the plantain tree was untouched. One of the windows in the upper part of the house was burned but no longer burning freely, embers glowing in the darkness. The street was relatively empty and littered with debris from garbage to tear gas canisters. *Tear gas canisters?* he thought. What had happened here since he'd left?

He knocked on the door. Adaora opened it. Without a word, he took her in his arms. If he let go, he was sure he'd fly into space.

CHAPTER 34

FISAYO

Fisayo was back on Bar Beach, watching the thing hovering over the water. It was undulating and glowing, and she could see other things in the water just below it. Large things that rolled beneath the alien lights. She had a chunk of cardboard on her lap. In her hand, she carried a permanent marker she'd found.

A cool breeze swept off the water, and it felt good in her short, damaged hair. She couldn't remember the last time she'd been outside without a wig. She normally wore long wigs of straight glossy black hair, usually expensive with lace-fronts. Her scalp suffered, but her pocketbook always prospered.

Her days of whoring seemed so long ago now. The world had changed. Lagos was eating itself. She took the cap off the marker. It looked new. Good. When she touched it to the cardboard, she felt such a strong tingle of emotion, she knew what she was doing was right.

Slowly, she wrote. Her hand was steady. Her mind was cloudy, though she thought it was clear. She didn't think she'd ever see her cross-dressing brother again. He would not be welcome in heaven and nor would she. Fisayo sat back and examined her work. In the moonlight and the dim beach lights, she smiled. Yes, this was perfect.

Her sign read, REPENT. LAGOS WILL NEVER BE DESTROYED!

Her pants were filthy. Her blouse was stained with blood—her own and someone else's—and the dirt of the earth. Her hair smelled of sweat and was stiff with sand and smoke residue. Her face was dirty with streaks from her own tears. Her bare feet ached and bled. She could not remember when she'd lost her shoes.

She stood up. She would tell everyone. She had seen aliens. And she knew for a fact that they could never ever be trusted. She would fight until there was nothing left to fight for because she loved Lagos. She'd shoved her wig cap into her bra and now she brought it out. She pulled the elastic string from her wig cap and tied each end to holes she made in her sign. Then she hung the sign around her neck.

When she reached the street, which was boiling over with confused, angry, fighting, laughing, destructive, terrified, driving, walking, running Lagosians, she raised her chin and then her voice: "Repent! Everyone! The end is nigh, o! Look to your left! Look to your right! Look up! Are they your friends? Your relatives? Or are they something else? Look closely, o! Repent!"

CHAPTER 35

CHRIS AND THE KIDS

It was past midnight and Chris was still stuck in traffic, but at least everyone seemed calm. He glanced in the rearview mirror. The white man was sitting in back, and Fred was looking at him with a great smile on his face. Kola sat in the passenger seat but had twisted around to look at the white man, too. He'd spoken in Yoruba-accented English and said his name was Oluwatosin. He wore a rather expensive-looking white buba and sokoto and white leather shoes tipped with gold. He certainly dressed and spoke like a Yoruba man of means. But there was more to being Yoruba than language and style of dress.

While driving, Chris had spotted the strange white man being harassed by a group of young men. He'd understood instantly that the strange white man was one of *them*. Chris had screeched to a stop and yelled for the man to get the hell into the car. They'd driven in silence for five minutes now, and Chris didn't know what to do. At least no one was dead. Those idiots harassing him had no idea how close they'd come to being hunks of bloody meat.

"You're one of *them*, aren't you, Mr. Oluwatosin?" Kola asked.

The man nodded and caught Chris's eye in the mirror. "I am."

Chris took a deep breath and muttered a prayer. He considered calling Father Oke and asking for his advice. Then he remembered he was through with that fraud of a holy man. "What . . . what is it you people will do?" Chris asked.

"We are doing what is already happening," Oluwatosin said.

Chris was about to ask another question when Fred asked, "Can he come with us? He can join us for dinner!"

Chris's body clenched. He'd wanted to drop the man-thing off the first chance he got and then speed away. He still didn't understand why he'd saved him. His actions were mad and he was endangering his children. But now his son had put him in a difficult position. Hopefully, Oluwatosin had other plans. There was always that chance.

"Would you like to come to dinner? A . . . a late dinner?" Chris asked.

"I would like that very much."

Chris cringed. *Shit shit shit,* he thought. Fred and Kola grinned widely at each other.

Kola squealed with glee and exclaimed, "This is the happiest night of my life!"

CHAPTER 36
FACE ME, I FACE YOU

The top right of Moziz's "face me, I face you" apartment building was smoldering, and there was a group of people outside it who seemed to be having a very wild party. Why, even Mrs. Ogbu was there, waving a bottle of Guinness, laughing raucously, and making lewd gestures at the slowly perishing building. She'd lived there longer than anyone, having moved there when her husband, the minister of education, left her and their two children for a young British white woman. Her two sons had since left, and she'd become an angry, hectoring fixture ever since. She was obsessed with the Lord Jesus Christ and believed everyone else should be too. She yelled at Moziz every time he left his apartment. When she wasn't at one of Father Oke Ikwuemesibe's services, she was outside her apartment, proving her devotion by bothering the other tenants.

Now she was drunk and doing a vulgar, undulating and grinding dance to some music playing from an SUV as her home burned. Moziz's home. Moziz's life. His online scamming was over . . . at least for a little while. He could always just use a cyber café later. *If any of them still remain after all this wahala don pass,* he'd thought.

But now Moziz was tired of thinking. Tolu, who was beside him in the passenger seat, said not a word. He just stared at the burning building. When Moziz looked in the rearview mirror, he met the eyes of the strange woman they'd saved. He looked away and met Philo's twitching eyes. Philo was not only stupid but she was shit during a time of crisis. For the third time tonight, he noted to himself that he needed to dump her as soon as he got the chance. He could do so much better than her. He met Jacobs's steady gaze. "Well?" he asked, again.

Jacobs sighed. "My place. Mek we go my place."

They parked on the side of the road, got out, and stood staring at Jacobs's apartment complex. It was five stories high and made of old concrete, but really, it wasn't a bad place once you got inside. Yes, inside. How would they get in? Jacobs felt ill. Ordinarily, there were vines growing over the garbage pile behind the building—but they seemed to have grown over the entire complex since Jacobs had left that morning. In fact, he could see them growing as he stood there, watching. Vines wriggled and undulated across each other, leaves sprouting and growing unnaturally large before his eyes. They bloomed bulbous red flowers, and those flowers must have been what were giving off the sweet, roselike scent Jacobs smelled.

"What de *fuck* . . . ?" Jacobs whispered.

Tolu sneezed.

"Na so you dey abuse my house, but see your place, na for bush you dey live," Moziz said, laughing.

"People dey there, *sha*," Tolu said. "Look."

He was right. Even from here, Jacobs could see rooms with lights on and people moving around inside.

Philo moaned and moved closer to Moziz, and he hissed and pushed her away. "No jam pack me," he snapped.

"I dey fear," she said.

"Wetin you want mek I do if you dey fear?" he said. "Nonsense."

"R . . . Rain," Jacobs said to the woman. She was still sitting in the car, serenely watching the building. She'd told Jacobs to call her "Rain" because, she said, she liked how it sounded. After seeing that her face had re-formed and this woman alien was not angry with them, Jacobs and the others were glad to have her with them. She was someone who knew more about what was going on than they ever would. Jacobs pointed at the building. "Is dis . . . what is dat?"

"I no sabi," she said.

"So dis no be de result of say una land here?"

"Dose people look to you like say dem from another planet come?" the woman asked.

"Dat no be wetin I mean," Jacobs said, frustrated. He frowned. He needed to get in touch with Fisayo. She wasn't answering her phone.

They all jumped at the sound of a gunshot nearby.

"Mek we go inside!" Philo said, grabbing Moziz's arm and pulling him toward the building. Tolu followed.

"You dey come?" Jacobs asked Rain.

She stood up and nodded. Jacobs smiled. "Good." But then he frowned. His third-floor apartment was clean, and he had plenty of beer and Fanta to offer them. His television was small, but it was high definition. But did he have his dresses laid out on his bed? He couldn't remember. The last twelve hours had been a blur, and it had started with his meeting with Seven and Rome. And before he'd gone, he'd spent two hours picking out just the right outfit . . . which meant he'd brought out his very best, tried them all on. Left them lying out. *Shit,* he thought as he and Rain joined Tolu, Moziz, and Philo.

They stood a few feet from the apartment entrance, which was draped with thick vines.

"Dem get poison?" Tolu asked.

"My brother, anything dey possible tonight," Moziz said. "But . . ." He looked at Rain and then looked away. None of them would talk to her. Only Jacobs. "I no tink so. No be as tings dey go."

"What of dat ting on de road?" Philo asked. "Dat one no dangerous? Why dis one no go dey poisonous?"

"No be you wan go inside?" Moziz snapped.

"I just dey talk . . ."

"Why you no jus close your mouth?" Moziz said.

"Oh my God, mek two of una stop am now," Jacobs groaned.

Tolu laughed and shook his head.

Rain stepped forward and pushed the vines aside. Jacobs held his breath. They all did. She turned to them. "I don die yet?" she asked sarcastically.

"Una people fit die, sef?" Philo spat, looking her up and down.

Philo was rude, but Jacobs was thinking along the same lines. The alien woman had reached out and touched the vines and the vines didn't hurt her, but that didn't mean they wouldn't hurt the rest of them. Did these aliens even die? Still, up close, the vines looked harmless enough. Jacobs opened the door with his key, and they all went inside.

The concrete steps to the third floor were uneven, and there was no light. Jacobs couldn't help smiling to himself as he heard one of the others stumble and curse. Philo lost her shoe when she mis-stepped on the stairs. "Wait, o," she said as she groped for it.

Jacobs turned and saw Rain was right behind him. He could barely see her in the darkness. He couldn't see any of the others at all.

"E dey for you back," Rain said.

"You dey see for darkness?" he asked.

"Yes. Why light no dey dis place?"

Jacobs shrugged. He'd never wondered why the stairwell had no light; it just didn't. As he unlocked the door, he began to sweat. He was suddenly sure that he'd left a pile of dresses on the chair. They all knew he didn't have a girlfriend. What the fuck was he going to say?

"Hurry up, my guy," Moziz said. "I wan piss."

"Bathroom dey down dat way," Jacobs said, pointing. "De next door for your right." He heard Moziz jog off as he opened his door. He stepped inside, purposely not turning on the lights.

"Mek I find light," he said as the others stumbled about. He took his time, wishing his eyes would adjust so he could see what he'd left out. But before he could do anything, the lights came on. Tolu had found a switch. And there, draped over his sofa, were the dresses.

Philo. The idiot empty-headed girl walked right to them. She had a big grin on her face. She looked back at Tolu as she picked up one of the dresses and held it to herself. It was bright green and silky with a drooping neckline. He didn't much like this dress because of its ugly color. Plus, he didn't have any shoes to match it. But he loved how it fell over his body, like a cascade of cool water. On hot nights, when he wasn't going anywhere, he'd slip this dress on, turn on a fan, open the window, and sit on the sill with the lights off.

"Na who get dis?" Philo asked, a knowing grin. She didn't wait for Jacobs to answer. She looked at Tolu. "See, wetin I dey tell you since? Jacobs get bottom power."

Tolu looked at Jacobs with openmouthed disgust.

"I no be gay," Jacobs said, his entire body going cold. How had *Philo* suspected? He'd always thought she was too stupid to notice anything. *Stupid olofofo poke-nose woman,* he thought. "I jus like to wear woman cloth."

"My God," Philo laughed. "E no even deny am!"

"Allah forbid!" Tolu shouted. "*Kai!* Whoo!"

Moziz walked through the open door and stumbled to a halt. Jacobs could hardly look at him. Moziz was glaring at Jacobs with real anger.

Jacobs just stood there, in the pool of light from his favorite lamp. The power in his apartment went out constantly. NEPA took the lights like God took human lives. Yet, now, during this terrible moment, the damn lights didn't so much as flicker.

"E just be like to fuck dog," Moziz said as he walked in. "You no like pussy? You prefer *animal?*"

"No be animal," Jacobs found himself saying. "I no even . . ."

Moziz turned to Tolu and Philo as he snatched up Jacobs's green dress and threw it to the floor. He wiped his hand on his jeans as if he'd just touched a sick man's shit. "*Kai!* So na sis man I don dey hang around since? A beg mek I ask, o. You dey worship deity too? You dey do juju?"

Jacobs glanced at Rain, who was watching quietly.

"You, you, you, dem suppose to stone you to death," Moziz said, stammering with rage. Sweat was beading on his forehead.

Tolu nodded vigorously. "How you jus fall our hand like dis, eh?" Tolu added.

Jacobs had known Moziz forever. They'd played together as babies and lived practically as brothers. Jacobs and Moziz were very different, but Jacobs had always been able to intuit Moziz's thoughts and reactions. Until now. He'd never have expected Moziz to do what Moziz did next.

BAM!

Philo screamed and ran behind Rain, burying her face in Rain's back.

"FUCK!" Tolu screamed.

Jacobs stumbled back. He blinked. Then he dropped to one knee. All his life, since his memories began, he had known Moziz. Their parents had lived in the same apartment building. Their fathers hated each other, and their mothers had been miserable together. What had happened? What had happened? Jacobs had never felt such pain in his twenty-three years of life. The left side of his chest simultaneously burned and felt drenched in water. Earlier today, as they'd driven to the woman's house to kidnap the alien, life had seemed so rosy. There was potential for such positive change. Now . . . now he didn't know what he felt. He coughed and tasted blood. He coughed again, suddenly unable to breathe.

Moziz blinked, the reality of his actions dawning on him. He looked down at Jacobs, his oldest friend, who was more brother than friend. He'd never known him. How long had he been dressing like a woman? Moziz couldn't believe it. Something had to give. Someone had to do something. His thoughts were cloudy when he looked up and met Rain's eyes. He raised the gun that he'd pulled from his jeans, that he'd shot his oldest friend with, that was still in his hand.

Paff!

Then Moziz felt no more.

Philo, who'd been standing beside Moziz, was looking at Rain just before it happened. Rain's face had twisted into an angry snarl, then it had shifted, and for a moment it wasn't even a face. There was a black hole where her head should have been—terrifying, bottomless, empty. Then her features re-formed, and she focused hard on Moziz.

The red dry blast hit Philo so hard that it blew off her dangling earrings. She had been to Germany once to visit her brother. She'd hated it and returned home a week early. No one could convince her to leave Nigeria again. What she'd hated most about Germany was the snow. On the day she'd arrived, there had been a snowstorm. The first time she breathed German air, it was accompanied by a blast of fresh snow. It had been cold and eventually wet.

What Moziz exploded into was not cold or wet, but it reminded her of that snow, the way the air whipped against her face. There was red and, for a moment, she couldn't see. She shrieked over and over. She couldn't stop. The shock was just too much.

Tolu ran out of the apartment, tears streaming from his eyes. He tore down the dark stairs, not missing a step. He burst through the door and into the night, not caring that he had to rip through a curtain of alien vines to get outside. He ran onto the street and then he just kept running. Cars passed him as he ran, and, once, he fell into a large deep pothole that he hadn't seen in the darkness. He got up and kept right on running.

Finally he stopped. He stood on the side of the road, grasping his hair. Then he started sobbing, his face turned to the sky, hot tears stinging his eyes. "Na God dey punish me," he moaned. "He dey punish we all!"

CHAPTER 37

THE BOY ON THE ROAD

Adaora, Agu, Anthony, and Ayodele were in Chris's black BMW on their way to the airport. Agu grasped the wheel and squeezed. The traffic hadn't moved an inch in over two hours.

Ahmadu Bello Way is the best road in Lagos. With its thick smooth asphalt, it is nothing like the deathtrap known as the Lagos–Benin Expressway. If that highway is full of ghosts (as Adaora's mother believed), then Bello Way is full of angels. At least on a normal day. Today, however, was anything but normal. Never had the road been so full of cars and people. On the left, just beyond a few buildings, was Lagos's lagoon, and on the right were the well-maintained buildings of the city's affluent Victoria Island community. This was supposed to be a beautiful place.

"We should just leave your car," Agu said. A boy was running through the traffic. He leaped onto the hood as he ran by, laughing. A girl carrying a tray of peeled oranges was going from car to car. Adaora glared at her. *Stupid girl,* she thought. *Or desperate.* The girl wasn't the only hawker trying to make some money from the chaos. Women and girls had emerged selling all sorts of foodstuffs, capitalizing on the chaos. But even *that* wasn't going well. As Adaora watched, two young men knocked over a girl who was selling boiled eggs. They ran off with her money and handfuls of her eggs.

Some people were indeed leaving their cars. They'd inch to the side of the road, get out, and walk away. Or run. Fights were breaking out all over, between and sometimes on top of the gridlocked cars.

"We leave the car, then it'll take us forever to get to the airport," she said. "And we're running out of time. It's already past three."

"Maybe. It can't be more than fifteen miles."

"We should stay with the car," Anthony said. He nodded toward the chaos outside. "Who knows what we'll end up doing if we go out there. It might go badly."

A woman selling bags of cashews was arguing with a driver. He got out of the car and knocked her tray of nuts to the ground. A truck driver leaped out of his car just as the first man slapped the woman.

"This is terrible," Adaora said, appalled. Another man and two women ran over and joined the truck driver in beating the man who'd attacked the cashew-selling woman. Another woman took the cashew-woman's tray and beat the man over the head with it.

"It's getting worse. Get out of the car!" Agu said, turning off the engine.

The four of them got out. Anthony took Ayodele's hand and Adaora ran around the car and grabbed Agu's hand, and they scrambled away from the fight.

Adaora felt it. A sort of swell in the air.

Pressure.

"That one! See?" a man who'd been staring at one of the fights shouted, pointing in their direction. "See him? That boy!"

Boy? Adaora wondered, meeting Agu's eyes. Then Agu was looking past her, in the direction the man was pointing. Adaora turned to look too.

The little boy stood nearby in a sea of people—men, women, children, everyone moving everywhere all at once. But *he* wasn't moving, and no one leaned toward him or reached for him or even brushed close enough to touch him. And in the vehicle headlights, he seemed detached. Not quite there.

He wore brown trousers and a dirty dress shirt.

Why is that little boy all alone? Adaora wondered.

"He is one of them!" a woman cried. She wore jeans and a red blouse. Her short hair stood on end, she had no shoes, and she was wearing a sign around her neck that said REPENT. LAGOS WILL NEVER BE DESTROYED!

Fisayo was sure of what she was seeing. She had already seen plenty of them. He stood out as Satan would stand out in a sea of angels. He'd been there when the three people were snatched by the sea, just last night. The first victims. She had a good memory for faces.

Lagos was flooded with evil; the end of days was here. Her throat was sore, her voice raspy from telling the News to all who would listen. There were fights going on all around her—people overtaken by devilry. But she focused on the boy and only the boy. The child-witch of Satan. The worst of them all. She wouldn't let him out of her sight. Not again. He would not escape. When she'd seen him on Bar Beach, she had instantly disliked him. He'd been clinging to a man, like a dog. Now only he stood still in the sea of chaos. She raised her gun. She pulled the trigger.

Agu saw it about to happen. He turned and started running.

The bullet smashed into the mute boy's left eye. He stumbled to the side and then sat down hard. He lay back. Comfortable now. His mind focused for the first time in his life. If he had had anything to say, he could have said it.

At the sound of the gunshot, the fighting stopped.

Fisayo turned the gun on a woman and pulled the trigger, stumbling back as it fired. The bullet hit the woman in the arm. *Lagos is hopeless.* She turned it to a group of fleeing people and pulled the trigger. A man fell, blood pouring from the heel of his foot where he'd been shot. *It is over.* She'd never shot a gun but it felt natural to her. Maybe that's why God had shown her the military man in the alley with the knife in his neck; had led her eye to the gun in the shadows a few feet away. It was not one of the big AK-47s that they normally carried; God had left her a weapon she could wield. In the name of Jesus; thanks be to God.

She pulled the trigger a fourth time and nothing happened. She smelled smoke. Her eyes stung with it. She'd done things. Terrible things. Her clients would have never guessed she lived in the "jungle," deep in the slums of Ajegunle, Lagos. That for the last month, she'd had to live on a human-made island of packed rubbish. She smelled too good. She walked too tall. She fucked with too much skill.

She hoped her brother would forgive her someday.

Poof! Ayodele blew into billions of molecules just as Fisayo pulled the trigger of the empty gun again. To Adaora, it looked like she became the kind of mist you see at the bottom of a large waterfall. Slow-moving and gray. And it smelled like the sea. Several people screamed. Adaora didn't blink. She wanted to watch.

But as she watched, Fisayo was there, surrounded by the mist, and then she was not. *No,* Adaora thought, horrified. *There was something.* She saw it only for a split second but she knew she'd seen it. In that moment, she had seen Fisayo, clothes and all, spread apart. She'd expanded as a photo expanded when only enlarged vertically and not horizontally. At the same time, Fisayo seemed to fade. Then she was gone. Adaora grasped her chest, understanding what she'd seen. Ayodele had pulled Fisayo apart on a molecular level. Adaora shivered.

Fisayo heard nothing. Saw nothing. And said nothing. She would never feel anything again.

A young man who'd been recording the chaos happened to point his digital camera at the boy just as the bullet hit him. He kept filming as the boy sat down hard and then lay back, blood pooling around his small head.

The young man squeaked with horror as three other men and a woman ran to help the boy. He continued filming as the three men realized there was nothing they could do. He got up close, not believing what he was doing. He'd never seen death. He'd always thought he'd run from it when he came across it, yet here he was, pushing his camera up into the boy's face. No one stopped him. He and his camera were capturing the boy's soul.

This young man with the recording camera would post the boy's death on the Internet minutes later using his phone. Millions would watch the boy's surprised but calm face turn toward the camera. The pool of blood spreading behind him like an expanding halo. Then the boy's face would go slack and the light would dim from his eyes, finally going out completely. The boy would join the group of murdered young people who became iconic figures of troubled times, like South Africa's Hector Pieterson and Iran's Neda Agha-Soltan. This child would become the Boy Who Died so the World Could See.

The mute boy never knew his father or mother. He was found in a Dumpster and then placed in an orphanage. No one ever bothered to name him, and he never knew how to name himself.

He was only eight years old.

Adaora threw herself back into the car and curled into a tight ball. Standing behind Agu, she'd seen the light go out in the boy's eyes. A hand took hers and squeezed.

"What did you do to that crazy woman?" she asked Ayodele, who sat beside her in the car now holding her hand.

"I took her to the water," Ayodele said. "That's all she wanted."

CHAPTER 38

UDIDE SPEAKS

Everybody saw it.

All over the world.

That was the real introduction to the great mess happening in Lagos. Nigeria. West Africa. Africa. Here. Because so many people in Lagos had portable chargeable glowing vibrating chirping tweeting communicating connected devices, practically everything was recorded and posted online in some way, somehow. Quickly. The modern human world is connected like a spider's web.

The world was watching. It watched in fascinated horror, for information . . . but mostly for entertainment. Footage of what was happening dominated every international news source, video-sharing website, social network, circle, pyramid, and trapezoid.

But the story goes deeper.
    It is in the dirt, the mud, the earth, in the fond memory of the soily cosmos.
    It is in the always-mingling past, present, and future.
    It is in the water.
    It is in the powerful spirits and ancestors who dwelled in Lagos.
    It is in the heads and hearts of the people of Lagos.
    Change begets change.
    Ayodele knew it.
    All her people know it.

CHAPTER 39

CODE NAME: LEGBA

I was there.

To be specific, I was in the Testament Cyber Café, not far from Bar Beach. The waters of the ocean were rising, and the government was trying to figure out who was attacking us. Yet there I was in the cyber café totally unconcerned, and up to no good. Okay, so I was good at it. I was good at being up to no good. I was good at 419. Nigerian Internet fraud.

My code name was "Legba." It was perfect because Legba is the Yoruba trickster god of language, communication, and the crossroads. I am Igbo and I peddle in words. I am American, born and raised. Igbo American, then. Or maybe American Igbo. That sounds better.

I'd come to Lagos to spend time with my grandfather. Two months. A good chunk of my summer vacation. Granddad was cool. I loved him. I was glad to come and be with him for such a long period of time. Before, I'd only come to Nigeria with my mom and dad and sister, and those times were only for a couple of weeks, or less.

This time, when I got here, I found my granddad was a spry old man who could still dance to highlife and liked to go for long walks every morning with his hands behind his back and a smile on his face. I was good at making Granddad laugh, too. He liked having me around. My major was engineering but my passion was acting. I could imitate *anything*. Any voice. Any personality. Granddad's

favorite impersonations were Grandma and the actor Nkem Owoh—
I could do them both perfectly.

Anyway, I had a lot of cousins, and I grew close to many of them.
They were shady and I could type fast. And not only could I imper-
sonate anything in voice, I could do it in writing, too. So, that's what
I was doing in that cyber café with my cousins Uche and Afam. Like
I said, I was up to no fucking good. Who would suspect an Igbo guy
who was American using the name of a Yoruba god? The stupid
American white woman was going to wire her "Nollywood lover"
another large sum of money, despite the fact that he hadn't been
there to meet her in Accra two weeks earlier.

My plan was genius. Seriously, the woman was an idiot. She
really believed her Caucasian blood and money made her irresistible
to one of Nollywood's top film directors. She'd even told me these
things in those exact words. She had no clue that she sounded like a
racist condescending asshole. There was a *very* pure strain of White
Privilege running through her. So why not capitalize on her idiocy?

There were many of us in the cyber café, despite the madness
outside and the strange woman appearing on our computer screens
and mobile phones earlier. We were all up to the same shit, mani-
pulating the same weaknesses. Classic 419. To those with mediocre
skills, it is like playing the lottery. To masters like me, it is like being
a superstar gymnast on a very narrow balance beam—risky but
sure. The payoff is only a matter of time. In my case, the payoff was
every few days. We were all in there trying to finish up our last bits
of business before the power went out. No one could say we were
not dedicated people.

I'd just sent one of my well-crafted love-letter e-mails to the
lady to ensure that she'd send the money ASAP. I told her that I
was in Lagos and needed the money immediately to get to Accra;
I'd return the money to her as soon as I got back to Lagos. I really
could have been a writer. I could make a woman think and do anything with a few well-chosen words.

"Now we wait," I said to Afam, leaning back in my chair. They were the cheap metal folding kind, but I felt like a king on a throne.

Afam grinned and we slapped hands and shook and snapped each other's fingers. I did the same to Uche. Afam brought out a cigarette and lit it. His hands were shaking. Beside his head the sign read, NOT ALLOWED: 419, PORNOGRAPHY, SPAM, OR SMOKING. I looked over his shoulder and could see the café owner at his front desk turn our way, a sour look on his face. He was a squat dark-skinned Yoruba man who wore cheap clothes and no wedding ring. I chuckled when he didn't get up.

There was a crash outside and, I kid you not, through the window I could see a group of youths jumping on an SUV like it was a trampoline. This was on the road right outside the café. They were shouting and laughing at the terrified passengers in the car. The SUV sped off, the guys on the car tumbling to the street. Most of them got up laughing. One of them was grimacing with pain as he held his knee. Everyone in the café looked worried, but most still turned back to what they were doing. It was scary, but I had a job to do, too.

"We should get the hell out of here," Afam said.

"Relax, dude," I told him. "We need to get a response first."

"How do you know the woman is even awake?"

"She's in the US. It's eight p.m. here, so it's afternoon there. Trust me, I know her. She's just sitting down at her computer."

Uche looked ready to piss his pants. I'd never have admitted it but I felt the same way. I wasn't sure if people were just wilding out or if it was murder-rioting like they occasionally did in the north when a Christian looked at a Muslim the wrong way. Uche bit his nails as he spoke, "But what if—"

"Afam, whatever the fuck is going on, we better wait it out here because some crazy shit's going down. Who knows, this may be our last chance to get online for a while."

"But what if . . ."

Ping! The white woman had responded. I could see the preview of the e-mail in my inbox.

"The money is on the way. Sent it to the same address. When we meet, we can . . ."

As I was reaching for the mouse to click the message open, the room shook and the computer screens flickered.

"Shit," Uche said, looking around. "Not that woman again. Please not again. What was that?"

"Don't know, *sha*," Afam said, his cigarette hanging between his lips.

We all froze. Not a good time for NEPA to take the power. *Just stay on long enough to let me read my e-mail,* I thought, my heart beating fast with excitement. But I already knew it was good news. The money was on the way.

An old man walked into the café and stood in the middle of the room with his hands on his hips. He was wearing a long black caftan. With the door open, the noise of the riots was loud. Several people ran out, cautiously moving past the old man. The room rumbled again, and I looked out the café window. A large truck passed by, and people in the street leaped out of its way.

Keeping one eye on the man standing in the middle of the café, I clicked the message open. Before I could even start reading, the room began to shake like crazy! We all fell to the floor. The lights went out. Monitors crashed down around us. You couldn't hear anything but breaking, cracking, falling, and yelling. Pieces of the cement ceiling began to collapse onto us. The old yellowed floor tiles buckled.

I was going to die.

The lights flickered. The door had fallen off and the doorway was now lopsided. A table had fallen on the three of us, and we peeked out from beneath it. People coughed and moaned and lay sprawled on the floor or beneath chunks of ceiling or wall. A woman shoved a computer off her, and it crashed to the floor. The owner slowly stood up from behind his counter. Those of us who could turned to look at whatever the fuck was entering the gaping hole that used to be a doorway.

It was massive. Taller than the room. But there was no longer a ceiling. So it could fit. It did not touch the ground, so the rubble, glass, and bodies made no difference to it. Everything was still shaky and I'd been whacked on the head pretty hard by the table, but I know what I saw.

It was a masquerade.

This was not some guys dressed up in an elaborate costume to perform Nigerian theatrics to celebrate the spirits and ancestors; this was the *real thing.* You'd have to truly *see* what I saw to understand. Its tiers of wooden platforms could have been twelve or fifteen feet in diameter. And it stood over thirty feet high. Bamboo sticks and canes stuck out of the top half, and it was covered in ceremonial cloth decorated with colorful geometric shapes and magical designs . . . and the designs were spinning and moving. Alive.

There were forty, maybe fifty brown-skinned human figurines on it. I could see them running around it like fleas, no, like fairies or little people. I could see the mother, father, the one in police uniform, the horses, the trees, the palm-wine tapper. I knew all the characters because since I was a kid I'd enjoyed the performance of masquerades. The theater of them. But never could I have imagined something like this. The upper and lower parts were even divided by the giant yellow serpent, the sign of Igbo pride and mightiness. And it was looking around curiously.

The creature was every color of the rainbow, glowing deep and powerful in the night. And it made music. The creature's cloth quivered with the beat it sent into the ground. The sound was impossible, I swear. The sound of life, the beginning.

Holy shit, this was Ijele. The Chief of all Masquerades, Igbo royalty. Ijele does not ask the small or big masquerades to leave the village square when it wants to enter. They have to. Ijele is the climax and it performs alone. If this thing wasn't Ijele, then I'd gone mad. It shook, hovering over the ground, and began to move toward the one computer that was still standing. Oddly enough, this computer had a lit screen . . . and the old man in the black caftan was standing in front of it.

Nobody dared to move as Ijele, the grand masquerade of masquerades, one of the greatest spirits of Nigeria, slowly danced toward the man in black. And the man in black didn't move. All this under the dark night sky, for the power in the area was completely out, even in the places that had generators.

They stood before each other. By this time, my two cousins had run off, as had anyone else who could. But I stayed to bear witness. This was something I could tell my grandchildren about, if I lived. I was witnessing a miracle. My days of fraud . . . Even as I knelt there under the table, I knew they were over.

It all became clear to me in that moment. All that had been happening for the last several hours. The terrorist who'd hijacked all the computers and mobile phones. We'd all watched her speak, but still we were focused on our own things, on getting what we could get. I was so focused on getting the white woman to pay, even when the madness washed into the streets.

But this woke me up. The coming of Ijele. I am not being melodramatic and I am not crazy. And I am not out of danger. But I will never practice fraud again. Never. I swear.

As I cowered under that table and watched Ijele and the man whom I now believed was one of the aliens look at each other, I felt this great swell of pride and love for Nigeria. I felt patriotism. I would die for it. I would live for it. I would create for it. This was *real*. Tears were streaming down my face.

"Ijele," the man in black said.

Ijele bounced, and as it came down, a drum beat deep like the bottom of the ocean sounded, shaking the husk of the building.

GBOOM! It was like the sonic booms we'd heard twice within the last twenty-four hours, except much louder, much closer. The remaining café walls shuddered and some crumbled. No one groaned. Those who were able to had fled. Except me.

How do I explain what I saw next?

They went into the computer. Does that make sense? Ijele became like gas and the man in black became like smoke and, together, they dissolved into the computer.

After several minutes, I got up and walked over to the computer. It was still on. I don't know why, but I logged into my e-mail account. I was surprised when I could access it. But I wasn't surprised to find all the e-mails and my contacts erased. And I was glad.

CHAPTER 40

ROAD MONSTER

I was there.

My wife, sons, and I were stuck in the go-slow. The hour was past midnight, but the place was like an angry party. The Lagos–Benin Expressway is a shit road. People get robbed there constantly. When I started my job, I would drive to work using that road, but I was robbed so many damn times that I started taking the bus.

Then I heard about that luxury-bus-robbery-turned-bloody-disaster last year, and I went back to driving. The place is full of Area Boys, even military men and police who waylay you like bandits or trolls from European fairy tales. And then there are the horribly maintained roads with potholes that will swallow your vehicle. No, let's not call them potholes; they are closer to *craters*.

But this night, they were not the problem with the expressway. It was just packed. We were all fleeing Lagos. My wife has one of those nice mobile phones. We all watched the broadcast on it. I did not believe it was an alien. It had to be Boko Haram or some other idiot terrorist group from the north, finally making a play for Lagos. Those *mumu* shout that Western technology is blasphemous, yet they use it to enact their plans. Hypocrites.

Before the strange woman giving a speech on my wife's phone finished, my wife and I agreed on one thing: We were getting the hell out of Lagos, immediately. Something was going to blow. Lo and behold, not minutes after the woman finished speaking, BOOM! Something did blow! We didn't know what, but we heard the sound. We threw the kids in the car with all the naira we had, some clothes, food, and our laptops, mobile phones, chargers, and got moving.

We made horrible time because people were already trying to escape the slowly rising water. We managed to head northeast on the expressway, and after about an hour, everything stopped. Nothing could move. Many tried to drive through the grass and dirt on the sides of the roads, but they got stuck there as well. People turned off their cars and climbed out to stretch their legs and talk, and soon the road became a market. Hawkers kept our bellies full with spicy suya, groundnut, cashew fruit—those girls were making a killing. But they were providing excellent service. Young men blasted music and eyed women. Babies cried and slept. Mosquitoes sucked blood.

Both sides of the road where we had stopped were flanked by shallow bush. There was nowhere to go until the gridlock broke up. I was sitting in the car and the boys were in the back sleeping. My wife was standing close by, talking to two women she'd just met. One was very tall and dressed like she was about to walk onto a Nollywood set, her tight pink-gray dress matching her pink-and-gray platform-heeled pumps. The other looked more like my wife, in black pants, heels, and a white top.

"We'll be stuck here for three days," the black slacks woman said.

"It'll be fine," the tall Nollywood woman said.

"I pray, o," my wife said.

"I heard it was getting crazy on Victoria Island," the black slacks woman said, nodding. "Riots, idiots burning everything; people are posting it all on the Internet. I was watching with my BlackBerry."

My wife sucked her teeth. "Well, how different is all that from what happens every day? Didn't that 'luxury-bus-robbery-turned-tragic-accident' happen near here?"

She was right—it *did* . . . right where we were parked, actually. Well, maybe about an eighth of a mile up the road, but that was close enough. I knew this because I had seen it with my own eyes. I'd never told my wife the truth about it. I'd been coming home from work when I drove past the scene that night.

Mangled, twisted bodies all over the goddamn road. I am not exaggerating. Traffic was routing through the grass and dirt to get past it. Unlike most, *I* didn't slow down. I moved quickly. *I* didn't want to see. Even in the dark, that swift passing was bad enough for me. My window had been open, and the air had reeked of blood and fouler things. I must have been overwhelmed because I felt faint, my vision blurred for a moment and the road before me undulated, and I could have sworn that I felt the car jump. But I hadn't driven over anything. Then I was past the scene.

My wife later heard about the accident and asked me if I'd seen anything. I told her that I must have passed the area right before it happened. I don't normally lie to her, but she didn't need to know that I'd been there. If I'd told her what I'd seen, she would have demanded details, I'd have told them to her, and then she'd have cried for hours over the dead. Then my sons, who are always listening behind doors, would have had that sick look on their faces that they always get when they learn something they are not ready to learn. My white lie was to *protect* them . . . at least, until the photos came out in the papers and on the Internet showing the brutal scene. There were torn-up bodies littering the road, blood, intestines, skid marks of skin, twisted torsos, body parts broken off. The photos would make anyone want to vomit.

These roads are full of ghosts. I'd always known that. That's why I'd have preferred to be as far from the expressway as possible at midnight on a night like this, when something was attacking Lagos.

But we were stuck.

I was looking down at the road when I saw a large black spider dart by and disappear into the grass. I shuddered. I hate spiders and this one was huge . . . and very fast.

"You're a *what?*" I heard my wife screech. I'd tuned out of their conversation and now I tuned back in. My wife and the woman in the black slacks were staring at the tall Nollywood-looking woman.

"You've been talking to me for the last half hour," the Nollywood woman said. "Do I look dangerous?"

I made eye contact with my wife before turning to look at the tall woman. She was . . . one of them. She looked so normal. Except . . . it's hard to explain. There was a flicker of oddness about her if you looked long enough. Like she was more than what she was and less than what she was presenting, like a double-exposed photo. My wife took a step toward the car, and I was about to leap out when the ground shook.

The boys woke up. "Daddy, what w'dat?" Loteh asked, slurring his words from sleep.

"I don't . . ." I looked toward the Nollywood woman. She was looking up the busy road. So was my wife.

The ground shook again. This time harder. My wife came running to the car, the two women behind her. I watched the Nollywood woman, waiting to see her change into a monster or something.

"Udeh! What is going on?" my wife shouted.

I could only shake my head. I didn't know where to focus. My children in the back seat, the shuddering road, my wife, or the "woman" standing behind her?

"Get out of the car!" the Nollywood woman shouted. "Hurry! It's not safe!"

My wife and I stared at her. The boys started scrambling out. I opened the door to get out. The woman in the black slacks ran around the car and up the street stumbling and pointing back at us, shouting, "I've seen one of them! Back there! Back there!" People leaped out of their cars and ran up the road with the woman, away. Away from us.

I grabbed my bag and my wife's purse. One of the boys snagged a bag of food, the other, my wife's phone. And that's when the road began shaking like a snake fighting a feisty rat.

"Get off the road!" the Nollywood woman screamed. She was right beside me. Everything was shaking, but even in the darkness I could see right into her eyes—clearly, steadily. They were brown but glowed like the sun was behind them; a sun from another world, maybe. In that moment, I understood in my gut, she was not human. She was not earthly. She was something completely other. *But* she was not evil, either. I felt dizzy but I had to stay alert. For the sake of my family.

I dragged my wife and kids into the grass, completely forgetting about the tarantula I'd seen run in there, and the Nollywood woman followed. If she said get off the road, then it was best to get off the road. We were the only ones to do so. It was dark except for all the headlights. Who would want to run into the tall grasses, bushes, and shadows in such darkness? So everyone else ran up the road.

At least they ran away from . . . it. To this day, I will never really know *what* "it" was, o.

Not far from where the accident took place last year, the road was undulating. Then it began to stretch like hot plastic. Something beneath it groaned, deep and cavernous, "OOOOOOMMM." The air stank of tar, and I felt a blast of heat on my face.

"Don't move," the Nollywood woman said. We didn't. But everyone on the road did. They screamed and ran. People started their cars and tried unsuccessfully to drive out of the gridlock, into the grass. "OOOOOOOOOOMMM," the road said as it began to move beneath the vehicles. My nostrils stung from the stench. My wife pressed the kids close to her as she watched the Nollywood woman. My sons were crying as they looked up the road where something enormous was heaving and piling over itself.

The road was rising up in a huge snakelike slab of concrete, the faded yellow stripes still in view. Then it rippled into a concrete wave. It knocked cars off itself as it rolled toward the fleeing people. When it got to them—well, you heard nothing but shrieks of agony. I covered my sons' ears. They were too far and it was too dark for us to see what was happening. I was glad.

And then it went quiet.

"OOOOOOM," the road said. This time it sounded almost as if it were in ecstasy. The screaming had stopped. Had it eaten everyone? That was when the Nollywood woman ran into the road. She ran at the road monster, her heels sinking into the soft concrete.

"Stay here," I said. My wife only looked at me, and my children were pressing their faces to her legs.

Quickly I crept alongside the road, afraid to touch it but also not daring to go too far into the grasses. I slowed down when I was close enough to see the Nollywood woman. The monstrosity was so terrifying that I changed my mind and moved deeper into the grasses, getting on my knees and crawling. Snakes and tarantulas were nothing compared to what I could see.

Let me tell you something—that woman, she was from outside this earth, yes. But that thing, that thing that was haunting the road, it was from *here* and had probably been here since these roads were built, maybe even before then. I am not a Christian or a Muslim, or maybe I am both. But I also believe in the mysteries we can never understand, especially in my country. This thing was one of them.

"Bone Collector," the Nollywood woman said as she looked up at it.

It piled up before her, reaching five stories into the sky. I swear to you, this is what I saw. Concrete that smelled like fresh hot tar . . . and blood. It smelled like blood, too.

"Why?" the woman asked it. "Why do you do this? Why now?"

"I collect bones," it said. The voice sounded blistering and wet. I felt the vibration of it deep within me. It made me feel like nothing but meat, like it could shake that meat from my bones, the bones it wanted. "I have always collected bones. I am the road."

"Collect my bones and then never collect again," the woman

said. "I am everything and I am nothing. Take me and you will be free of your appetite."

Everything around me seemed to go silent. I couldn't even hear the grass rustling. Can you imagine? Never in my entire life had I witnessed such a selfless act. She was not from earth. Yet still. I thought of Nigeria's worst diseases—pervasive corruption and unsafe roads. The one who had spoken through my wife's phone was right. She and her people were indeed agents of change. I could feel the change in me then, while I knelt there. I'm sure I was not the only one, either.

I feel it now.

I watched it take her. I owed it to her to not turn away. I saw the pain on her face as she was pulled into the road's hot flesh, as it turned to mush beneath her high-heeled platform shoes, pulled her down, her pink-and-gray dress pushed up around her as she sank. She never screamed, never made a sound, just let it take her. The road shuddered, the road stretched, but in the end, the road was satisfied. It laid itself back down, and became still. And when it was done, I heard the relieved sigh of millions of ghosts.

Not long after, the gridlock cleared up. Some people came back, got in their cars, and drove away. My wife and I got into our car with our sons, drove around the abandoned vehicles, and left Lagos.

After the road ate that woman, I do not think any other people died on the Lagos–Benin Expressway. Not that night.

CHAPTER 41

AFRICAN CHAOS

I was there.

Though, maybe I shouldn't have been there. Maybe my mother was right. She'd warned me not to travel to Nigeria. She said that of all the African nations, this country was the one she heard the weirdest things about on CNN. Internet fraudsters, Christians and Muslims killing each other in the streets, a government that openly robbed its people blind. To her, Nigerians were a race of trouble-makers. "You ain't no African," she declared the night before I left. "You American. They gon' eat you alive." Then she hugged me and gave me five hundred dollars and a bottle of cod liver oil capsules.

My mother hated hip-hop, too. She called it "successful trash" and "crass ghetto bullshit." She'd always felt I should have been singing in church. She said she didn't raise a rapper. But I am what I am and I be what I be. I can sing well enough but the church isn't for me. My mother can deny it, but she *raised* me to be free. A sharp thinker who goes after her dreams. And despite her issues and the fact that my father left us with nothing but debt when I was a baby, she did a good job.

For years, I'd been digging on Anthony Dey Craze, the lyrical genius rapper from Ghana. A Ghanaian friend of mine turned me on to his work, and then months later I saw Anthony live. His performance . . . How can I describe it? It *changed* me. Listening to him in my car or on my phone was one thing. Live was something else entirely. It was in the bass of his voice, the flow of his words.

There was a rhythm to his performance that swayed the entire audience! You could practically *see* waves of it rolling over everyone. I'd never experienced anything like it. That shit came straight from the soil of the continent, I just knew it. I wanted to learn how to do *that*. So when I opened for him at a show in Atlanta and he asked me to go on tour with him in Ghana and Nigeria, all expenses paid, of course I said, "Hell yeah!"

The show that night in Lagos was amazing. I was the opening act, and I don't think the audience was expecting me. I don't think they were ready for a six-foot-tall African-American woman in a glamorous evening gown with a shaved head who could both rap *and* sing. I took the stage like a dragon. I wrapped things up with a freestyle session. I was so deep in the zone that I don't even remember what I was spitting. It was just coming and coming and coming. I should have known there was something in the air. Backstage, Anthony came up to me, gave me a big hug, and said that I was officially his protégée. I was speechless! Everything in my life was coming together.

I grew up in Athens, Georgia. Up until three years ago, the farthest I'd ever gone from home was Jackson, Mississippi, to attend Jackson State University and study psychology. I was the first in my family to go to college. And by my junior year, to my mother's horror, I also became the first to record a hip-hop album. Never in a million years could I have imagined I'd wind up on the streets of Lagos during some sort of riot.

I'd gone out looking for Anthony after the concert. His producer told me he'd slipped out and that I'd find him down the road at some place called Bar Beach. That's why I was out there. I really didn't plan to go anywhere alone. I just wanted to see if maybe he hadn't left yet.

There were some guys milling about near the entrance of the nightclub. I leaned against the door and watched the road. The club was on the corner of a busy intersection, and I watched the traffic and enjoyed the night air.

This was how I actually saw it. I *saw* the sonic boom. I swear to God, the very air shivered. I saw it coming up the street. At first, I thought I was just tired and overwhelmed from such a wonderful night. I wondered if I needed to go and eat something. I can never eat before a performance, and now I was starving.

But the air really *did* shiver. And as I stood there, it came right at me. There was no physical breeze; it came like a ghost. Then it washed over me like a great wave of water. When it passed, I felt drenched, heavy.

There was a brief silence, like the moment after an intake of breath.

Then *BOOM!* Deafening noise that made my head vibrate!

People dropped to the ground, a man fell off his *okada*, windows shattered, car alarms sounded, two cars went over curbs. For a full minute, the constant traffic of honking, beeping cars, trucks, *okadas*, red buses, beat-up orange *danfo* mini vans, motorized tricycles in front of the nightclub completely *stopped*. I should have gone inside. Instead, I stepped into the sea of people, holding my ears. In those first few minutes many others did too. And soon the sides of the roads were full of people like me, curious, afraid, excited people who were scared of being indoors.

We were all wondering the same things: What blew up? Was something else going to explode? My head throbbed and I struggled to ignore it. I stood on shaky legs at an intersection, pressing close to a streetlight to avoid getting knocked around too much. The traffic started moving again, but people were clearly scared. You could see it on their faces.

"Did you see that?" Someone tapped roughly on my shoulder.

Rubbing my temples, I turned. An old bent man in a long tan caftan and a wide-brimmed hat leaned on a dark wooden cane. He stank of many cigarettes and had a bushy gray beard and tufts of wiry hair on the sides of his head.

"I . . . I don't know."

"Yes, you do," he said. "You saw it. *Na wao*, the first thing you say to me is a lie, *kai!*"

"I . . ."

"Maybe you know what it was, then?"

"The noise?" I asked.

"No, the shivering air. Was it a bird?"

"I don't think so?"

"A plane?"

I frowned.

The man grinned. He didn't have many teeth. Then he laughed wheezily and said something in another language. Could have been Yoruba, Hausa, or complete gibberish. I don't think it was gibberish. The man had a glint in his eye and it put me on edge.

"What do *you* think it was?" I asked.

"You assume that I think."

"I need to get back to the club," I said, turning to leave. This was too much weirdness for me. Plus, the car alarms and exhaust were increasing my headache. I turned back to him.

"Where are you from? Atlanta, Georgia, United States of America, right?" he said.

"How did you know that?"

"I can tell, o. I got an American cousin," he said with a smile. "I got cousins all over the world."

"Um . . . wow," I replied. An *okada* passed dangerously close to him as he stood with his back to the road. He didn't seem to mind or even notice.

"Yes, you saw what you saw and I saw it too," he said. "It's going to get really interesting here soon, you'll see. It's a great time to be in Africa! And at least you can say that you saw it all begin." He pointed a gnarled finger at me. "You can say you were there. That is not something most young American girls can say. If you ever make it back to your country, make sure you tell them about your country here. Just because you are American does not make you American. *This* is your home."

I smiled, despite the fluttery feeling in my chest. I needed to get back to the nightclub. "Okay," I said. "Well, have a good night, sir!"

"Scratch," he said. "Call me Scratch."

"Okay, Scratch. Be safe."

"No worry about me, o," he said. He winked. "This my kine of night."

I turned to run back up the street to the nightclub. I looked over my shoulder but the man was gone, already swallowed up by the late-night bustle. I took one last look at the busy street. *What* was *that noise?* I wondered. It was almost midnight, and the street was busier and more frantic than ever.

I'd see Scratch again, twenty-four hours later when I was running for my life after we'd had to abandon our car on the way to the airport. I was with several band members and Anthony's manager, and we were all terrified, having witnessed riots downtown (we couldn't find Anthony). Scratch was dancing with a crowd of market women in the middle of a dirt road as the women sang songs to the Lord Jesus Christ. When I saw the old man reveling with the women, I lost my fear. They reminded me of my mother and her church group on Sundays.

I'd have a heck of a story to tell my mother. Papa Legba, the god of the crossroads was alive and well in the country of his origin. That's epic. Even now, I wonder how much he had to do with what was going on. Papa Legba loves trouble. I just might write a song about all this, too, if I survive. I'll call it "African Chaos." And if there is one city that rhymes with "chaos," it is Lagos.

CHAPTER 42

MMIA

Agu drove, Adaora sat in the passenger seat, and Anthony and Ayodele were in the backseat. They were all quiet. Adaora was nibbling at toothpaste. The travel-sized tube was all she had in her purse that could fight off her nausea. Whenever she went scuba diving, she always liked to brush her teeth right after her return, so carrying it was a habit.

The last "dive" I did was nothing like the others, she thought hysterically. Her mind moved to the incident on Ahmadu Bello Way. She could still see the little boy's eyes as he died. The mad woman. *Why* had she done it? Ayodele said that the woman had lost hope. That wasn't good enough for Adaora. That poor boy. She wiped her eyes and sucked down a bit more toothpaste.

They weren't far from the airport. It was nearly six a.m. They had minutes. The closer they got the fewer cars they saw. Agu said the airport had probably been evacuated. But it looked flat-out abandoned.

Whirrrrr!

At the sound they all leaned forward to peer through the windows into the dark sky. In a few hours the sun would come up. And what would it reveal? Adaora pushed the thought away and focused on the plane above. There was only one in the sky.

"Shit!" Agu said, speeding up.

"You think that's them?" Adaora said.

"Of course it is," he said. "Who else would it be?"

"Tonight?" Anthony asked. He'd opened his window to get a better look. Then he laughed. "*Chale*, could be a lot of things."

"What does this man look like?" Ayodele asked.

"Like a taciturn old yam farmer," Adaora said.

Agu chuckled. "He is tall and skinny like Anthony . . . but not healthy. He has many ideas but he hardly follows through on any of them."

"Baba Go-slow," Adaora muttered.

A minute later, they arrived. Agu stopped at the gateway that led onto the tarmac. Up ahead was the ramp that led to the drop-off and pick-up section of the airport that Adaora knew well. Even from here, she could see people milling about outside. Confused. No one was going into the airport; most likely the doors had been locked. But there were a few people leaving the building—running out and hopping into waiting vehicles.

The entrance to the tarmac was deserted and the gate was up. Agu shook his head with disgust. They drove in. It was easy to spot the president's small jet. It was the only plane labeled "Nigerian Air Force," and it was the only moving plane on the tarmac.

"Shut the lights off," Adaora said.

They crept after the plane as it taxied to a stop on the far side of the tarmac. Agu parked the car in the darkness between two stair-trucks and got out. Adaora's legs were shaking. Had they done the right thing by bringing Ayodele here? What would she say to the president? What would she *do* to the president?

The plane stopped. Nothing happened for several minutes. But through the round windows, Adaora could see the lights on and people walking up and down and looking out into the darkness. She spotted the president.

"I see him! Do you?" She pointed.

"I do," Anthony said.

"The window near the center," Agu said.

The president of Nigeria was looking outside. A soldier pulled him away from the window. Adaora could see two of his wives, too. Hawra was the junior wife who was in her early forties. People called her "the smart one" because she was a lawyer who also carried a PhD in political science and was rumored to be one of the president's closest and mouthiest advisors. Zena was the senior wife and in her late fifties. People didn't call her much of anything.

Finally, the door opened, lowering into stairs. The first to come out were three military officials. Guns up, they looked around. They must have deemed things safe because they stepped aside to allow Hawra and Zena to exit. The two wives, Zena a tall woman of nearly six feet and Hawra short and plump, wore white garments and veils. Then two older men in fine suits emerged—the president's advisors. Then the president came forth. Two young soldiers were holding him up. He looked weak and semi-conscious. They half carried, half dragged him down the stairs, his legs barely touching each step. When they got to the bottom, one of the soldiers patted him on the shoulder as if in apology for the rough treatment.

This shriveled, sickly man was to lead the country during a crisis. Adaora had never felt so ashamed and conflicted. If he was this ill, why didn't he step down, or at least delegate responsibility until he got better?

Adaora was the first to realize Ayodele was moving.

"Wait," Adaora said, running after her, Anthony and Agu following. "Wait for us!" But Ayodele was swift. Though she appeared to be walking, she was covering the distance impossibly fast.

The soldiers raised their guns as Ayodele approached. She didn't slow down. "President," she said loudly. "I am here to speak with you."

"Stop right there!" one of the soldiers shouted, when Ayodele was a foot from his gun. "I will shoot!" Three other soldiers joined him, guns raised.

"Who are you?" Zena asked in her shrill voice. She stepped in front of her husband. "What are you doing here?"

Out of breath, Adaora, Agu, and Anthony came to a stop behind Ayodele.

"I am Private Agu, Amphibious Division, sir," Agu told the soldier, snapping a salute. "We are only here to help."

"Has the airport been shut down? There was no one in air traffic control! We nearly died landing!" Hawra said. "How can an entire airport be empty and dark?"

"Aren't you aware of what is happening?" Agu asked.

"We know only what we've heard," the president said, his voice weak.

"You," one of the soldiers said, pointing at Anthony. "Are you that rapper from Ghana?"

"Yes."

"Eeey, *na wao*," one of the other soldiers said, lowering his gun. "I have all your albums, *jare!*"

"Say it, *sha*," the first soldier said, grinning. "I dey craze!"

Anthony rolled his eyes.

Adaora stepped forward. "My name is Adaora," she said. "I am a marine biologist. This is Ayodele. She is one of them, one of the . . . the extraterrestrials. She is their ambassador. She was the first to make contact and she seeks an audience with you, Mr. President. We've gone through a lot to get her here."

The soldiers pointed their guns at Ayodele as they moved to shield the president.

"Oh, move aside," the president snapped at the soldiers, becoming a little more animated. "Do any of you think you can save my life? Look at me! I'm nearly dead already!" He muttered something in Hausa. "Come," he said, looking at Ayodele.

She stepped up to him. Her long braids blew in the soft breeze. Both of the young soldiers holding up the president looked terrified. Above, the dark sky was warming as sunrise approached.

"Are you truly a stranger? An extraterrestrial? An alien?"

"Yes."

"You look like a woman from Igboland."

"Looks can be deceiving."

He chuckled weakly and then coughed. "Prove it."

She paused. Then she said, "Watch closely."

Even as she spoke, her words were falling apart, disappearing into the din of metal balls on glass, shifting and reshaping along with her body. The soldiers guarding the president dropped their guns, the wives screamed, and one of his advisors fainted. The pilot fell to his knees and began to vomit. The president watched with wide eyes. Thankfully the two soldiers carrying him did not drop him, though one of them started to sob, and the other seemed to be having trouble breathing.

Ayodele was now a broad-shouldered, stocky white man in a blue uniform with bushy gray hair and beard and haunted eyes. He had a mustache like a handlebar. Ayodele-the-man put her hands on her hips and cocked her head.

The president's mouth fell open. *"Karl Marx,"* he whispered. "I . . . I . . ."

"I know," Ayodele said in a manly voice. She stepped closer to him, graceful in her man's body. "You believe in Marxism, yet you are too powerless to enact it."

The president whimpered.

"I can read the air you breathe," she said. When he still could not speak, she changed back to her brown-dress-wearing-vaguely-Igbo-looking woman form. Her second transformation was too much for the guarding soldiers, the pilot, even the advisors. As one, they turned and ran. One of the soldiers holding up the president started praying to Allah under his breath; the other continued to sob.

"Does this help?" she asked, watching them run.

When her gaze returned to the president, he licked his lips and took a deep breath. "Y-yes."

"Would you like me to look more Hausa?"

"It's . . . No, you are fine."

"I did not mean to frighten you."

"You are evil!" Zena shouted from behind him.

"I am not," Ayodele said flatly. "I am change."

"How did you take over all the mobile phones?" the president asked.

"It wasn't just the mobile phones and it wasn't just me. They helped," she said, motioning to Adaora, Anthony and Agu. "So did Adaora's offspring," Ayodele continued. "As did my people. As did your people. It is a matter of connecting and communicating." She grinned. "And your technology is simple, easily manipulated."

"And yours is not?"

"We *are* technology, Mr. President. And no, we are not easily manipulated."

"What do you want?"

"We do not want to rule, colonize, conquer, or take. We just want a home. What is it *you* want?"

He paused. "To be alive again."

"I will make it so."

ACT III
SYMBIOSIS

THIRD EYE BLINDED

The bat is thoroughly shaken.

She has eaten fifty mosquitoes. Fifty-one. Fifty-two. Her belly is full of insects. Her soft brown fur rustles as she flies. She knows where everyone else is; they are there above the gathering humans on the beach. This place teems with mosquitoes and gnats, who are attracted to their lights and body heat and blood. She discovered this earlier in the week, and other young bats followed her. Now, they flit about so fast, the humans aren't even aware of their presence.

She feels great. The moment before it happens, she catches and eats a mosquito and then does a barrel roll, pushing high into the sky, loving the humidity and the cool air. It makes her feel light and powerful. She drifts on the warm breeze. As she does, she sends a series of ultrasonic squeaks that show all the other bats the beauty of the evening.

Then the thick soupy haze lights up the horizon where it meets the ocean. Like the rotten inside of a crushed fruit. The haze rolls, folds, and expands. It is heading right toward her.

BoOm!

Visceral, thick, but not quite substantial. She sees it perfectly because, for her, sound is as near solid as a sound can be. Deep and ample and spreading. Fast. Then it washes over her as the waves wash over the sand below.

She feels it like she felt the first breath of life when she was born. She remembers the moment of her birth clearly. She had opened her eyes and seen little. But then she chirped, and the sound found her mother. Then the others. Then the cave. And a few weeks later, when she echolocated the night, she thought she'd die from the beauty of the trees and the land.

Now she is in the middle of . . . of red, pink, green, yellow, blue, periwinkle. She has no words for color because she is a bat and bats do not see colors. But she sees them now. She sees a thousand of them. She can taste them. They are meaty like mosquitoes, leafy like palm fronds, fruity like mangos. She tumbles in the air and then falls to the sand. She struggles to stay conscious, stretching her wings and twisting her head. She looks into the sky and sees . . . lights. At this moment, she is the only bat on earth seeing the stars in the sky. But she doesn't know what those are either. Her echolocation will never reach that far. The stars become many. They seem to grow closer, too. It is overwhelming.

Then everything is dead quiet. No air. No sound. No earth. She is in space. Farther, deeper. She sees a planet of stone. Red oily stone and liquid air. Then an aqueous world of blue, blue waters. Then a yellow fast-spinning sphere lit by three suns. World after world. She wakes in a tiny warm cave of darkness, but there is energy here, too. She is being jolted by sound, by rhythm. What kind of higher echolocation is this?

This is what awakens her. Jars her back into her body, back to life. Then the darkness opens into the night, and she is hurled into the sky. Grateful to the Supreme Being that she has been given another chance at life, she flies into the night, her mind buzzing, her perspective changed.

Nevertheless, sound *and* sight—now she has both. She looks up and sees the stars. She echolocates for miles. Her world is suddenly huge.

She does not eat a thing. She only wants to fly and see with her new senses. She has grown an eye in the middle of her forehead but she doesn't know this. And if she could, she would not know what to make of it. She flies higher than she's ever flown before. Maybe she is trying to leave the earth. She isn't sure. She isn't thinking about it.

She's far in her mind, deep in her own thoughts. The air on her wings feels amazing. She is swimming, rolling through the air as if it's water. She lifts her head as she flies and lets out a series of loud chirps. And that's when she sees it. The largest bird ever. Flying faster than any hawk or eagle or owl. Roaring like some sort of monster. She doesn't know the human word "dragon," otherwise she would call it that.

There is no time to flee. No time to turn. No time to shriek. And no pain. It is like being thrown into the stars.

The pilot of the Nigerian president's plane has no clue that the plane he is flying has just killed the most enlightened bat on earth. After obliterating this bat as it passes, the plane flies on toward the airport on the strangest night in the city of Lagos's history.

CHAPTER 43

YAWA DON GAS

"AHHHHHHHHHHHH!"

Adaora pressed her head to the car seat and shut her eyes. For the first time in years, she prayed. She prayed to her father, who'd been crushed to death by a speeding truck on the Lagos–Benin Expressway, she prayed to all those spirits she knew lived deep in the polluted soil of Lagos, she even prayed to the Christian god she didn't believe in and the Muslim god she'd never learned about. Lastly, she prayed she was doing the right thing by getting in the car with Agu, Anthony, the president's wives and the two security guards, and leaving the president of Nigeria out there with Ayodele the alien.

"GAAAAAAAH!" the president continued to scream.

Agu was holding down Zena, and one of the soldiers was holding Hawra.

"LET ME OUT!" Zena screeched, tears streaming from her eyes.

"Ah-ah, what is she doing to him?" one of the soldiers moaned.

The screaming stopped. Adaora listened with all her being, but there was no sound to indicate whether the man had died or run off or fainted or ceased to exist. Moments passed. Adaora opened her eyes to find Anthony staring at her, sweat pouring down his face. The minute Agu let go of Zena, she leaped out of the car.

Adaora went after her. Hawra ran a few steps, her thick legs carrying her as fast as they could, and then slowed down. The president and Ayodele were seated face to face on the tarmac in front of the plane. Zena had stopped, standing over them.

"My love, are you okay?" Zena asked.

Adaora stepped up behind her, staring at the president. Even in the darkness, she could see that his eyes were clear, no longer rheumy. The lines on his face were still there but his skin had cleared up. He was sitting with his back straight, unbent. He was smiling.

"I'm fine," he said. Even his voice was louder. Clearer. Stronger. He chuckled, looking up at the sky with a smile on his face. "I'm fine."

"What did she do to you?" Zena cried. "It sounded like . . ."

"She healed me, Zena."

"Praise Allah," Zena whispered, tears running down her cheeks. She bent forward and put her hands on her knees, attempting to catch her breath. Hawra came up behind her, her eyes wide.

Ayodele said nothing. She was looking up at the sky with the president.

The others got out of the car and slowly approached.

"The air is so sweet," the president said. He inhaled and exhaled. "Allah is great." Slowly, he stood up.

Zena blinked and then cocked her head, frowning suspiciously now. "Help our husband," Zena said, pushing Hawra forward. "You are stronger." Hawra moved toward the president.

"My mind . . . it is clear," he said, his arm around his second wife. He chuckled again and Adaora looked at Agu, who shrugged.

The president turned to Ayodele, who'd also stood up and was looking at the airplane. "Take me to your leader," he said.

Ayodele turned around and smiled. "Leaders."

"Where will I meet them?" he asked.

"In the water."

Agu moaned.

The president looked at him. "Private Agu, where can we get a boat?"

CHAPTER 44

NARRATOR'S WELCOME

The sea always takes more than it gives.

Right now, as I weave, the sea roils and boils with life.

About a day and a half ago, the oceans were ailing from pollution.

Today, as the sun rises, there may as well be a sign on all Lagos beaches that reads:

HERE THERE BE MONSTERS.

This has always been the truth, but today it is truer.

They must understand this. But I hope they do not understand any of it. If they do, then they will not step on to that boat, and the story will not continue. My strong webbing will snap. The story will stop growing and spreading. Let them venture forth. I will throw out a strong thread, maybe three. Then I will anchor it firmly to Lagos. That way, I can continue to narrate this tale while I enjoy it.

I am Udide, the narrator, the story weaver, the Great Spider.

I live in this great cave beneath the city. I have been here for centuries, and I will be here for centuries more. This metropolis is just getting started. The coming of these new people is indeed a great twist to Lagos's tale. Who saw it coming? Even I did not.

I roll onto my back and place my hairy feet to the earth above me. I feel the vibrations of Lagos. This way, I see everything. What a story this has been. The sun will soon come up, and I will watch everyone see what they have done. The chaos will be on display.

The sun rises.
Dawn is here, and the dust settles.
The streets are full of mayhem's terrible fruits.
Burned vehicles. Smoldering buildings. Dead animals.
The waking giant of the road goes back to sleep, leaving a trail of terror.
The death of the boy on the road has already been seen by over three million people around the world and will be seen by millions more.
There are new people among the old people.
And the digital ether has gone wild.
The great Ijele leads the wildness, and the tricky Legba laughs.
The Bight of Biafra's waters are teeming.
The president is healed.
His eyes are dry and white. His skin is clear and brown.
His mind is strong and free.

I revel in it all.

I am stronger than ever. I approach the end of this leg of the tale.
And here, I greet you.
Welcome, listener, welcome.
I press my sensitive feet to the cave's ceiling.

Na good good story.
I go continue to listen, o. Quietly . . .

CHAPTER 45

ON THE WATER

The president of Nigeria walked along the narrow path outside his mansion, inhaling the scent of lilacs and lilies. The small garden between the mansion and the guesthouse in the back was his sanctuary. Well-paid gardeners tended to these flowers daily, and it was worth the cost. This was where the president usually came in the morning to think. Nevertheless, this particular morning was not the usual morning at all, so he walked swiftly past the flowers toward the guesthouse.

He'd dressed in a white sukodo and buba, his finest attire. Granted, if he fell in the water, he suspected his clothes would make swimming hell. But he didn't plan to fall in the water. He imagined that the aliens would come to his boat on whatever contraption they used as transportation and talks would ensue. Talks of what? He'd cross that bridge when he got to it. The fact was that the woman Ayodele, who was not a woman, had healed him. She was a child of Allah. So everything was good.

"I'm not going," Zena said, holding her delicate black veil over her face as they stood outside the guesthouse. She'd stayed here since they'd arrived. She didn't want to be in the same house as "that creature in women's clothing." Nor did she want to be near her husband, who'd surely been infected with whatever the creature was spreading. Though Zena had hated watching her husband deteriorate, there had been comfort to be taken from his illness. It was Allah's will and she'd come to terms with that.

But there had been more to it than she'd admit. When he'd been healthy, he'd married two other wives, and slowly her role in his life had dwindled. With the onset of his illness, Zena had become his support system again; she'd become his mouth, his confidante. His third and youngest wife, Caroline, had even grown jealous and moved to their home in Abuja. Now, with him being healed, all that would change.

"One of us should stay here," Zena snapped. "Let Hawra go." *And may she never come back,* she thought. Zena was tired of the overeducated, PhD-wielding, cheeky Hawra. *Let her go and never come back.*

Hawra dressed in fitted jeans and a T-shirt, and then donned her veil. All her life she'd dreamed of being a part of something huge. Something that would bring a change to all things as she knew them. She wouldn't miss what was going to happen next for the world.

CHAPTER 46

THE GLASS HOUSE

Father Oke rested his back against the wrought-iron bars of the gate that surrounded the Glass House in downtown Lagos. He had a pounding headache. But at least he was alive. When he'd come back to himself on the lawn of Chris's home, everyone was gone and the house was on fire. They'd left him there. His flock. Maybe they'd even joined the aliens.

He shoved the thoughts away as he looked at the road. It was a bright early morning. Quiet, too. Not only were there no people in the area, the power in the city had been completely knocked out by the last sonic boom. Once in a while a group of young raucous boys or a car would pass, but otherwise the road was empty. Here, Lagos was desolate, except for a smoldering car down the road. Most likely all the worst madness was in Oshodi or near Mile 2.

Along with his head pounding, his face burned from where he'd been slapped. He'd thrown off his filthy white robes long ago. Then, wearing his gray pants, white shirt, and gray tie, he'd walked the streets for a while. He'd seen a woman laughing as a man ravaged her from behind against a stalled vehicle. She'd been screaming and laughing that an alien was probing her. Father Oke had helped a young woman with three young children cross a busy street; they'd all nearly been run over, but he'd gotten them to safety. He'd seen several go-slows so solid that people had abandoned their vehicles. He'd seen Area Boys carrying branches and palm fronds that they used to threaten people, moving in on the abandoned vehicles like vultures. And worst of all he'd seen many of *them*.

It wasn't something most people around him noticed. Everyone was too busy doing whatever they were doing. But Father Oke wasn't going anywhere. *He* was not lost. For the first time in his life, his eyes were open. So *he* noticed those people who seemed a little off. Their faces didn't carry as much emotion as other people's. Or they seemed too calm. Too comfortable. Too adapted to the situation. They walked with too much grace. And they were everywhere.

He saw them helping people escape Area Boys. He saw two putting out the flames in a burning truck. He saw one helping a little girl find her father. He saw them watching as so many people of Lagos made fools of themselves.

"Oh Lord," he said, rubbing his temples. "Oh my Lord, save us, o."

"Excuse me, sir. Did you say something?"

He looked up. The woman was standing in the parking lot, looking at the building. She was curvy, wearing tight blue jeans and a white short-sleeve blouse that barely contained her large breasts. On each of her wrists she wore a shiny silver watch. Their faces sparkled in the moonlight. Only watches encrusted with diamonds did that. Father Oke remembered admiring the watch of a rapper once while he was in the United States at a fund-raiser. Yes, those were very large breasts and very large diamonds.

"Uh, no, no, I didn't say anything," he said, his eyes taking all of her in. He regularly bedded his house girls and paid them to keep quiet about it. They were sexy, docile, pliable, and certainly sweet. But this woman was something else. This woman was mysterious. And she reminded him of a woman he'd loved years ago.

She sashayed over to him. She wore those high-platformed heels he saw all the Nigerian actresses wearing in their films. Shoes that lifted them up but could never make them truly tall. He loved to watch them walk in those heels.

"Oh, I thought you did," she said. She spoke like she was from the Niger Delta region. She was still looking at the building with a grand smile on her face.

He smiled too. "Are you looking for someone in there?"

"No, no, I just love this building," she said.

"Well, this is not the best time to come out and see it."

"It's crazy, yeah?" she said. She looked up at the bank. Father Oke frowned at the beautiful woman's strangeness. She chuckled and looked at Father Oke. "The city is breaking itself," she said. "But not one single pane of this building is broken."

Father Oke looked at the Fin Bank and winced. The Fin Bank was one of Lagos's most artistic structures, a gigantic trapezoid with arched wings made entirely out of square panes of glass. A few were red, but the majority of them were an ocean blue. It had gone by many names over the years, but Lagosians had always called it the Glass House. He hated this building. He was sure that it was evil. Not surprising, with all the evil that was flooding the city tonight, that the Glass House should be spared.

"Do you want to come with me?"

He smirked. "Come with you where?"

"Answer my question first."

Father Oke looked from her to the building and then to the sky. He could hear someone shout nearby and the sound of tires screeching. The worst night of his life had melted into the worst day. The night and day that everything fell apart. He turned to her. "Fuck it," he said. "Yeah, I'll go with you." He laughed, imagining her heaving breasts bouncing above him as he took her right there on the deserted beach. He was already soiled, why not soil himself more? Might as well get some pleasure from the night.

"You know the mythology behind this place, *sha*?"

"Yes, yes," he quickly said. He didn't want to think about it "Let's go."

"They say that because this building is so shiny and the color of the water, it creates an aura that attracts the sea. You see, the Atlantic always overflows at Bar Beach and that's close to this building. So this place is always flooding."

"Okay, o," he said, wanting to get moving before she said more. He took her arm and pulled. But she wouldn't move. He frowned. She was like a heavy stone. He shoved her hard and still she didn't budge.

She chuckled. "You know what they also say? That it's not the *ocean* that is attracted to this place. That it is Mami Wata who loves this building. Do you know Mami Wata?"

"Yes," he said. Mami Wata was the goddess of all marine witches.

She looked squarely at him. "This is my favorite building, o."

Many things happened to Father Oke at once. He felt his heart break. Why had he slapped that woman so hard yesterday morning? Why had he slapped her at all? Twice in one night he had conversed with a woman who was not really a woman. The first had been from outer space. This second was from the earth's water. For the first time in his life, Father Oke truly realized that he lived in a glass palace, while others around him lived in a ghetto.

He gave up.

Father Oke gave in.

What a relief.

They left the Glass House, crossing the empty street. They were heading toward the beach.

No one ever saw Father Oke again.

CHAPTER 47

FEMI

Adaora, Anthony, and Agu led the way as they walked along the beach, the president and his second wife behind them, flanked by his guards, Bamidele and Chucks. The morning sun was just warming the sky. The president was excited to get some fresh ocean air, but there was a greater purpose in their long walk to the army boats.

"What is that?" Anthony said, pinching his nose.

Adaora pressed her hand to her chest. The sight of it was worse than the stench. A giant carcass stripped of all skin, putrefying in the increasing morning heat. "That used to be a whale," she said. "It must have beached itself. Probably got scared. Poor thing."

"I saw it before," Agu muttered. "They have taken most of the meat." There were still a few people carving out pink slivers of unspoiled or semi-putrid meat. All were young men, many with desperate looks on their faces. To make the situation sadder, there was a camera crew filming them, and several well-dressed journalists interviewing people. There were even youths standing around holding their mobile phones up as they recorded the pathetic scene and probably posted it on YouTube. Adaora felt her gorge rise in her throat as she thought of the little boy on the monster road. Hadn't these people gotten enough last night? Someone pointed at them, and the president's guards raised their weapons.

"Na de president!" a man carrying three slabs of stinky meat shouted.

"Oh my living God! Na dream I dey dream so."

"How e go be de president? Dem been don deport de president."

"And him been don die before dem deport am!"

Several of the people laughed hard.

"Na him be dat, *sha*. See him flat-chest wife, na."

"Na him!"

Soon the president and his wife were surrounded by journalists, camera technicians, and chattering civilians.

"I'm fine, I'm fine," the president snapped. He frowned, wanting them to understand. He switched to Pidgin English, which he hated speaking. It was the ignorant-man's language. "Nothing do me," he loudly proclaimed. "See me well well!"

The five journalists jostled to get a statement from him.

"Do you have anything to say about last night?"

"Where have you been?"

"How come you did not—"

"Last night," the president said, switching to Standard English, "our biggest city ate itself. Now it is full and ready to give birth to itself. That is all I have to say on that."

"Where have you been?" a male reporter asked.

"Sick. But now I am well."

"Where are you going?"

"To see if I can make this better. You may follow us if you like. But do not try to follow us once we are on the water."

"Oh my God," a woman reporter said, pointing at Ayodele. "Isn't that the woman extraterrestrial who got into all our technology yesterday?"

As one, the crowd forgot the president and focused on Ayodele. A cameraman swung his camera into her face and moved it down her body. Adaora shoved the camera away. "Enough," she said. "She is not a piece of whale meat."

"We don't know *what* she is," the cameraman muttered. He stepped back a few paces as Ayodele turned to him.

"I am taking them to the Elders," Ayodele said. "Your leader will meet mine."

"Why can't we come along?" one of the male journalists asked. Adaora recognized him immediately. Femi Adewumi. He wrote features and a column for the *Guardian*. She'd always thought he looked handsome in his column photo—her husband used to get annoyed whenever he saw her reading Femi's writing—and he was just as handsome in person. Adaora frowned at the direction her thoughts had taken. *What am I becoming?* she wondered.

"You may," Ayodele said, after looking him over. "But only you."

Femi grinned and stepped beside Agu.

"Be careful what you wish for," Agu told him.

"This is the story of a lifetime," Femi said excitedly. "Sometimes a man must throw caution to the wind!"

"Madam," said a female journalist. "Please. Can I come too?"

Ayodele looked her over. "You can't swim. You stay here."

The woman's face fell but she didn't argue.

Several others asked after that, including two men carrying rotting meat. Ayodele said no to them all.

"Let's move on," Ayodele said.

Agu nodded. "This way."

There were nine of them: Ayodele, Adaora, Agu, Anthony, Femi, the president, Hawra, and Bamidele and Chucks. The sleek white speedboat was made to take ten, but this didn't set Agu's mind at ease. The boat, like most government-issued equipment, was a piece of shit, with leaks and a faulty motor that backfired randomly at high speeds.

"You can drive this thing?" the president asked Agu.

"Yes, sir," he said. "Usually it takes two people, but I can drive it. My job is to patrol the water. Amphibious Division 81, five years." As he watched everyone climb aboard, Agu shuddered. After his experience in the water, he was not in a hurry to get back out on it. How much was Ayodele going to be able to protect them?

"Put your life vests on," he said. He undid the rope and got in. "Adaora," he whispered.

She looked at him and said nothing. But she took his hand.

"Ayodele," he said. "Where are we going?"

"Take us far out," she said.

Agu started the motor.

Adaora looked out into the water as they left the shore. The morning sun was warming up, its rays penetrating deeply into the water. So deeply that she could have sworn she saw the bottom, over thirteen meters below. But that was impossible. She should have been delighted, inspecting and studying the water and its inhabitants with her biologist's eye. But she just couldn't muster up any delight. No water was that clear when it was that deep. Adaora sat down and focused on the horizon. The water's unnatural clarity was the least of her worries.

The trouble started minutes after they fired up the engine. The boat kept lurching up as if it were driving over wide speed bumps. The fifth bump was a big one, and Hawra screeched and grabbed the president. But his attention was already elsewhere.

"What is that?" he shouted, pointing.

"God of Abraham," Femi exclaimed, his camera up as he snapped photos. "No, no, video, video's better," he muttered, looking at his camera, his hands shaking.

Bamidele and Chucks were looking into the water directly below the boat, their guns drawn. But the president was pointing into the distance. Adaora followed the line of his arm just in time to see something break the surface.

It was black and looked about the size of a house. As it fell back into the water, all three of its huge tentacles slapped the surface, creating large waves that rocked the boat. Adaora shuddered. She could name most cephalopods down to their local and scientific names. But what she'd just seen didn't have a name.

239

The president's guards scrambled to the center of the boat. "Oh my God, oh my God! Oh my God!" Bamidele babbled.

"Don't do that," Chucks said as Femi held his camera over the boat's edge.

"It looked like a giant swordfish," Chucks said. "The size of a bus!"

"Ayodele," Anthony said. "What is all—"

The boat lurched again and everyone held on.

The flash of Femi's camera as he photographed Ayodele made her frown. He lowered his camera and smiled sheepishly. "Sorry. There usually isn't a flash in sunshine like this."

"It's the people of the waters," Ayodele said. "They are tired of boats and human beings."

"Then why'd you bring us out here?" Hawra shouted.

"Your leader must meet the Elders," Ayodele said matter-of-factly. "The world is not yet safe."

"Meeting the Elders is fine, but tell the fish to leave us alone!" Adaora cried.

"*They* do as they wish. They won't listen to me. Some of my people have even mixed with them. Once we make it to the ship, we'll be safe."

Femi's camera beeped as he took another photo of Ayodele.

CHAPTER 48

HERE THERE BE MONSTERS

Fifteen minutes later, a three-tentacled sea beast leaped over them, spiraling wildly through the air. It splayed all its thick purple fifty-foot tentacles wide for full effect, splashing loudly into the water.

"Keep going," Ayodele said. "This creature is too strong. I will catch up." Then without a word, she leaped into the water and was gone. They all looked at each other for several moments. Then Agu pushed the boat to top speed.

No one spoke, no one moved. Everyone watched the water. For several minutes, the surface was calm.

"That thing is the . . . ship?" Hawra asked, pointing at the undulating black-and-brown mass hovering above the water miles away.

"Yes," Anthony said. "When they brought us into it last time, it was under the water."

"Wish it stayed there," one of the soldiers muttered. "Dat ting, na wor wor. Look like sometin' rotten."

BONG! The entire boat vibrated from the impact of whatever had just rammed it. Agu and Adaora fell against the stern; the president and the two soldiers tumbled onto a pile of coiled rope. Femi screamed as he tried to grab Hawra, who was dangerously close to the boat's edge. Something slammed into the boat again, and Hawra toppled over the side, grabbing the railing at the last moment.

"Help!" she screamed. "I can't . . . I can't!"

"Coming," one of the soldiers called, trying to get to his feet.

Adaora looked into the water. "I see it! It's a swordfish, it's . . . oh God! Hold on!"

The swordfish monster rammed the boat again, and Hawra dropped into the water. Her terrified shriek was abruptly cut off as her head went under.

The president ran to the edge of the boat and looked over the water. He was sure it was full of disease. Look what it had done to the sea creatures! "Hawra!" he screamed, holding on to the railing. "Hawra!" He let go of the railing as though to jump in after her. Anthony grabbed him. "No!" the president shouted as he strained to free himself from the other man's grasp. He slapped at Anthony. The water now roiled with hundreds of glistening, eel-like fish. "Leave me! Leave me to save my wife! LET ME SAVE MY WIFE!"

Agu stumbled over and grabbed the president's other shoulder. "No! Don't jump in there!" Agu shouted. "You can't—"

"Let me die, too! Let me DIE!" he screamed hysterically. What if the water did something worse than death to her?

Agu wanted to tell the president to stay calm, that his country needed him to remain on the boat, meet the Elders, but reason was a stupid thing to request. If Adaora had fallen off the boat, he'd do the same thing the president was doing, and nothing anyone said would change his mind. So Agu held the president of Nigeria with all his might. Anthony put his arms around the two of them and did the same.

Thump, thump, thump.

It was coming from the back of the boat, where Adaora crouched. She listened. *Thump, thump, thump.* "Help!" The word was nothing but a whisper. But it was human. *Thump, thump, thump.*

"Agu," Adaora said. "Do you hear that?"

"Hear what?" he said from the other side of the boat.

"Please," the voice wheezed.

Adaora took several breaths, working hard to ignore Femi, who was right beside her. They were under attack; a woman had fallen into the water, and yet this man was recording everything.

"Please, stop it," she said to him calmly.

"No," he whispered.

Fine. She had more important things to do. She stood up and looked into the blue waters. There was Hawra, clinging to the side of the boat. She was soaked but okay. "How . . ." Then Adaora saw something below Hawra swimming up quickly. Something huge, black, with too many fins. Adaora threw herself forward. "Agu, come help me, o. Hurry!"

She could see the thing more clearly now. A mouth. Opening. Full of teeth. Adaora dug deep within herself. Within all that she was. Her love of logic and science. Her love of the water. Her love of the sea. She came to the story of her birth she'd heard so many times from her parents.

That.

She hung on to that.

It was in the knowing. She knew. She stepped over the side of the boat, out onto the water.

"No!" Hawra said. "What are you . . . ?"

Adaora's feet landed on the water and the water held her up.

"Shit!" Femi shouted, camera pointed and recording.

Hawra clung to the side of the boat, eyes wide, her mouth hanging open. "Agu!" Adaora yelled back. "I need you!"

Then she knelt down and spread her hands, palms flat on the water's surface. It felt solid and warm. She pushed, and felt something emanate from herself. Something solid. The enormous creature with the mouth full of teeth below slammed against Adaora's invisible force. Adaora felt it push against what she'd sent. It was the same thing she'd done when she was fighting with Chris, except this time she did it to save another person. She took one hand from the water and reached out to Hawra. The other woman grabbed at her.

"Are you . . . ?" Agu was staring at Adaora, mouth agape, as she knelt on the water, holding Hawra up and pushing the thrashing monster down.

She looked into his eyes, needing him to understand, to trust her. "Remember how you got through the riot?" She motioned with her head to the waters behind her. "Do that again but keep all the monsters away while I help Hawra into the boat."

Agu just stared at her.

"Go!" she shouted. "Don't think! No time! Agu, go!"

To her relief, he blinked, twitched, and then threw himself in the water. Something big was coming at them from her left and Agu swam right for it. He dropped beneath the water's surface. Adaora saw the huge gray sharklike creature collide with Agu. A moment later, the creature was flying out of the water, hurled a hundred feet in the air. Adaora could see its great toothy jaws gape. Then *splash*!

Agu's head popped out of the water. He looked around until he spotted them. He waved and Adaora waved back. Then he dove back down.

"Come, come, come," Adaora said quickly, hoisting Hawra up until she, too, was standing on water.

"This is blasphemy," Hawra whispered. But she giggled.

"I don't know what it is," Adaora said.

"Take my hand!" the president said. Chucks stood beside him, ready to help.

Another large creature, this one like a ropy, pink-purple squid, wildly flung itself out of the water. And from the front of the boat, Bamidele was shooting at something. "That one, *chale*! Shoot that one!" she heard Anthony yelling.

Just as Hawra got one leg onto the boat, a tentacle flew out of the water, past Adaora, and slapped around Hawra's other leg.

"Argh! Get it off!" she screamed. "It hurts! It—"

The president grabbed at the tentacle and then fell backward, smoke rising from his hands. He must have received a horrible electric shock from the monster. Adaora felt the current trying to lock up her muscles, but her force field must have dampened the impact. She stumbled back, still on the water's surface, as the tentacle dragged Hawra under.

Agu saw Hawra dragged toward the deep. The tentacle belonged to a great octopus. It glowed a smooth purple and was the size of two horses. He could feel the electrical current the creature put out. It tickled him, even underwater.

And it seemed the entire ocean had decided to come after them. Large fish, armored fish, spiked fish, monstrous sharks, a giant swordfish; he even thought he saw something that looked like a whale. All were bearing down on the boat, on him.

Why? What had they done? He knew the answer. He, Adaora, Anthony—everyone else—they were human. They didn't belong here in the deep. So they would die here and it would be right. Best to leave these waters to the ocean animals, and the aliens.

A large shark was coming at him from his right, and the huge swordfish and a school of smaller fish were coming at him from his left. He couldn't fight them all off. He was losing air. He needed to swim to the surface. But he didn't want them to see him torn to bits. Better to stay down here. He would keep them safe for as long as he could.

Suddenly, Anthony torpedoed into the water. He looked right at Agu. As he swam he motioned frantically to the boat. For a moment, Agu didn't understand, then he did. He propelled himself up, to the boat. Just before bringing his head above water, he looked back. In the morning sunshine, just below the surface of the water, Anthony was in clear view. He floated there. Then he thrust his arms and legs out.

Agu felt a hand grab him, and he was hoisted up by the president and his soldiers. They all fell onto the deck and jammed their fists to their ears as a huge wave shoved them farther out to sea.

MOOOOOOOOOM!

The boat rocked and swayed this way and that but thankfully, somehow, it did not capsize. Everyone felt the itchy buzz in their heads as their eardrums popped. Adaora felt as if she were covered with ants. Then there was nothing but the sound of lapping water against the side of the boat. After several moments, they got to their feet. The surface of the water was littered with the bodies of hundreds of tiny dead fish. Larger fish roiled in the water farther away, all swimming away from Anthony. Away from the boat.

"Did he explode?" one of the guards asked, his gun still in his hand.

No one answered.

A head surfaced from the water at Adaora's water-walking feet, and then Hawra was flailing and coughing. Adaora dropped to her knees, pressing them down. Soft and warm, the water held her as she snatched Hawra's shoulder then arm.

"Relax," Adaora shouted. "Stop!"

"Oh praise Allah! Praise the Most High!" Hawra gasped as Adaora pulled her up to also stand on the water.

"Wife!" the president shouted, leaning over the side and yanking Hawra onto the boat. "Oh, my wife, my wife, my wife." They sat on the floor, cradling each other.

The air smelled sweet, with a hint of blood. Something slapped at the side of the boat, feet away.

"Someone, pull . . . me up."

"Anthony!" Adaora said. Without a thought, she ran over to him, her feet supported by the water like those of a water-skipping insect. She and Agu helped him crawl back onto the boat. Agu gave him the only towel on board, and Anthony wrapped it around himself. Once on the boat, Adaora ran over and hugged him tightly and kissed him on the cheek.

"You are *amazing*," she said.

Anthony laughed weakly.

"What *are* you three?" the president asked. He was holding Hawra tightly, and she was resting her wet head on his shoulder. The wig she had worn was gone, revealing her short Afro.

"We're Nigerians," Agu said. "Just Nigerians." He looked at Anthony and added, "And one Ghanaian."

There was the sound of metal balls rolling in a glass bowl and there Ayodele stood beside Adaora. "That is what I was telling them," Ayodele said, motioning toward the water.

"Why did you leave us like that?" Adaora snapped. "Why—"

"If I hadn't handled the larger creatures, none of you would be here," Ayodele said. "That's where I went. You think what you dealt with were the biggest?" She shrugged. "You saved each other but I saved you all. The going should be smoother from now on."

Agu stumbled to the motor and breathed a sigh of relief when it started. He got them moving again. His skin felt prickly and tight. He'd gulped down several mouthfuls of salt water and felt that if he didn't belch soon he'd throw up. Anthony was probably full of the water too. And Hawra and Adaora.

Beep beep! Femi lowered his camera, his eyes wide, his mouth agape. "Wow." He reached into his pocket and brought out his BlackBerry. Within ten minutes the footage was on YouTube.

CHAPTER 49

RESPECT YOUR ELDERS

Once they were back on the boat, everyone who'd been in the water threw up copious amounts of it. When there was none left in their stomachs, they dry heaved. Anthony was in the worst shape, breaking out in hives and plagued by a throbbing headache. Femi ran back and forth between Anthony and the side of the boat, dipping a cup in the water and then pouring it on Anthony's arms and legs to help soothe the itchiness.

"Sorry," Ayodele said. Adaora didn't think she meant it at all, but she was too weak to tell her so.

"Is it the water?" Femi asked. "I mean, I'm fine, and so are the president, Bamidele, and Chucks. None of us were in there."

"Yes, I think it is."

Adaora felt her stomach lurch again. "What have you people done to it?"

"Nothing that didn't want to be done."

Done by whom? Adaora thought. She knew the answer. The sea creatures. They wanted the water to be "clean." "Clean" for sea life . . . which meant toxic for modern, civilized, meat-eating, clean-water-drinking human beings. *Shit,* she thought. *I'm going to die out here.*

Adaora didn't know how much time passed. All she knew was that when she next opened her eyes, the sun was somewhere else in the sky and the boat had stopped. She sat up. She felt a little better but she'd broken out in the same rash that Anthony had and her head pounded miserably. Anthony was lying on the boat's floor, Agu and Femi beside him.

"Is he all right?" she whispered.

"He's still breathing, but he won't open his eyes," Femi said. He got up and walked past Adaora.

"Agu?"

"Yes, Adaora," he said.

"Are you—"

Splash!

Adaora was looking at Agu's face. He was looking behind her, at the others at the far end of the boat. At the sound of the splash, his jaw dropped. She felt her heart sink. The president, Hawra, Ayodele, the guards. She didn't want to turn around and see what had happened to them. She'd had enough.

"Wait," Agu said, getting up. He stumbled, grabbing hold of one of the seats. He started moving to the other side of the boat. "Wait!"

Adaora turned around. At first she didn't know what she was seeing. Water? But it was solid. Solid enough for the president to step on, as Adaora had stepped on it. She dragged herself up.

"Wait a minute!" she said. She nearly fell to the floor as the world swam around her. Her belly cramped and she dropped to one knee. Agu was on the floor a few feet away. "Do . . . What . . . Where are you going?" Adaora whispered.

She fought hard to focus. Ayodele was standing with the president on the water. Femi was still on the boat, snapping photos.

"I'll be all right!" the president shouted as he was lowered below the side of the boat. By what? And into the water? Adaora couldn't see. Hawra was clinging to one of the guards, weeping. Femi was doing something with his mobile phone. Agu was coughing. Anthony remained silent.

Adaora couldn't stand any longer. She sat down hard on the boat floor and gazed out at the ocean, whose water was clear as crystal. In the distance, she saw something huge leap up and then splash back in, and a group of flying fish passed by yards from their boat. Below the glasslike water, she imagined there was a great, great metropolis of ocean life—giant, reaching, dark brown structures bloomed up from a flat surface beneath that she couldn't see the end of. And the structures had slowly shrunk and expanded even as she watched, sea creatures darting, wiggling, spiraling everywhere.

She closed her eyes and everything went away.

Water is life.

Aman Iman.

Water.

Adaora had spent fifteen years studying creatures of the water. Now, Adaora was in water.

Her hair was floating around her face. Yet . . . ? There was a rushing sensation in her neck that happened involuntarily. Her lungs didn't hurt. She felt the rushing of water again. She brought her hands to her chest. She could feel her heart beating. Several yards below her was a brown crusty coral-like surface covered with green swaying seaweed. She could see a group of red crabs the size of small children plucking the seaweed and delicately munching it.

She shut her eyes, trying to focus. She touched her neck. Instead of smooth skin, her fingers slipped into large grooves, the edges of flesh loose and thick. She twitched, realizing what they were, then she shuddered and screamed. But no sound came out. Because she didn't have lungs any more . . . she had gills. She tried to swim up. But which way was up? She opened her eyes and watched bubbles float past her. Upward. She followed the bubbles with her eyes. Upward. A glowing pink dot. The sun. The surface was more than a hundred feet above her.

Adaora realized several things at once. She was breathing water. She was not alone. She could see what was happening. She could hear it, too.

She focused on what was happening in front of her. The president. He was suspended in what looked like a giant bubble of air. He hung before five humanoid figures that reminded her of something out of *Star Wars*. She frowned. Hadn't she read somewhere that the president loved the *Star Wars* movies? Adaora did too, though she preferred the earlier films. But she'd watched the later films enough to recognize the aliens she was seeing. All of the creatures she saw now were whitish-blue-skinned, with huge black eyes and long long arms, legs, and necks. They even moved with the same fluid motions as they had in the movies.

The president was talking to them. She moved toward the bubble of air and then stopped. What would happen if she tried to enter it? She touched the gills on her neck. They felt like several numb hairy flaps of skin. The flaps pumped up and down, but the more she thought about it, the more she realized she could do it voluntarily, too.

Okay, she thought. But then she looked down and her mind reeled. Her legs were no longer legs. This part of her body had become the body of a giant metallic-blue fish. *The upper and lower lobes of it are equal in shape and pointy*, she thought, twisting for a better look at herself. *A lunate caudal fin, like that of a sailfish, marlin, or swordfish. I was made for speed.* Something tapped her on the shoulder. She turned and came face to face with Ayodele. Adaora swam back, surprised. The motion pushed water through her gills, and her mind sharpened.

"*Relax*," Ayodele said.

Adaora heard Ayodele's voice in her head.

She opened her mouth and tried to speak. Again, no sound.

"*Think your words*," Ayodele said. "*Move your mouth if it helps, but think your words.*"

Adaora moved her mouth as she thought, "*What is happening? What have you done to me? Is this permanent? Where is everyone else? Agu and Anthony? Where are they? Are they okay?*"

She heard Ayodele laugh. *"Calm down,"* Ayodele said. She reconfigured her body. Ayodele was now a dolphin. No, she was too long to be a dolphin. And dolphins did not have such large eyes. Ayodele swam in a circle around Adaora.

"Swim with me," she said. *"I will explain."* When Adaora didn't move, she laughed again. *"Your Agu is fine. Anthony is fine. They are all fine. Your president is meeting with the Elders, as you see. You cannot join them. Now come."*

Adaora hesitated. Beyond the president and the Elders, she could see a very large swordfish monster hovering in the background. Was it the same angry swordfish that had nearly killed them all? She shuddered.

"Come," Ayodele said again.

Adaora followed only because Ayodele was swimming in the opposite direction from the swordfish. Ayodele moved fast, and Adaora was surprised to find she could keep up easily. As she swam, she realized that all around her were bone-white edifices that were at least thirty feet high. As Adaora and Ayodele passed, some collapsed, and others grew. Sea creatures from fish to crabs to sea cucumbers clung, swam through, crawled, and wiggled past. Adaora could not tell which were the aliens and which were the earthlings.

"Everything you see here is the ship," Ayodele said as they swam through a yawning cave. Some kind of fish with a sucker mouth clung to the lip of the cave above them. *"The longer we stay here, the more we shift and become like the people of the water."*

"What about on land?" Adaora thought. This time, she didn't move her mouth.

"Yes, there, too."

"Why am I not sick anymore?"

"Why is your body part fish?"

Adaora paused. *"Because this is . . . what . . . I wanted?"*

"Is it what you wanted?"

Adaora had always loved the water. And she didn't want to die of whatever pollutants were in the water. Yes, it was.

"Is this place your ship?" Adaora asked.

"Yes," Ayodele answered. *"One of them."*

"How far does it extend?"

"Many many miles, I suspect," Ayodele said. *"That may change."*

"If I swim beyond, will my body change back?"

"I don't know. I think you will change back when you reach land. Isn't that how you imagine maidens?"

"Mermaids."

Ayodele laughed, shifting into a mermaid herself. Her face looked nearly identical to that of Adaora's friend Ayodele Olayiwola, the one Adaora had named her for. Adaora found herself smiling.

"Will you take me to see Agu?"

"That's where we are going."

Agu and Anthony were trapped in a bubble. They'd woken up inside it, at what they thought might be the bottom of the sea. They stood on hard white stone and above swam monsters and sea creatures. Most ignored them, but a few came for a curious look before moving on.

Anthony paced back and forth, muttering in Twi. He was no longer sick, and he was viciously hungry. He rubbed his hands over his rough wet hair. Images of being underwater as all those monstrous creatures came at him kept crowding his mind. When he pushed these away, he would look around and see *more* such creatures swimming about, watching him, perhaps even plotting revenge. Which was crazy. If he didn't get out of here soon, Anthony realized, he'd go mad. "What are we even doing here?" he muttered.

"No clue," Agu said, sitting down in the center of the white stone. He rested his head on the palms of his hands. "Don't even know how we *got* here." He looked at his hands. He had punched that kid so hard when he was twelve that the boy had lost consciousness. Less than two days ago, the power had boiled up again and he'd nearly killed Benson. And, last night, when he'd run through Lagos trying to get back to Adaora, he was sure he *had* killed some people.

"You are useless," Agu said to his hands. "I am useless."

Now he and Anthony were imprisoned at the bottom of the sea, to starve to death or eventually be eaten by the first sea monster aggressive enough to bite into the bubble. He noticed two figures swimming toward them. They were not as large as some of the other creatures lingering around the bubble, but they were moving fast. He got up and moved a few feet back, as far from them as he could.

Agu and Anthony were trapped in a bubble. Its shimmery surface made it difficult to see inside, but she was sure it was them. It was a dome the size of a small room. She waved her hands as she swam toward them and they both waved back.

"*How did they get in there?*" Adaora asked.

"*The same way you got to where you were.*"

This answered nothing and Adaora sucked her teeth, frustrated with Ayodele's vagueness. Sucking her teeth yielded no sound, and this annoyed Adaora more. When they got to the bubble, she hovered before Agu and Anthony, unsure of how to communicate with them. She waved her hands and moved her lips, and she tried to say, *Are you okay?*

"What?" she heard Agu shout, the sound of his voice muted by the water.

Anthony was frowning deeply and pointing at her fin. Agu looked at it and then his face went slack.

Adaora thought for a moment, then she turned to Ayodele. She wanted to ask, *Will I drown? Will I die if I go in there?* But she didn't. There was only one way to find out, and she wanted to find out for herself. *If I can't breathe . . . I will just crawl back in the water.*

She put her hand through the bubble's surface into the dry air. Then she pushed herself in up to her waist. Anthony and Agu quickly pulled her in the rest of the way.

As they laid her on the dry ocean floor, Adaora felt fully disoriented. Up became sideways and sideways became up. The dry air bit at her skin and the inside of her gills. Worst of all, she couldn't breathe! Her body arched as she fought for air. *Put me back in the water!* she wanted to scream. But her new body was not capable of speech. She bucked, hoping Agu would drop her and she could crawl back through the bubble.

Agu struggled but managed to hold her tightly. "Can she—"

"Throw her back in the water!" Anthony screamed.

Adaora twisted again, turned her head to the side, and vomited water. It felt like she was heaving from the very tip of her tail. Then she threw her head back and inhaled loudly and long, air rushing into her lungs like the wind itself. Lungs. She had them. Now.

She shut her eyes and felt her neck. The gill flaps were still there. "Who am I?" she whispered. Her voice was her own, albeit rough. When she opened her eyes, she was looking into Agu's. A tear was falling down his cheek. He was shaking from the strain of her weight.

"Something new," he said.

"Something old," Anthony said. He laughed. "Something borrowed, more than gold, something true, never sold, goddamn aliens too fuckin' bold. *Chale*, see I spit am!" Then he grinned and shouted, *"I dey Craaaaaaze!"*

Adaora was so surprised that she burst out laughing, which made her cough,

"Oh my God, the man dey craze," Agu muttered, but the corners of his mouth quivered as he fought his laughter.

"You should have plenty of new material for a new album," Adaora told Anthony.

"Artist is artist," he agreed.

"Agu, you can put me down now. Before you pass out. I know I'm heavy."

Anthony put his arms beneath her and helped Agu lower her to the sea bed. Once seated, she crossed her arms over her bare chest. Her fin felt heavy and useless.

Agu sat beside her and Anthony sat across from her. For a long time, they were silent, Adaora more than aware of her strange naked mermaid body and the cold dryness of the air. Anthony thinking and thinking about all he'd discussed with the Elders when they were first pulled into the ocean, only two nights ago. And Agu looking out into the water.

"I thought it would kill me the first time it happened," Anthony said. He'd spoken in Twi, so the others didn't understand. He switched to English. "I call it the rhythm." He recounted the story of the day he'd discovered his power. A story that he'd never told a soul.

Agu laughed hard and clapped him on the shoulder. "Do you believe in God now?"

Anthony chuckled. "Yeah."

The three of them burst out laughing and didn't stop for the next minute. Adaora's eyes watered and her fin slapped the damp stone. Agu rolled on the sea bed as he guffawed. And Anthony held his cramping belly. In the water outside the bubble, clouds of fish wiggled toward the surface, and a giant pink squid spiraled by. This sent them into more hysterics.

Several minutes passed and they calmed.

Then it was Agu's turn. "I have no name for it. But the first time I used it was to save a boy we called Stick Boy." He told them about punching the other boy unconscious and how as the boy lay there, he decided to become a soldier. Then he told them about nearly killing Benson. Then he told them everything that had happened in the streets of Lagos. As he spoke, he watched Adaora's eyes grow wider and wider, especially when he spoke of possibly killing people in the streets during the riots.

No one laughed when he finished.

Adaora knew they were expecting her to explain the origins of her powers, just as they had. But her story was different. "Okay," she said. She looked around. They were at the bottom of the ocean in a bubble created by aliens, surrounded by sea monsters. She shut her eyes, still aware of her fin. It was drying out, and her scaled skin was starting to sting. She opened her eyes and looked at both of them. "I don't know what this is," she said. "Mine wasn't something that kicked in when I was a girl, as it did when you were boys." She paused, fighting the voice that told her never to speak of such taboos. The knowledge that made her feel like she was evil. The stigma that burned brightest when she thought about her husband's constant accusations of witchcraft. And the fact that after all her denials, maybe she *was* a witch. Well, she was certainly *something*.

"I was born with webbed feet and hands," she blurted. "And my legs were joined together by flesh." Even after everything they'd been through, she half expected them to recoil in disgust.

"That's . . . that's disgusting," Anthony said. But he smiled as he said it.

Agu was laughing.

"My father . . . He said that if it were the old days, they would have thrown me in the bush," Adaora continued. "He liked to remind me of that whenever my grades were too low in school. It always worked." She sighed. "Anyway, they surgically separated my fingers, toes, and legs. Still, from the moment that my mother first took me to the ocean, I could swim. No one ever taught me. I was . . . like a fish."

Both Agu and Anthony burst out laughing. Adaora wanted to cry, but she laughed too. "I've always loved the sea. I am fascinated by it, the smell, the creatures, its size and depth. It is no surprise that I became a marine biologist. But that's all there is. I don't have any childhood stories about doing amazing things. All this"—she gestured to her tail—"is completely new. Two nights ago when I was fighting my husband, that's the first time anything ever happened!" She frowned. "But . . . maybe it's always been there. Beneath the surface."

Agu nodded. "I was about to say that."

"What are we?" Adaora asked after a moment.

"We're people," Agu said. He looked at Anthony. "You can make a sonic boom." To Adaora, he said, "You can create some sort of force field. I have superhuman strength. And we all walked into each other's lives just as aliens invaded Lagos."

"Not a coincidence," Anthony said. "*Na* the work of de universe."

"It's the work of something," Agu said.

Adaora shivered. "My father would have said it's the work of the gods."

As Adaora finished speaking, she felt a terrible pressure, enough to make her ears hurt. She looked up and saw the bubble's bowl shape distorting, as though something were pressing on it. The air pressure dropped. The temperature dropped. Adaora's fin stung horribly as her sleek fish skin continued to dry and began to turn brown.

They all saw it at once.

Adaora screamed.

Anthony whimpered.

Agu began to cry.

The spider standing above them was the size of a mansion. Rough hair covered its eight endlessly long legs and bulbous body. It—*she*, Adaora instinctively knew—was looking right at them, down at them. With all eight of her intense black eyes.

"*Even in the corners of palaces, spiders dwell,*" she said. "*Remember that, if you ever find yourself walking the halls of the great and powerful.*" Then she was gone.

"What the *fuck* was that?" Anthony asked.

There was a wet splashing sound behind Adaora. It was Ayodele flipping water into the bubble as she hovered outside it. *"They are ready for you. Come."*

CHAPTER 50

SECOND CONTACT

Adaora, Agu, and Anthony met with the Elders.

There were five of them.

And that is all that Adaora, Agu, and Anthony will ever remember about those thirty minutes of their lives.

CHAPTER 51

THE MAGICAL NEGRESS

Anthony and Agu had been given bubbles of air, like helmets around their heads, and they'd all swum back to where Adaora had seen the president speaking with the *Star Wars*–like creatures.

Then her memory grew hazy, and she remembered nothing until her head was breaking the surface of the water beneath the late-afternoon sun. She felt as though she had encountered something enormous—something so far beyond anything she could have imagined—and that its presence threatened to force her out of existence. Whatever had happened with the . . . spider, with the Elders—it was all too huge to contemplate.

Hawra and the president, Femi, and the two guards were on the boat when Agu, Ayodele, and Anthony emerged from the water. All but Ayodele looked shell-shocked, and none said a thing as Adaora was pulled onto the boat, naked, half fish and half human. Hawra fanned Adaora's fin, and each burst of air was like a thousand needles against her scaly flesh. But soon the scales of her fin grew transparent and began to flake away, revealing her brown human legs.

"Can you imagine?" Hawra whispered over and over as she helped Adaora pick the peeling scales from her flesh. All the men had turned their backs to give Adaora some privacy.

"I can imagine anything," Adaora murmured.

Hawra leaned close to Adaora, smiling. "I spoke to a giant swordfish," she whispered. "I heard its voice in my head."

"What did it say?" Adaora asked, glad to focus on something other than removing her scales. She peeled away a large swatch. It left a patch of fishy-smelling slime on her skin.

"It spoke like a member of that group Greenpeace!"

Adaora laughed, her body aching. "Was it enormous? With spines coming out of its back?"

Hawra nodded.

"That swordfish hates us," Adaora said.

There was an extra army uniform in a compartment on the boat. After Adaora had slipped into the garments, Hawra helped her to her feet. She was shaky. Air didn't hold her the way water did.

The president was talking on Femi's mobile phone. "Have the set ready for when we arrive," he said. "And make sure I have a change of clothes."

"Us too," one of the guards added.

The president nodded. "And, and, bring two army uniforms. Pressed. Crisp. I'm not having these two guys leave my side, even while I am on camera. These guys have kept me alive, o!"

Still leaning on Hawra, Adaora stepped up to Agu, Anthony, and Ayodele. They'd been quietly discussing something, but she didn't want to know what. "Is there a plan?" she asked instead.

"We're going to Tin Can Island," Agu said. "Trust me, it's the easiest, safest port to use to get ourselves, and the president, back to land. We need a place that's safe from the monsters."

Tin Can Island, a mostly industrial area and one of Lagos's main cargo ports, took its name from the biscuit tins used to transport mail to and from the island by strong swimmers, who would ferry them to and from passing ships. Vessels couldn't dock at the island as it had no natural harbor or wharf—only a small creek, whose waters were far shallower than the open waters where the alien ship rested. And because of that, Agu reasoned, if there were beasts there, they wouldn't be nearly as huge as the ones in the deep.

★ ★ ★ ★

They heard the gunshots long before they arrived at the island. A mobile phone in Femi's pocket went off. "Your phone, Mr. President," Femi said, frowning and handing it to the president. The president grabbed it. "What is going on?" he shouted.

He listened and frowned.

He turned to his guards with wide eyes, and then to Agu. "Ssss, sss!" he said, waving a hand at Agu. "Stop the boat! Femi, give me your camera."

Agu brought them to a halt, as Femi handed it to the president. The president continued to hold the phone to his ear as he fumbled with the camera. "There's something—"

More gunshots rang out from the island.

"What's going on?" Adaora shouted. She squinted, barely able to make out a large group of men waiting at the dock. *Bang bang bang!* She could see a man firing. At the water. Beside the shooter, several men seemed to be trying to drag something out of the water. *No,* Adaora realized. *Someone.*

"Please," Adaora said to the president. "Give me the camera!"

"Why?" the president asked, frowning as he continued fiddling with it. "What do you—"

"Just let me have it!" She snatched it from him and held it up to Femi. "Make it zoom in."

When he handed it back to her, she held it up. She focused on the men. There was something in the water . . . and it was trying to drag a man under. Then two red tentacles shot out of the water. One smashed a window of the black car behind them, and the other slapped at one of the men. He fell back. Adaora could have sworn she saw blood spatter. More men began shooting into the water.

"Shit!" she screamed, nearly dropping the camera.

The president grabbed it from her just as Femi's phone buzzed. "What is going on?" the president shouted into the phone.

"There's something in the water, attacking them," Adaora said.

"Oh Jesu Christi," one of the guards moaned. "Will we never get out of this infested water?"

"We will, cousin, we will," the other guard said.

"Are you people stupid? Stay away from the water!" the president shouted into his phone. There were tears in his wild eyes.

"I think it's some sort of octopus or squid," Adaora said.

"*Chale*, those things are smart," Anthony said. Adaora had been thinking the same thing. Cephalopods were the smartest invertebrates on earth. One that was alien-enhanced . . . Those men didn't stand a chance.

"Ten men? You let it . . . oh my God." The president sat down on the floor of the boat, the phone pressed to his ear. "Oh my God. Okay . . . yes, save them."

The boat started moving. The president turned to Agu. "What the hell are you doing?"

"I'm not letting more soldiers die," Agu said. "I'm getting us close enough for me to swim to them."

"Why'd they station themselves right in front of the water?" the president moaned. Hawra sat beside him, her arm around his shoulder. "It got ten of them before they realized what was happening."

"I will go, too," Anthony said.

Adaora hesitated. Agu had super strength, Anthony had his rhythm. But she could levitate, walk on water, and protect herself with a force field. If she got into the water, would she grow her fin back?

"It will kill you both," Ayodele said. "I will go."

Again, she jumped into the water before anyone could protest. Agu pushed the boat faster. He had a bad feeling about what was going to happen. When no one argued, it was clear that he wasn't the only one who felt it.

Finally they were close enough that they could see what was happening perfectly. There was a body floating in the water. Some soldiers were behind a black car, firing wildly. Others were standing on the dock at the edge of the creek, screaming and shooting. As they drew into view, some yelled at them; a few frantically waved them away.

When the boat was less than ten yards away from the island, a deep moan came from beneath the water. And then it surfaced. The monster was a bundle of slimy red tentacles, ridged with horrible black, bony spokes. The tentacle ball tumbled and rolled on the surface of the water and then parted to reveal an enormous, gaping, pink, parrotlike beak. Adaora had to tense every part of her body to keep herself from screaming. The creature's beak snapped open and shut. And then it plunged back beneath the water and disappeared.

All was silent as they stared at where the monster had been and now was not. They waited, but it didn't return. The water rippled gently, and then was still. The soldiers on land slowly stood back from the edge of the dock. The others emerged from behind the car.

Adaora leaned over the side of the boat. "What did she . . . ?"

"Ayodele!" Agu called.

The boat bumped softly against the dock, and everyone jumped off except Adaora, Anthony, and Agu. They leaned over the side, looking into the water. Femi jogged toward the soldiers, who were also watching the water. He was taking pictures as he approached, saying, "Gentlemen! Hello! Excuse me, can I ask you some questions? I am with the press. . . ."

"This way, Mr. President," one of the soldiers said, leading the president to the black car. "Sorry about the window."

"Don't worry about it," the president said, clasping Hawra's hand as they walked. "We saw everything."

"What of the others?" Hawra said, looking back.

"They're coming," the president replied.

"No, they're not." Hawra pulled her hand away.

Adaora knew the creature was gone. Had it eaten Ayodele and thus been satisfied? Adaora whipped around, her head pounding. Too much. Too fast. *There* she was. Ayodele was pulling herself onto the far side of the dock, a hundred feet away. Right in front of the soldiers. Adaora felt relief flood her body. Then she saw one of the soldiers roughly grab Ayodele by the arm and yank her onto the concrete, bring his huge booted foot back, and, with all his might, kick her squarely in the side.

Adaora could hear the meaty sound of the boot smashing into Ayodele's flesh even from where she was. The man kicked Ayodele again, another man joining him. He smashed at her face with the butt of his AK-47, and Ayodele's head flew back to smack against the concrete, her nose spraying red blood. Adaora jumped off the boat. Everything went silent as all the blood rushed to Adaora's head. What was she seeing? Why was Ayodele *letting* it happen?

Anthony was already off the boat and running toward the men. Adaora ran after him, Agu behind her.

"Stop!" he shouted, waving his hands about. "STOP IT!"

But they didn't stop anything. Ayodele did not get up, nor did she do anything to protect herself. It all happened in seconds. There were five soldiers now, all dressed in green-brown-and-black fatigues with black shiny boots and dull black guns. These men rained blows on every part of Ayodele's body with their boots, the butts of their guns, their fists.

"Winch, I kill you!" a man growled as he punched Ayodele in the face.

"Kill am!" another man shrieked as he kicked.

Her white dress was splotched with spreading patches of red as they stamped on her torso, chest, legs, and arms. They crushed bone and mashed muscle and organs. One man brought his foot down squarely on her exposed neck.

Bang! The gunshot tore open Ayodele's side.

Another man smashed his gun into her lolling head.

Anthony had stopped, yards from the chaos, swaying on his feet. Even as she ran, Adaora could feel everything around her being pulled toward Anthony.

"Anthony, don't!" Adaora shouted as she ran up behind him. "DON'T DO IT!"

"Why?" Anthony asked calmly.

"No more killing," she said, panting. She turned to Agu behind her. He had murder on his face. "No killing! They don't know what they are doing, they don't know what she is, they are confused. . . ." She was confused, too. What was she saying? She shook her head at both Agu and Anthony. She wiped the tears from her eyes. "Let me," she said, and ran to the mob of soldiers surrounding Ayodele.

She didn't hesitate. Adaora plunged into the melee and began to shove aside the men beating Ayodele. Someone kicked at Ayodele but missed, landing on Adaora instead. Ignoring the pain, Adaora fell to her knees and threw her arms around the limp Ayodele. Then she flexed what was hers.

It felt like staticky heat bursting from her back and washing over her, and then toward the soldiers, shoving them all away. When they tried to press forward against it, the force repelled them, sending them flying back.

Adaora grasped Ayodele tightly, pressing her face to the alien woman's neck. She could feel Ayodele's warm blood seeping into her clothes. She could smell its coppery scent, mixed with sea water and urine. Ayodele was breathing in raspy gulps.

Why? Adaora thought. *Why why why?* Why was Ayodele bleeding? Why was she not changing? Why had she allowed them to beat her? Why *had* they beaten her? She continued to hold them back, as she pressed Ayodele's broken body into her own.

"Witchcraft," one of the men grunted.

Bang!

One of the soldiers must have fired at her. The noise was deafening, but Adaora felt no bullet. Just before the soldier could fire again, Agu ran up and punched the man so hard that he flew across the concrete, nearly tumbling into the deadly water.

Adaora brought her face close to Ayodele's. She held the alien woman's wide gaze. So different from the woman she had seen first on the beach less than two days ago. She'd experienced so much humanity in so little time.

"I saw you first. It started with you," Ayodele whispered. "My people sent me for a reason. I've known all along. . . ." Blood dribbled from her lips and Adaora shuddered. "Your people. They wanted to use me, kidnap me, kill me. . . ."

"I'm sorry," Adaora said. "We're better than that."

"The Elders sent me," Ayodele whispered. "We are a collective. Every part of us, every tiny universe within us is conscious. I am we, I am me. . . ." She coughed up more blood.

"But why . . . ?"

"You people need help on the outside but also within," she said. "I will go within. . . . Adaora . . . let go of me . . . cover your ears."

"Why?"

"Trust me."

"Ayodele, please."

"You'll all be a bit . . . alien."

Slowly, Adaora laid Ayodele on the ground. Then she looked up. Everything around her was slightly tinted periwinkle, the same color her fin had been. It must have been the effect of her force field. The soldiers were staring and staring, their guns raised, fists clenched. She could see Anthony and Agu not far behind the men.

Ayodele was looking up at her, and for the first time, Adaora could see how badly hurt she really was. Her neck bulged grotesquely, and Adaora could see the white of bone. One of Ayodele's legs was twisted in an impossible direction, as were both her arms. She had been shot in the abdomen; bright red blood was soaking through her white dress. Her face was swollen and bruised. Her eyes were battered nearly shut.

"Garden eggs. Nothing better." Ayodele chuckled weakly.

Adaora smiled, remembering how Ayodele had eaten the vegetables raw like candy.

"Close your ears," Ayodele said, placing a hand on her knee. Adaora put her hands over her ears. She looked across at Anthony and Agu. They did the same and dropped to the ground.

Ayodele mouthed something to Adaora and she understood. "Let go," Ayodele had said. And Adaora let the force field drop as she squeezed her eyes shut.

GBOOOM!

When she felt Ayodele's hand leave her knee, Adaora opened her eyes. In the space where Ayodele had lain a white mist swirled, as if a fog had rolled in off the water. It had the faint tomatoey scent of . . . garden eggs. As she knelt on the concrete, covered in Ayodele's blood, Adaora was overcome with a craving for garden eggs. For their crunchy cool fruit, sweet or bitter. "Oh," Adaora whispered. And instinctively, she knew that this fog was rolling like a great wave over all of Lagos. She could almost see it in her mind. And everyone was inhaling it. Everyone in Lagos was craving garden eggs. Ayodele. What had she done?

She felt hands on her shoulders. "Please," a man said. "Let me help." It was one of the soldiers.

"Leave her!" she heard Agu shout.

"Agu, it's okay, please," she said.

"Are you all right?" Anthony asked.

She nodded. She could see the soldiers who'd beaten Ayodele standing all around her. She didn't want to look into their guilty faces.

Ayodele was gone. Ayodele was here. "Lagos will never be the same," Adaora said.

CHAPTER 52
INFINITE POSSIBILITIES

The president of Nigeria sat in the middle of the backseat of the armored black Mercedes. Already he was writing his speech in his head. Originally, he'd planned to present the one named Ayodele as he gave his speech, but she'd died. He didn't understand what Adaora had said about inhaling her essence. That wasn't important.

Beside him was his second wife, Hawra. She had never been so proud and happy to be in Lagos. Her husband was thinking like a president, but she knew he had to think even more broadly. There were infinite possibilities.

Anthony sat to the president's right, his cheek pressed to the window. He would go home to Ghana. What had happened was only the beginning. The Elders had plans for him and his country.

Agu and Adaora were squeezed into the passenger seat. Agu held Adaora's cool hand as he thought it all over. He was a home-wrecker with superhuman strength that came from the Ancestors or the soil or whatever. And he had a new purpose in life—to be a proud soldier for the New Nigeria, whatever that was. When things calmed down, he would go and see his family in Arondizuogu. Hopefully, Adaora would come with him. They wouldn't stay long because they would certainly be needed in Lagos. But he would make sure they were okay and maybe tell them his story. He touched the cut on his forehead. It had finally stopped bleeding.

Adaora's mind was blank. Whenever she tried to think, she only saw Ayodele.

One of the soldiers from Tin Can Island drove the vehicle. Over and over, he replayed the memory of his *ahoa* being pulled into the sea by some sort of giant squid. And then how they'd beaten the woman, and how she'd disappeared. His hands shook as he grasped the wheel.

The other soldiers followed in a second vehicle. They were confused, afraid, and eager to see what would happen next.

How would you have felt?

CHAPTER 53

CASTING BROADLY

The drive was smooth. Many had left Lagos, and those who had stayed were safely in their homes, waiting to see what would happen next. The Area Boys who haunted the streets were waiting for the sun to set, which would be in less than an hour.

The president had never felt so calm. His body seemed to hum. His mind was clear. Ever since Ayodele had dissipated, he'd been feeling strange. Not only did he crave raw garden eggs, but he felt so calm, as if all that had happened was something he could understand. He had been in Saudi Arabia yesterday. He'd been more than half dead. Yesterday, he had felt his death in his bones. Today, he felt like he'd live forever.

The Elders. They'd told him the waters off the coast hid aquatic forests. All the offshore drilling facilities would be destroyed by the people of the water. Even in the delta, all was lost. Oil could no longer be Nigeria's top commodity. It could no longer be a commodity at all. "But we have something better to give you all," the Elders had said. Their technology.

The president smiled. *We will be a mighty nation,* he thought. He made a few phone calls as they drove, managing to reach one soldier on Victoria Island who claimed he'd tried to help Adaora's daughter when she was shot and that he now had the island back under control; his VP Wishwell Williams who was not surprisingly safe in Nigeria's capital, Abuja; and two governors in northern and southeastern Nigeria. All that each reported made him smile more. Things were settling down and things were looking up.

When they arrived at the television station, there were three men and a woman waiting for him. All were dressed in semi-casual attire, but three of the four of them looked nervous, staring at the president. The fourth, a short young woman with neat braids in a white blouse and a long black skirt, spoke first.

"You all can sit here," she said, motioning to some chairs set up outside the broadcasting room. She picked up three stacks of clothes. "We have everything ready for your speech, Mr. President." She handed him a stack and then handed the guards theirs.

He blinked at her for a moment, looking into her brown eyes. She looked to be in her early fifties, but she had the alertness of someone much younger. Her calmness reminded him of . . . Ayodele. "Oh," he whispered, understanding why. "Em, Miss . . . I need a room where I can . . ."

"Get your thoughts together?" she asked, finishing his sentence.
"Yes."

"Come, I'll show you."

"Honey, do you want me to go with you?" Hawra asked.

"No," the president said. "Thank you."

"We will stay outside your door," one of the guards offered.

"That is all right. You need to change your clothes too. I will be fine."

The president glanced at Agu, who was watching him intensely. The president nodded reassuringly at him. Agu didn't nod back.

They followed the woman to an office down the hall. The guards were shown into one room, the president into the one next door. He shut himself inside. The space was plain, with an old computer on the desk and some filing cabinets against the wall. It smelled of face powder and perfume; it was probably usually used by a woman. But he didn't care. Not tonight. He sank into a cheap leather chair and sighed, glad for the solitude. It felt good to be alone for a moment. He'd composed his speech in his head, but he needed to just be still.

"This is all happening," the president said aloud. "Just hold on." Everyone needed him to do this right. Everyone in Lagos. Everyone in Nigeria. Maybe everyone in the world. He worked best when people needed him. And as it always did, this knowledge calmed him down. Since taking office, he'd found himself powerless to fight against Nigeria's soul-crushing corruption. Wherever he tried to make changes, people around him were always trying to drain some sort of shady profit from his efforts. If he tried to create a program to improve schools or hospitals, someone set up a fake contract that would bleed money from the program. When he tried to address unemployment, health care, inflation, electricity, education, agriculture, any time there was money to be spent, it was the same result: The vampires always came. This had worn him down. It had made him feel futile, useless. Now, for the first time, he felt like a president. And this speech would be his first real act as Nigeria's *true* leader. Oh, it was exciting.

He removed his dirty clothes and stood in the room in his boxers, looking down at his body. He'd filled out since the alien woman healed him. His ribs were no longer so prominent. His skin was smooth instead of splotchy. Months before he had left for Saudi Arabia, he'd been so thin that he'd resorted to stuffing his clothes to appear bulkier. He slipped into the fresh white caftan and then the white pants. He filled them out nicely now. He truly was cured. They'd done this to him. He thought of Ayodele and wondered what else they'd done to him.

Someone knocked at his door. "Are you ready, sir?" It was the calm woman who reminded him of Ayodele.

"Yes. I'm coming."

His guards followed behind him as he walked with the woman. "When the broadcast goes live," she said, "it will appear on all of your people's screens. As it did before. Everything with a screen will turn on, whether it is plugged in to anything or not."

He stopped walking, looking at her. She stopped too, and smiled a small smile. "Mobile phones," she said. "Computers, desktops and laptops, televisions, e-readers, all things with screens."

"How?" he asked. "How do you do that?"

She laughed. "The knowledge is in you. Ayodele made sure of that. We will explain, later. But for now, just be aware, you are reaching everyone in this city." She paused. "Unless you'd like it to reach farther?"

He considered it. "Can you make it reach all of Nigeria?"

"It won't be exact, there will be some spillover into other countries, but sure."

"Okay, do it." He considered his speech. No, he wouldn't have to change much of what he was going to say. He hadn't been thinking only about Lagos. He'd been thinking of his entire country.

Yes, it was right.

A leather chair nicer than the one in the office where he'd changed clothes was set behind a wooden desk. The Nigerian flag hung behind it, over a full bookcase. He sat down, and his guards stood behind his chair in their fresh, spotless uniforms.

Technicians rolled the camera in front of him, and someone applied makeup to his face. He smiled when she didn't linger. He didn't need much. Before, he'd needed thick makeup to make him look less sick.

"I don't need the teleprompter," he said. He tapped his forehead. "It's all here."

The technician nodded.

The president inhaled, watching the technicians. The woman who was not a woman stood on the other side of the camera. She placed her hand on it, and he saw the tips of her fingers sink into its black casing.

A technician said, "Five, four, three, two . . ." He motioned to the president, and the red light lit up. The president was on the air.

The woman who was not a woman's fingertips were in the

camera. Again it hit him. *Oh God,* he thought. He looked into the camera, his brilliant words escaping him. So much of Nigeria was seeing him right now. Even in the most rural places, these days more often than not *someone* carried a mobile phone or was near a television or a computer.

He sat up straight. This was his time.

"Greetings, Nigeria," he said. He was strong. He was healthy. His country was seeing him. The world would see him. This was the most positive thing to come out of Nigeria in a long time. *Let the world watch,* the president thought. *Let them see that we are mighty.*

"This is a historic moment for our nation," he began. "For it marks an important milestone in our march toward a maturing democracy."

The president had never been a great orator. But today, this early evening, he was feeling his words. He was tasting them. They were humming to the rhythm of his soul. He smiled as he spoke. "For the first time since we cast off the shackles of colonialism, over a half century ago, since we rolled through decades of corruption and internal struggle, we have reached the tipping point. And here in Lagos, we have passed it. Many of you have seen the footage on the Internet or heard the news from loved ones. Last night, Lagos burned. But like a phoenix, it will rise from the ashes—a greater creature than ever before.

"The occasion that has put me here before you tonight is momentous. It marks another kind of transitional shift. Now listen closely to me. This shift is cause for celebration, not panic. I will say it again: celebration, *not* panic. There are others among us here in Lagos. They intend to stay. And I am happy about it. They have new technology; they have fresh ideas that we can combine with our own. Hold tight. We will be powerful again, o! People of Lagos, especially, look at your neighbor. See his race, tribe, or his alien blood. And call him brother. We have much work to do as a family.

"Now let me tell you about my own adventure. Then we will get down to business. . . ."

The president spoke of his failure as a president and of the corruption he could not stand up to. He told of his pericarditis and fleeing to Saudi Arabia to die, away from his country. He spoke of his shame. Then he spoke of being healed by Ayodele. He said nothing of her subsequent sacrifice. He wasn't sure how the people would take it, especially the part about her dissipating into a fog that they'd all inhaled.

He mentioned Adaora, the marine biologist, who would serve as his scientific expert because she'd been up close and studied their . . . guests. He spoke of Anthony the Ghanaian rapper, explaining that he was the man who "eagerly offers celebrity endorsement from a neighboring country." The president knew Anthony wouldn't mind because Anthony didn't think the world needed to know *what* he planned to do, he just needed to do it. The president spoke of two soldiers, one named Agu who had interacted closely with the newcomers and developed a rapport with them, and the other the soldier he'd spoken with at length via phone. His name was Hassam, and he'd restored order on Victoria Island. These were the trained officials he was appointing to take the lead in keeping everyone safe. All were part of the old world, the president explained, and part of the new world. However, he didn't say a word about the fact that despite it all, he *still* felt Agu, Adaora, and Anthony were witches. Good witches, but witches nonetheless. Old outdated ways of thinking don't die easily, and sometimes they don't die at all.

He warned people to stay away from the waters for now. And then finally he told of his meeting with the Elders. He spoke of aliens among the people, and he spoke of them as friends.

"Listen to your own hearts and look around you," he said. "We tore at our own flesh last night, as we have done many times in the past. Now, as we hurt from the pain and loss, let our minds clear. And see."

Then he spoke of alien technology and how the land would be pure and palm nuts, cocoa, and other crops would grow as they never had before. Extinct creatures would return and new ones would appear. Nigeria would have much to give the world—and to show it. "In the coming months, we will set up solid programs. The change will be both gradual and swift." He paused. "Corruption is dead in Nigeria." Then he smiled.

The red light went off. The broadcast had ended. The president felt his entire body relax. He was drenched in sweat. His armpits were soaked. He felt damn good.

CHAPTER 54
SPIDER'S THREADS

As the president gave his speech, Adaora stood at a window, looking outside. There were speakers all around the studio; one could hear the broadcast in every room. The others had stayed to watch, but Adaora needed to be alone and gather her thoughts.

There would be meetings with reporters, local, national, and international. There would be meetings with government officials and scientists. She'd collect a group of oceanographers, and they would go on dangerous dives, document and research in labs, collect samples and creatures (at least the ones who would allow themselves to be collected). *Maybe I will even call Moctar Ag Halaye,* she thought. The Tuareg diver was one of the best, and he'd gone on dives to study great whites many times off South Africa's False Bay, so monsters didn't scare him much.

She'd used the office phone to call Chris and the kids, speaking briefly to Chris's mother before losing the connection. She hadn't been able to reach them again. There were a lot of people trying to make calls.

But in their brief discussion, her mother-in-law had assured her that they were all okay. In the background, Kola and Fred had asked when she was coming to be with them. "Soon," she said, and she was telling the truth. But she wouldn't be able to stay because she had things to do that went beyond motherhood. She would risk never returning to them, every time she explored the dangerous waters. She sighed. *What kind of mother am I? And what kind of wife?*

"I am a marine witch," she whispered.

She'd work it out, as her city would work out its alien issue. Adaora leaned against the window frame, and her eyes fell on three women standing at a corner beneath a palm tree. They were huddled together, all watching their mobile phones. When the president finished his speech, Adaora observed closely.

The women looked up from their phones and stared at each other. Finally, one of them said something and another nodded. The third was pointing at the ground and laughing.

In the town of Arondizuogu, Agu's younger brother Kelechi looked out the window of his uncle's house and watched as the truck full of thugs drove away into the sunset. The thugs must have had mobile phones too. They must have seen the president's speech. Maybe they finally understood that people like them were no longer going to rule Nigeria's present and future.

"*Kai!*" his father exclaimed, sitting back on his plush chair. He pulled at his short salt-and-pepper beard. "Part of me wants to think that this cannot be good, but I think it is!"

They had all watched it on his uncle's television. Kelechi had gazed in astonishment at his cheap mobile phone. He'd seen people in Lagos with their BlackBerries watching videos on the small screens, but he'd never had the privilege of such a thing. What he remembered most was how clear the president had looked, even on the small screen of his flip phone, and how he'd sounded like he was right in the room, speaking personally to Kelechi.

"How can this be good? Aliens?" Kelechi's wife muttered, setting a bowl of okra soup and gari on the portable table in front of him. Kelechi's father leaned forward and smiled at the food. He was in a good mood. "They are probably devils," she added.

"You're a child," his uncle said irritably. "What can you know about devils except what those silly churches pound into your head?" He pounded his own head to illustrate his point. "What we just

heard that normally brainless president say—that was the most wonderful thing I have heard *any* politician say in decades!"

Kelechi's aunt came out with another bowl of okra soup and
gari for his uncle.

"Have they gone?" his mother asked Kelechi.

"Yes," he said. "I think so."

"Thank God," she said.

Kelechi laughed. "Well, thank something."

"No, thank God."

"If those idiots had not left, I'd have gone out to handle them,
damn the consequences," his uncle growled.

Kelechi's father winked at him and nodded. "As we did during
the civil war."

"No one could stop us."

"Not bullets, not armies."

"If all the other rebels had been like that, we'd be citizens of the
Republic of Biafra."

They both laughed, sharing a knowing look as they ate their
okra soup. Kelechi's father bit into an excellent piece of goat meat.
Still chewing, he said, "It is a good, good night."

"Devilry," Kelechi's wife muttered, adjusting her wig.

The woman who looked straight out of a Nollywood film showed
up at the door just as the sun set. Chris didn't want to think about
how she had gotten past the high concrete wall and locked gate of
the community where his mother lived. The woman wore high
heels, had the body of a goddess, and spoke with a confidence that
reminded Chris of the best lawyers. In a firm voice that Chris found
impossible to disagree with, the woman invited herself in for a cup
of tea. As he showed her to the kitchen, followed by his curious son
and daughter and his anxious mother and two aunts, she said that
a road monster that called itself the Bone Collector had eaten her.
"Your roads are safe now," she said.

Then, not even ten minutes later, there was another knock on the door. This time, it was an older Yoruba man with smooth onyx skin who said that he'd been inside the Internet for hours and hours talking to Ijele. No matter Chris's religious beliefs, even *he* knew that no one spoke directly with Ijele and lived. Not even one of . . . *them*. Still, he stepped aside and let the black-skinned man into his home. After that another seven aliens came. What was attracting them to his mother's house and why, he did not know. But something deep in him had broken open, leaving him warm and curious. He wanted to be a part of whatever was happening.

His aunts were excited to have so many to cook for, and they happily went to the kitchen to get to it. Nevertheless, his mother's face looked pained. She must have had a feeling that this situation went beyond the family. Beyond their beliefs. Beyond their religion. His mother was a Pentecostal Christian widow who gave much of her ample savings to the church and fell over with the Holy Spirit regularly during mass. Still, she retreated to the kitchen and helped her sisters cook a feast. They cooked egusi soup, okra soup, pounded yam, fried fish, and stew and rice. His mother even made chin chin. There was nothing left in the house's two fridges when they were done. And when the strange guests had eaten their fill, there was no prepared food left either.

Kola and Fred served the visitors, and then after the visitors had eaten, Kola and Fred asked them questions. They joked and laughed and told them about Ayodele and about life in Nigeria.

Chris kept his distance, talking only to the Nollywood woman who called herself Stella Iboyi. And the only reason he talked to her was because she wouldn't leave him alone. After a while, his blood pressure began to rise.

"Why did you people allow your roads to be so dangerous?" Stella asked.

"We didn't 'allow' it," he said. "Our government—"

"Your wife's father was eaten by the road monster, though.

You never went to the road and asked it to give her father his life back."

"That doesn't even make any sense!" he snapped. "When a man dies, he goes to heaven or hell. He doesn't . . ." He frowned. "Her father was hit by a truck. He wasn't eaten by a road."

The television, his mobile screen, and his mother's computer all came on at the same time. On their screens was the president. Everyone in the room grew quiet. Chris watched on his phone, everyone else watched on his mother's most prized possession—the wide-screen television. Adaora had bought it for her last year when his mother had broken her ankle and had to stay in the house for three weeks.

When he heard his wife's name mentioned, Chris felt his heart flip. Then a surprising emotion washed over him. He was *proud*, deeply proud. His witch of a wife was part of something that was going to be grand.

"In the name of Jesus," he whispered.

In the city of Accra, Ghana, several people in a street market had stopped walking. They were looking at their mobiles. The sun was setting in a beautiful display of orange, pink, and indigo but few noticed. Music drifted from the MP3 player of a man selling women's dresses, then it stopped and began playing the voice of Nigeria's president.

A woman who'd been walking down the middle of the busy dirt road that passed through the market wanted to throw her mobile phone away. She'd never liked mobile phones. She knew it sounded crazy, but she had always been sure that they could do more than anyone let on. She had a feeling that they could watch you. That they could speak to you at night when you were asleep and brain-wash you. "Maybe this is why Ghana is still the way it is," she'd proclaim. "Because we all use phones and they all control us."

Nevertheless, her boyfriend insisted she carry one. She'd only agreed because he was a sweet, sweet man and she liked the way he spoke Ewe, the language of her mother, whom she missed very much. She'd done exactly what he asked her to do, which was to carry the phone. When he called she answered, but that was as far as it went. She never used it otherwise. She wrapped it in tinfoil and kept it deep in her purse where it wouldn't harm her.

She'd never set her phone to vibrate, but vibrate and vibrate it did as she walked through the market. Finally, she brought the thing out and unwrapped it. It was talking. And it was showing the Nigerian president. It wasn't made to do any such thing! Her boyfriend had assured her. And what the Nigerian president was saying made her stop and stand still for many minutes. When he finished talking, he disappeared from her phone's tiny screen and there was the date and time again. Like normal.

She frowned, her nostrils flaring. She squeezed the phone. Then she wrapped it in tinfoil and put it back in her purse. She started walking very fast, wanting to get home to check the news on her boyfriend's computer. For the first time since the Internet and mobile phones had come to Ghana, she wasn't afraid.

A young man named Waydeep Kwesi slung a plastic bag over his shoulder as he stepped out of the fast-walking woman's way. He watched her pass and then looked around. He didn't have a mobile phone, and he hadn't been near any sort of screen in the last few minutes. He was more interested in the people around him, anyway. His belly growled. He reached into his bag and brought out one of the smaller garden eggs he'd just purchased. He'd been hungry for them for hours.

No one noticed as he bit into it like it was the sweetest mango and continued on his way.

CHAPTER 55

GOOD JOURNALISM IS NOT DEAD

Femi didn't think he'd ever see his Honda Civic again. He sat in the gray, well-worn driver's seat and sighed deeply. His car smelled faintly like his girlfriend's perfume. Laughing, he'd sprayed the driver's seat just before he left their apartment two days prior.

"God, that seems so long ago," he whispered. He laughed. He was actually in his car again. They'd let him go. But he was planning to return to the president as soon as they called him. He took another breath and looked around. He was parked close enough to Bar Beach to see the water . . . and the part of the shape-shifting alien ship that hovered above the water, far out from shore. A few cars passed on the street, and there were one or two people on the beach but no one nearby. *Good*, he thought.

He reached over to the passenger seat and undid the latch underneath. Then he flipped the passenger seat open. Quickly, from among various cables, chargers, batteries, SIM cards, and mobile phones, he removed his car charger and his laptop. He'd owned this car for six years. He had bought a Honda for more than its plain, unassuming look. Hondas *lasted*. Even on the roads of Nigeria. And for this reason, he'd spent thousands of naira to have this secret hiding place custom-made for his car. He kept absolutely nothing else inside it. This kept him mobile. A journalist needed to be mobile.

He plugged his phone into his car charger, placed it on the armrest, and then opened his laptop. Its background was black, and there was only one icon on the screen. He kept all his links and folders inside and then opened his browser.

When he checked his YouTube account, his heart began to pound like crazy. The footage he'd posted of Agu, Adaora, and Anthony saving him, the guards, the president, and one of his First Ladies on that boat had already gotten over three million hits. He'd named it "The President of Nigeria Saved by Witches and Warlocks!" That title, coupled with his reputation as a respected journalist who'd once worked as a CNN correspondent, plus his substantial following, might have gotten the ball rolling.

"Okay, Femi," he whispered, opening his laptop wider. "This is happening. So make it happen."

His inbox had over a thousand messages. Many were from Nigerians threatening to kill him for involving himself in witchcraft. Some were from Nigerians who called him a disgrace to journalism. The majority were from Lagosians asking him to please report more. He spotted several e-mails from newspapers around the world demanding more news. And there were some e-mails that accused Nigeria of being too backward, undeserving of an alien visitation.

He found at least ten from news services including CNN, Fox News, the BBC, the *Guardian*, Reuters, the Associated Press, and Al Jazeera.

He read and then closed all of these and clicked on the one from the *Nigerian Times*. This one wasn't asking to buy his story. It was his editor asking where he was. He typed a quick response: "I'm fine. I'll have a story to you soon. Watch your inbox." He paused. He still had the footage from Tin Can Island where the one called Ayodele had sacrificed herself. He clearly understood that this was what she'd done. He'd inhaled the fog like everyone else, and he'd immediately felt a shift. In perspective; in memory. He'd only smoked weed once in his life, when he was seventeen. Within minutes he'd felt everything around him open up like a flower. He'd been horrified by the experience and never gone near the stuff again. This was how the perspective shift had felt, though smoother, more integrated with his own point of view. He felt it most when he looked at the sky.

Of all that had happened, of all he'd seen, Ayodele's sacrifice was the real story. That was the story CNN and the BBC would really want. But that story wasn't for sale. At least not to any foreign buyers. He quickly added a bit more to his e-mail: "I'm fine. I'll have a story to you soon. Watch your inbox. This isn't a story for print. It'll have the best effect if posted on the Web. I have video." Then he clicked send.

He settled back. All he needed to do his job was his car, his laptop, and his mobile phone. He sat back and began to write:

> My fellow Nigerians, my fellow humans, let me tell you about all that I have seen. I was there! . . .

It was the most honest piece of journalism he had ever produced. He did not write it hard-news style; he wrote it as a memoir. He was a reporter sharing *his* experiences. He ended his fifteen-thousand-word article with what had happened on Tin Can Island.

> . . . She saved them all and then they beat her to near death. But can you blame them? After all they had probably been through? Even before getting to Tin Can Island? What must they have seen during that night when Lagos burned, rioted, ate her young? So they beat her. I saw them stamp on her chest, kick her in the head, and worse. I was too far away to help. So the only way I knew I could help was to keep recording. This is what happened next. Do you all remember that fog? You should if you were in Lagos; wherever you were, whether you were inside or outside, you inhaled the fog. This is where it came from:

Then he embedded the footage he'd posted on his YouTube page. When his editor posted the story on the website, he'd make the YouTube footage live.

He reread his story, editing, adding where he saw fit. He didn't censor a thing. He read it out loud. He read it aloud again, and then he played the footage. The combination gave him the shivers. The world as he knew it had changed. He'd been sent out to cover the dead whale on Bar Beach. He never could have imagined what would happen next.

He clicked send. Then he sat back and waited for his world to turn yet again. His thread of story would join the vibrating of the great natrrator's rhythm. He smiled. And it was good.

CHAPTER 56

THE SWORDFISH

She swims around the alien home that was in the water three times. Three is a magic number to her. Her most memorable moments happen in threes. She'd never seen the massive ones in her entire life, until one day while swimming far from land she saw three of them. Though they could stay underwater for a long time, they could not breathe it as she could. She'd enjoyed watching them meander to the surface and blow water out of a hole in the top of their heads. On the best day of her life, she'd eaten not one, not two, but three of her favorite fish in a row. And it had taken her three tries at spearing the dead snake thing in the water to make the dry creatures go away for good. They are gone for good. Yes, she is sure of this.

So she swims around the underwater part of the visitors' home three times. As she does so, she inhales the sweet, sweet water. Her gills are enormous now. Her body is huge. She matches perfectly the golden light filtering through the clear water. Then she swims away. South. She swims out to sea, to see what she can see.

CHAPTER 57

SPIDER THE ARTIST

I am the unseen.
For centuries, I have been here. Beneath this great city, this metro-polis. I know your language. I know all languages. Legba is my cousin, and he has taught me well. My cave is broad and cool. The sun cannot send its heat down here. The damp soil is rich and fragrant. I turn softly on my back and place my eight legs to the cave's ceiling. Then, I listen.
I am the spider. I see sound. I feel taste. I hear touch.
I spin the story. This is the story I've spun.

I am Udide Okwanka.

I have been spinning these stories in this cave for centuries. I've spun the birth and growth of this great city. Watched through the vibrations that travel through my webs. Lagos. Nigeria. I know it all because I created it all. I have seen people come from across the ocean. I have seen people sell people. I've knitted their stories and watched them knit their own crude webs. They came in boats that creaked a desperate song and brought something I'd never have created. Lagos has fed me. Fast life, fast death. High life, low life. Skyscrapers, shanty towns. Flies, mosquitoes. The roads rumble as paths to the future, always hungry for blood. The Bone Collector will always be one of my favorite children. Ijele is my cousin.

I have watched, heard, tasted, touched these new people.
Shape-shifters of the third kind. Story weavers of their own time.

I respect them.

They brought Agu, Adaora, and Anthony together. Adaora the brave. Agu the strong. Anthony the energetic. I know their stories as I know all stories. Do you want to know how their stories end? Do you want to know what happens to Chris? Does he get back together with his wife? Or will Adaora stay with Agu? What of Kola and Fred? What is Anthony's place in the new world? Yes, you want to know. We all want to know things.

But I feel the press of other stories.

I wove that which Adaora draws from to practice her witchcraft. I wove that which gives Agu his leopard's strength. Anthony's life became part of my web when he first set foot in Lagos. I know the one who wove his rhythm. Anansi is my cousin. Anthony has always been within my reach. Fisayo's destiny was written. The boy with no name had no destiny until I wrote that part of the story. Father Oke was destined to meet one of my cousins. The young man Benson and the other soldiers—they are all part of my great tapestry.

And now the world sees what is happening inside of Lagos and her waters. What is that sweet taste I feel with my feet? It is patriotism, loyalty. Not to the country of Nigeria but to the city of Lagos. Finally. Maybe it will flow and spread like a flood of clean water. What a story that would be. The waters off the coast are treacherous. They are clean. It is beautiful. But there is a problem. Other people in other parts of the world—they see what is happening here. And they fear it. They are agreed. Lagos is a cancer. They wish to cut the cancer out before it spreads. I will not let them. I don't know who will launch them, but these people are all in communication, so all are involved in the decision.

They will burn it away before it spreads.

I will not let them.

For the first time since the birth of Lagos, my glorious city, I will pause in my storytelling.

I will leave my web.
I become part of the story.
I will join my people.

And we spiders play dirty.

SOME NIGERIAN WORDS, PHRASES, AND PIDGIN ENGLISH TERMS

419—a highly successful strain of advance-fee Internet fraud popularized in Nigeria, which appears most often in the form of an e-mailed letter. The number "419" refers to the article (sectioned into 419, 419A, 419B) that deals with fraud in Chapter 38 of the Nigerian Criminal Code Act ("Obtaining Property by False Pretences: Cheating").

Adofuroo—a derogatory term for homosexuals in the Yoruba language

Ah-ah—for goodness' sake

Ahoa—Nigerian foot soldiers

Am (Pidgin English)—she, he, or it

Anuofia—an insult that literally means "wild animal" in the Igbo language. *Anu* means "animal," *ofia* means "forest."

Area Boys (also known as Agberos)—loosely organized groups of street children and teenagers (mostly male) who roam the streets of Lagos

Chale (Ghanaian Pidgin English)—a terminal intensifier that is similar to the exclamation "man" in American-English slang. Pronounced very similarly to the name "Charlie."

Chin Chin—a snack consisting of sweet crunchy bite-sized bits of fried dough

Chineke—the Igbo Supreme Deity. To exclaim it is the same as saying, "Oh my God!"

Chop (Pidgin English)—to eat

Comot (Pidgin English)—to leave a place

Danfo—a commercial minibus or van. They are usually orange or individually painted and very old, beaten up, and have been repaired a million times.

De (Pidgin English)—the

Dey (Pidgin English)—this means "is" or "are" . . . most of the time. Other times, it means "something else."

Face me, I face you (Pidgin English)—a type of building where a series of single-bedroom apartments have their entrances facing each other to form a compound with a main entrance leading into a square in the middle. This type of building is common in urban areas in Nigeria, such as Lagos.

Gari—a creamy white, granular flour made from fermented, gelatinized fresh cassava tubers

Go-slow (Pidgin English)—heavy traffic

Gragra (Pidgin English)—a show of bravado (often false)

Ibi (Pidgin English)—it be

Igbo—(1) the third largest ethnic group in Nigeria and name of the language of the Igbo people (note: the author of this book is Igbo) (2) Nigerian slang for cannabis (unrelated to the Igbo people or language, and not capitalized as a proper noun)

Kai (Pidgin English)—a sympathetic exclamation

Kata kata (Pidgin English)—trouble of the sort that only the poor experience

Kparoof (Pidgin English)—to manhandle

Marine witch—who the heck really knows? Certain Nigerian evangelical Christian sects believe many of the world's ills are perpetrated by witches, and the most powerful is the "marine witch"

Mek (Pidgin English)—make

Mumu (Pidgin English)—an idiot

Na (Pidgin English)—it is

Na wao (Pidgin English)—the equivalent of exclaiming, "Wow!"

NEPA—pronounced "neh-pah." An acronym that stands for the National Electric Power Authority. Usually to blame when the power goes out. Now called PHCN (Power Holding Company of Nigeria), people still refer to the governmental electricity company as NEPA.

Nko (Pidgin English)—an interrogative pronoun used for emphasis at the end of sentences (believed to be of Yoruba origin)

Nyash (Pidgin English)—ass

O—a terminal intensifier. One sings and prolongs the sound more than speaks it.

Oga—a term of respect toward men, equivalent to "sir." The term of respect for women is "madam."

Okada—a commercial motorcycle or motorcycle taxi

Peme (Pidgin English)—to die

Pure Water—a sachet of drinkable water, often sold on the street

Sabi (Pidgin English)—to know or know how

Seke (Ghanaian Pidgin English)—craziness

Sha (Pidgin English)—a terminal intensifier that is similar to the exclamation "man" in American-English slang. It can mean "anyway" or "like that."

Ting (Pidgin English)—thing

Una (Pidgin English)—you guys

Wahala (believed to be of Hausa origin)—trouble

Wetin (Pidgin English)—what

Winch (Pidgin English)—witch

ACKNOWLEDGMENTS

Thank you, Lagos, Nigeria, for being Lagos, Nigeria. Two decades ago, I knew I'd write about you someday. And someday, you *will* be the greatest city in the world.

I'd like to thank Nigerian Pidgin English extraordinaire, Taofik Yusuf, for his help with the grittier Nigerian Pidgin English sections of the novel and insisting that I change the title of this book from *Lagos* to *Lagoon*. Thanks to Nollywood director and friend Tchidi Chikere for his meticulous help with the Pidgin English sections, as well. Thanks to my ambitious UK editor, Anne Perry, for convincing me to keep these Pidgin English sections as I originally intended them, as opposed to toning them down. Thanks to Beegeagle for all his firsthand information on the Nigerian military. Thanks to the Ethiopian-American rapper and visionary Gabriel Teodros and New Orleans artist Soraya Jean-Louis McElroy for being *Lagoon*'s first readers. Both of them loved the opening swordfish chapter, and this fact meant a *lot* to me.

Thanks to the South African science-fiction film *District 9* for both intriguing and pissing me off so much that I started daydreaming about what aliens would do in Nigeria. This novel was birthed from my anger at *District 9*, but it quickly became something else entirely.

And of course, last but not least, I'd like to thank my daughter,

Anyaugo, who was the first person to hear the summary of *Lagoon* (back when it was still titled *Lagos*). She loves Nigeria as much as I do, and she thought the story was utterly hilarious (especially the road monster parts).

MEANWHILE, BACK IN CHICAGO . . .

Douglas Hall's Room 217 was the warmest classroom on campus. In the dead of Chicago's winter, one could comfortably wear a T-shirt and jeans here. It was the perfect place to thaw out after trudging through the snow, and there weren't any classes in it between twelve p.m. and three p.m. Thus, pre-med sophomores Shaquille, Jordan, and Nature made this their study room on Mondays, Wednesdays, and Saturdays.

Today was Saturday, and the plan was to study, study, study. They were all taking Chem 101 and the class was no joke; best to get ahead while they were ahead. Nevertheless, their plans had changed in the last day. The whole world's plans had changed. Quietly so. Nature had been the first to hear about the latest footage on YouTube. Minutes before, her sister had sent the link to her phone. She couldn't wait to watch and discuss it with Shaquille and Jordan. Every few hours, more weird news came out of Nigeria, and it added a spicy element of excitement to everything— a nice change from the mundane routine of school and work at the Harris Bank.

"We're Nigerians. Just Nigerians," the one who the people in the video called Agu said. Agu looked at the guy with supersonic powers and added, "And one Ghanaian."

"Wow," Nature whispered as she refreshed the screen so they could watch it yet again. "Apparently, they on some X-Men shit in Africa." She took off her coat and sweater. "I don't think any of this is real." She wore an orange Baby Phat T-shirt underneath with a shiny pink cat design on the front. The many thin gold bangles on her wrists jingled as she sat down in front of her laptop.

"Yeah man, this can't be real," Shaquille said, sitting back at his desk as he watched his laptop screen. He waved a hand. "Don't play it again yet. I need to think." He picked up his hefty red headphones and then put them down, a perplexed frown on his face. He rarely took off his headphones, not even during class; he liked his world to have a soundtrack. But *this* warranted taking them off. Anything linked to what was going on in Africa did. He needed to hear the audio as clearly as he could, even if the audio was shit. He was still wearing his heavy leather coat, the chill from outside still in his bones. "Shit's totally fake," he muttered.

"'The President of Nigeria Saved by Witches and Warlocks!'" Jordan read, bending forward and bringing his face close to the screen. He laughed. "All right, the title's kinda fucked-up *but*, oh my God, come on, Shaq. What'chu think all this is, then?" Jordan wore a black T-shirt with a drawing of a marijuana leaf in the center. Being skinny and quite tall, he was more comfortable standing than sitting at a cramped, hard-seated desk.

He stood up straight and stamped a Timberland boot on the floor. "The kid dying in the street—*dying*, man, *you see him die*—people there tweeting and posting claims about seeing aliens and shit, folks reporting fear and crazy-ass riots, this X-Men in the ocean craziness . . . You think it's some Orwellian shit?" Jordan asked. "Like that *War of the Worlds* radio broadcast back in the day that caused all that panic? You think Nigerians are that gullible? In this day and age? And look at the 'stars' of the show. They black. Even the heroes are black. You think they gon' spend they money to put somethin' together that looks this *real* and actually allow black folks to star in it? Real *Africans*? And then set it *in* Africa?" He guffawed with glee and shook his head. "Nah man, not gonna happen. This shit real. That's the more likely scenario."

Nature sucked her teeth and pulled up her low-riding skinny jeans. "Man, I don't care about no uppity Africans anyway. What's Africa ever done for me?" She sucked her teeth again. "I think Shaq's right. Or . . ." She shrugged. "I dunno."

"Ey, I hear you, Nature," Jordan said. "Africa ain't done nothing for us but enslave our ancestors. Won't disagree with you there." He grinned. "But look, come on, if anyone gon' be flying around, shootin' lasers outta they eyes or jumping in the water and making shock waves because they *can*, it would be a bunch of *Africans*."

The three students had a good laugh at this, and then watched the footage again. No matter how hard they looked, even their Hollywood-level-special-effects-accustomed eyes could not spot a flaw or an anomaly in the footage. Even the great sharklike beast that the guy Agu supposedly punched out of the water looked real. This along with the mainstream news reports of terrorist activity and rioting in Nigeria and the significantly different, more individual reports circulating on various social media outlets of an "alien" invasion had caught the attention of many Americans. These three students were certainly not the only ones bothered and confused by the stories and footage coming out of Africa.

Nature opened and closed a textbook. After a moment, she opened it again and brought out her syllabus from her backpack. She looked up. "I'm just glad it's all happening over there. It's freaking me out."

The two boys nodded.

"You think it's gon' stay there, though?" Jordan asked.

Nature shrugged.

"Whatever's going on, it'll probably make more sense tomorrow," Shaquille said, placing his big red headphones back over his ears. He turned on his iPod and clicked on Drake's "Successful." He didn't care for Drake, but he loved this particular song. It was a rare moment of real hip-hop from a shitty whiny rapper. He took his coat off.

They took out their pens and highlighters and opened their textbooks to chapter 1 in *Chemistry: The Central Science.* Spring semester was going to be tough, and they had to get ahead to get more ahead. In the meantime, the world would take care of itself.

INSIGHT INTO THE LAGOON

Some readers have told me that though they enjoyed *Lagoon*, they felt they were missing some things on the cultural/political/societal side. Understandable. Fair enough.

I admit (and don't apologize for) the fact that my flavor of sci-fi is evenly Naijamerican (note: "Naija" is slang for "Nigeria" or "Nigerian"). You can read more about what I mean by this in a recent interview I did with VenturesAfrica.com. Thus, I'm going to explain a few things.

WHAT's 419?
In *Lagoon*, there are 419 scammers working out of cybercafés. The number 419 is the name given to the "Nigerian scam.". . . You know, when Nigerian Prince So-and-So sends you an e-mail claiming he's got billions sitting in the bank, but he needs "you" (a total, complete, gullible, and greedy stranger) to send him a minimal fee to get it out of the bank, and gosh, when he does, he'll send "you" a nice cut for helping. The number 419 is a reference to the section of Nigerian law that the scam violates.

If you want to know more about this practice from an objective perspective (as opposed to one that solely sides with the victim), I highly recommend Alan Dean Foster's nonfiction book, *The Phisher*. He wrote this book after responding to a 419 scammer's e-mail and actually striking up a conversation with the guy who was, indeed, in Nigeria. (No, I do not recommend trying this for yourself. Just delete the e-mail.)

Note: Don't joke to me about Nigerian scammers and princes. This happens to me on Twitter far too often, and people think they're being clever. It's terribly irritating. If all you know about one of Africa's most powerful and innovative nations is that there is an abundance of 419 scammers from there, that's on you, not me.

DOES "WITCH SLAPPING" REALLY EXIST?

There's a "witch slapping" scene in *Lagoon.* Are there self-proclaimed holy men slapping the so-called witchcraft out of women? Yes. See for yourself at: youtube.com/watch?v=bfeGpcmfMBA.

Witch slapping is just one symptom of the strong strain of Christian fundamentalism running through Nigeria's veins. Such things can be found all over the world, you say? True. However, what worries me about the particular strain that's been running through Nigeria in recent years is not that it's teaching people extreme and bizarre forms of Christianity. It is that it's teaching Nigerians to hate their own indigenous traditions, spiritualties, and religions. It's one thing to move past what was there before; it happens. People evolve, change, and move on (and sometimes they return to the old ways or create new hybrids). However, it's another thing entirely to move past what was before because of a nasty form of hatred of one's self in the guise of religion, brought or imported by outsiders and foisted upon people who are simply looking for God.

WHY FIRST CONTACT WITH A SWORDFISH INSTEAD OF A HUMAN?

Because (1) If aliens came and were interested in Earthlings, Earth has many citizens (human and nonhuman) who'd be of interest to them, and (2) I felt these environmentalist swordfish deserved to be immortalized and empowered for their efforts. (Reuters did a brief news story about swordfish attacking an Angolan oil pipeline.)

WHAT'S UP WITH THE ROAD MONSTER?

The roads of Nigeria are unsafe, often scary, and in poor shape in far too many parts of the country. They're monstrous and they've swallowed many lives. I'm not going to lie; I have seen terrible things on Nigeria's roads. I've seen death there multiple times.

Pause to remember the dead on the road.

More specifically to *Lagoon*, there was a supergraphic photo circulating the Internet back in 2010 of a horrific accident on the Lagos-Benin Expressway. (If you really must see it, you can find it, but I warn you, it's quite awful.) There were several explanations that explained the photo; most of them were inaccurate, but all of them very possible. The incident caught my writer's eye, and it made it into *Lagoon*.

WHAT THE HELL ARE THEY SAYING?

There's a lot of Nigerian pidgin English in *Lagoon*. Really, more people should have been speaking it in the novel. However, I knew I wanted to go 100 percent when the characters spoke it, so I limited the pidgin to certain characters. Nollywood director Tchidi Chikere (my favorite of his movies is *Stronger Than Pain*) and self-proclaimed pidgin English expert Taofik Yusuf worked closely with me to get it as accurate as possible.

To those with no background in any kind of African or Caribbean—even knowing African American–English should provide you with the necessary tools for hearing pidgin English—my advice is to just relax your mental ear, chill, and remind yourself that there's English in there. Some of it will start coming through.